The Mirage Guild

GABI SALAS

ISBN: 979-8-9889056-4-6

To the girls who didn't find themselves until they were thirty-something; may you get railed by a much younger man of your dreams

TROPES, TAGS, AND TRIGGER WARNINGS

Tropes:

Brother's best friend, he loved her first, reverse age gap, a *tiny* bit of good girl behavior, he gets a bit bossy but is a golden retriever

Tags:

MF, good girl, sex club, chosen family, sex positivity, public sex, small business, horoscopes, romantic comedy, friendships, consent-focused

Trigger Warnings:

This book uses explicit language and very descriptive sex scenes. Sex happens both privately and in spaces where other people are in attendance. **There is an element that may be triggering for some but is a spoiler.** You can skip to just after the *Epliogue* to read it if you'd like. It has nothing to do with violence.

ONE
ISABELLA

I had two problems: One, the neon pink cocktail umbrella stashed in my weathered brown leather tote bag, a relic from my last tequila sunrise on the beach, was laughably insufficient for the torrential downpour brewing outside. And two, I was undeniably, unquestionably late for my introductory meeting with my new boss.

The boss of the job I'd flown 6,337 miles just two days ago for.

The drizzle of New York City seemed a world away from the sun-drenched days of Bora Bora. Now it was time to put the crystal-blue lagoon waters, endless papaya, and island-hopping behind me. According to my mother, I needed to "grow up" and "start my real life."

At thirty-five years old, with a stamped passport thicker than my resumé, I had to beg my baby brother for a job. Apparently, racking up more miles than Phileas Fogg didn't count for shit, and world travel alone wasn't enough to impress potential employers. Luckily, Dominic hadn't hesitated when he offered me the waitressing position at the club he cofounded with his best friend, Liam.

And, no, I would not dwell on the fact that my own brother got me a job at a sex club. Nope, I preferred to consider it more Liam's business. I rolled my eyes at the thought of my quiet, elusive brother—the sibling who always seemed to have it together—going off to UCLA and coming back with a best friend and a business idea. Dominic, whose new business was taking off like hotcakes, at least had direction.

The black town car pulled up—thank you, rich Mom and Dad—and I scurried out from underneath the awning of my parents' building in Gramercy Park, making a beeline for the passenger door. The storm clouds hung around me like a foul smell—or was that just New York? They wanted to engulf me, to snatch me up and remind me of how little progress I'd made in life. I told them no.

The sounds of the city, and my depressing thoughts, were cut off as I settled into the soft black leather seat and shook off the rain that had pelted my skin. I shivered as the cool breeze from the air-conditioned car hit me, and I tilted the vents away. My dress already had dark spots of rain staining it, the tight material stretching over my skin. I wasn't made for depressing weather like this.

Isabella, or Izzy, as my friends called me, thrived in the sun. My favorite temperature was "hot car." You know, the suffocating heat you feel when you first slide into a car after it's been trapped in the sun all day? The kind that takes your breath away and cooks you from the inside out. The kind of temperature they warn you about not leaving puppies or babies inside cars for too long. Yeah, that one.

My high school graduation gown had barely hit the ground before I enrolled in online college classes, pulled my passport out of my parents' safe, stuffed clothes into a suitcase, and booked the first flight out of JFK. My first stop was Amsterdam, then Barcelona, then I popped over to Athens. I made a little money nannying or waitressing, but most of my income came from the inheritance I'd uncorked when I'd turned twenty-three.

But I had never needed a lot. I could find the most luxurious hotels, which somehow stayed hidden from the tourist crowds and cost nearly nothing. I could tell the street vendors apart—there were the ones who had bright food stalls with red umbrellas that would give me the most delicious meal of my life and then their yellow-clad competitors who would treat me like a rich American foreigner and force me to cut the line at the outdoor toilet outside the Eiffel Tower with my hands covering my butt. But as my friends got picked off one by one—no, they weren't murdered, just engaged—I caved to my mom's plea, for the billionth time, that I move back home.

I longed for days lying on pristine beaches and exploring ancient cities. But now, back in the Big Apple, I swapped flip-flops for heels, beachy waves for sleek ponytails, and wanderlust for the Prism Society's 5 p.m. to 3 a.m. hustle.

The fact that it was an adult club was only a fraction of the reason for the nerves in my belly. Honestly, the nude beaches in France had numbed me. Seeing naked bodies no longer brought out giggles or made my face flush. No, the main cause for the nerves in my belly was that I knew, without a doubt, I would be the grandma of the Prism Society. The rest of the staff were all around my brother's age, except for the one receptionist, Maureen, and that seven-year age difference between me and Dominic felt more significant than the Trans-Siberian Railway.

Still, I had no regrets for the magical years of travel with the fleeting romances from Amsterdam to Australia. I wore the callouses earned on cobblestone paths and my newfound culinary snobbery, thanks to countless hole-in-the-wall discoveries, with pride.

New York was the real world which was why I'd avoided it for so long, but now that I had returned, I had to get serious. The town car stopped in Brooklyn outside a three-story brick building with large arched windows on both sides. I was surprised, if not slightly disappointed, the Prism Society didn't have a flashy neon light hanging off the corner. From the outside, it looked like it could be an event space for weddings or birthday parties for wealthy people.

As the car splashed to the curb, my phone buzzed with an incoming message. Glancing down, I found a picture from Natalia, my friend who was still annoyingly basking in the sunny bliss of Bora Bora. In the selfie, Natalia grinned widely, the blinding sunlight casting a halo around her golden curls. Beside her was a bronzed Adonis whose name Nat most likely didn't remember.

It was a few minutes after eleven in the morning where

Nat was, and she already had the glassy-eyed look of too many Aperol spritzes. I rolled my eyes at the picture. The contrast between Natalia's beachy nirvana and my own rain-soaked reality made me homesick for a place I wasn't even from.

"Beach bum," I muttered, my thumbs flying over the screen as I sent back an eye roll emoji and a middle finger one. But then, feeling guilty, I typed back, Nice tits. With that, I swiftly slid my phone back into my bag and steeled myself for the task at hand. I was in the real world now, so no more beachside frolics or carefree flirtations. I scooped up my bag, took a deep breath, and stepped back outside into the rain.

With a rhythmic drumming of my heart echoing the downpour around me, I reached for the roughcast iron handles affixed to the imposing wooden doors of the Prism Society. Adorned with intricate scrollwork, the cold iron clashed with the warmth of the building's aged brick. Despite their ornate appearance, they remained stubbornly immobile under my insistent tugs.

My dress, a tight cream number more suited for a beach-side bar than the dreary NYC weather, grew clingier with every passing second. The rainwater snaked its way down the fabric, staining it a darker shade of taupe and making me shiver from its icy touch. A stubborn stream of water raced down my back, slipping under the material and tracing a cold line along my spine.

As I gave another frustrated tug at the door, I looked up and was promptly drenched by a gush of water cascading from an overflowing copper gutter lodged above the door.

The deluge doused me, matting my hair to my face and eliciting a startled squeal as the cold water seeped into my dress, running rivulets down my skin.

With a screech, I pushed myself into the doors, and they finally gave way. Push, not pull. The doors could've used a sign. The glimmering skyline of New York City and the towering structures, now hidden behind heavy, ink-black clouds, disappeared behind the curtain of rain and the thick door as it slammed shut. I took a deep breath, held my arms out from my body in a hopeless attempt to keep myself dry, and pushed through thick velvet curtains into the club.

As I stumbled into the Prism Society, I could hardly see through the droplets clinging to my eyelashes. I stood there for a moment in the grand entrance, water dripping from my hair and down my face, mixing with the salty tears of frustration that had welled up in my eyes.

With a deep, steadying breath, I wiped the rain off my face with a drenched palm—not exactly a towel, but it would do. I blinked and squinted my eyes, trying to adjust to the club's softer, moodier lighting. My nose picked up an odd cocktail of leather, musk, and a hint of pine. The latter made me smile. Leave it to my brother to keep a high-end sex club smelling like a forest.

As sophisticated as it was seductive, the Prism Society resembled a burlesque Narnia with its wallpapered nooks, cozy chairs, and winding staircases. I pictured Dominic, my practical, numbers-oriented younger brother, poring over lighting options and discussing the merits of satin versus silk.

I bit my lip to keep from laughing at the ridiculous mental image.

In the middle of the entrance to the Prism Society, I stood like a drowned rat—an on-brand welcome for New York, to be honest. I wanted nothing more than to crawl back to the screened-in porch Nat and I had fallen asleep on four nights ago. Instead, I held my head high and walked through the dimly lit lounge, my wet feet sliding in my Chloé wedge heels.

I grabbed a handful of cocktail napkins off a small table to soak up as much rainwater as possible. The paper napkins dissolved into a wet ball in my hands. I took a deep breath, mentally restarted "my morning", parted another set of velvet curtains, and headed toward the bar spanning the back of the lounge.

My fresh resolve cracked as I gaped at the sight in front of me. A man—no, scratch that—a *gorgeous* man stood shirtless on a wooden ladder against the shelves high above the bar like a goddamn smutty Beauty and the Beast. Hozier played quietly from the bar speakers as he reached to pull down a fresh bottle of red wine.

His back muscles flexed—who has back muscles anyway? —as he plucked bottles from the shelf, added them to a box, and began his descent. I shook my head clear, swallowed, and masked my face with indifference as he turned to face me.

The guy, who could definitely moonlight as a romance book cover model, took notice of me as he turned to heave the box on the bar top. Maybe he'd take pity on me and crack open the seal of one of those expensive-looking tequila bottles and pour me a shot. His eyes flared with something I didn't understand as he scanned me from head to toe and back again, his lips parted in surprise.

The sharp peaks of my nipples pushed against the rough fabric of my dress. I was soaked, and it was freezing in here. I only had to put two and two together along with the blush that crept up on his face to know I was showing off way more than I intended to.

I had had enough. "Are you gonna help a girl out or just keep staring at my tits?"

"Iz!" Dominic's voice made me turn before the male model could answer. "Jesus Christ, do you own a bra?" Dom's hands flailed in the air as he tried to physically block my appearance from his vision. "Goddammit, Iz, your nipples are out!"

I heard a chuckle come from the male model, but I ignored him. Currently, I took zero pity on the scars I was undoubtedly inflicting on my baby brother. "They're just nipples! We all have them!"

I crossed my arms over my chest, feeling the wet fabric press into my arms. I couldn't wait to take this stupid dress off. "In case you couldn't tell, it's a fucking monsoon outside, and for some reason, you keep it set to Arctic tundra temperatures in here." Aware of the male model's gaze, I asked Dom, "Do you have a sweatshirt or something? A parka? Even a Snuggie would do."

"No, Iz, I don't keep my winter gear here, just"—Dom started to walk away, his eyes to the ceiling, avoiding any glimpse of me—"cover yourself or something. I can give you a tour of the place real quick before I leave."

"Oh my god, thank you so much for your overwhelming hospitality. How can I ever thank you for your generosity?" I rolled my eyes and picked up my tote. Maybe I could carry it across the front of my chest and protect my baby brother from the offense of my nipples. But the leather was soaked, and I'd have to spend an hour conditioning the material of my Celine tote bag to try to salvage it from ruin.

"Here, this might help." The male model spoke, and his voice was deeper than I expected it to be. He tossed me a hoodie from behind the bar, and it was still warm, like he'd just taken it off. "Not that I'm complaining," his eyes shifted down my chest, and my eyebrows shot up at his brazen attempt to check me out, "but it is cold in here, sorry."

And this is typically when I would fall in love.

Another version of me, a past version of me, would take a whiff of this man's hoodie and be convinced the pheromones it emitted were that of my soulmate. Another version of myself would smile a lazy grin at this man, lock eyes with him, and allow the film reel of our future to roll through my mind. Izzy of the Past would replay this moment repeatedly, analyzing how his full lips parted when I leaned over the barstool to pick up the hoodie. I would take note of the way his brown eyes didn't leave mine as I stuffed my arms into the sleeve and tugged the thick fabric over my head.

But that version of myself had been dropped off some-where between Spain and the Netherlands. That version of myself hadn't made it through customs.

Instead, I picked up the hoodie, snuck a quiet sniff, and quickly said, "Thanks."

"Oh," Dom had turned back to me, "I guess before we move on, Iz, this is Max, your new boss. Max, my sister, Isabella."

I pulled the oversized hoodie further down, making a half-baked attempt to shield myself. Not only did it give me an extra moment to channel my inner Zen, but it also allowed for one more deep inhale of his intoxicating firewood scent. As I peered out, it hit me. Max was the living embodi-ment of every "Too-Hot-to-Be-Real" meme I'd ever shared. Naturally, my new boss had to be a model-esque heartthrob with probable delusions of Hollywood grandeur. I'd known the staff would be young, but no one warned me about navi-gating a sea of under-thirties looking like they'd leaped out of a cologne ad.

I set my face in a small smile as I said, "Hey, hi, hello." Every laugh line I'd recently noticed forming around my eyes waved hello too.

Max had picked up a wineglass and was buffing it with one of those lint-free towels whose texture gave me the heebie-jeebies. But his eyes were locked on mine, and the corner of his mouth was turned up slightly like he could read my inner panic. Because, of course, guys who look like him know how they make women feel, with his dark hair swept back and smoothed down, and his stupid black t-shirt that was too tight across his arms.

I pulled my eyes away and turned to my brother. "Are you going to show me around this brothel or what?"

"Iz," Dominic said as he rolled his eyes and started walking, "it's not a brothel. Whatever, come on."

Dominic walked me around the entire bottom floor of the Prism Society and pointed out various areas where members could sit and enjoy drinks so I could get an idea of my section. There were cozy nooks scattered throughout the entire first floor. Pairs of small cream, fuzzy-looking chairs swiveled in toward each other in the main lobby, curved high-back velvet booths lined two walls, and of course, high-top chairs ran the length of the entire bar.

I heard the pride in his tone as he walked me through the spaces, and even though I felt like a soggy newspaper thrown out on someone's lawn, I couldn't help the big grin that spread across my face. My brother had always been the one to slide into a situation, totally unequipped, only to massively succeed. Dom was the kind of person who would quietly watch how others went about their lives. He seemed to take notes on what to do better so that by the time it was his turn, he was immediately the best at it.

This trait annoyed me. It was something, as the oldest, I didn't get the luxury of doing. I was the kind of person to dive in headfirst and figure it out on the way down. While that personality worked in my early twenties, it was time for me to get some clarity. I craved the sureness Dominic had about where his life was heading. It definitely didn't seem like he tossed and turned every night, pondering all the missed opportunities and what-ifs.

I browsed the second floor with Dominic, my gaze darting curiously around. This was the Prism Society's inner sanctum, where members sought full-service sexual exploration.

"Jules is in charge up here," Dominic pointed out, indicating the bubbly woman with bright blue hair seated at the reception. A sign reading "reservations only" was prominently displayed.

I greeted Jules with a polite nod, noting the oxblood-painted doors behind her. I remembered Dominic mentioning them—the private rooms with ever-changing access codes. I could only imagine the activities they shielded.

Growing up, discussions about sexuality were commonplace in our household. However, hearing about Dominic's venture with Liam differed from actually being here, experiencing the ambiance and the hidden promises it held. We headed up to the third and final floor.

On the top level were the private offices for Dominic and Liam and a wide-open, skylight-lit room. Well, it would be on a day that didn't look like Dementors were about to fly down through the rain-pelted sky. I recalled Dominic mentioning a recent workshop—something about Sensual Food Play. I shuddered at the thought of misused sushi rolls.

Back on the main floor, Dominic showed me to my designated office, where I would be sharing a space with Max, Maureen, and Jules. I noted Maureen's age and wondered about her story. Maybe I could strike up a friendship with

Maureen, the sixty-something my brother hired for his front desk support. Apparently, she had been looking for something to spice up her life in retirement. I wonder what she thought about all the activities that took place behind my spot in front of the heavy velvet curtains.

"She's full of surprises," Dominic remarked, seemingly reading my mind.

It struck me that my own presence might be out of place here. Yet, what were my alternatives? My resume was certainly . . . unconventional.

Shaking my head, I was pulled back to a memory of Nikos. Our whirlwind romance centered around travel and adventure. But he'd chosen a different path, one that didn't include me. The breakup had been unexpected and had hit me like a ton of bricks. There were things Nikos had said about me during his long speech as to why we wouldn't work that still sat, sour, in my belly.

Dominic's voice interrupted my reflections. "You okay, Iz?"

I met his gaze, forcing a smile. "Just taking it all in. It's . . . different." My voice carried a touch of loneliness, betraying my feelings of being adrift amidst so many choices.

A brief silence settled between us, the weight of unsaid things hovering. The ambient sounds of the Prism Society filled the void—soft music coming from the speakers, distant chatter of other staff members showing up, and the clink of glasses as Max stocked the bar.

"All right, Iz," Dom broke the quiet, his voice more business-like now, "I got you set up in the system, so you should be able to clock in." As he slid on his coat, he added, "Be back here tomorrow, but closer to two so Max can walk you through everything."

"Where are you going?" I blurted, feeling a pang of abandonment. The idea of navigating the unfamiliar space without Dominic was daunting, and I wasn't ready to leave the comfort of my current surroundings.

"I have dinner plans," he said, shrugging his shoulders like it was no big deal.

"Dinner? But I just got here. I thought we could catch up or something." My voice came out more desperate than I had intended. How desperate would I really be if I practically had to beg my little brother to hang out with me? It had always been like this with them. Even as his sister, I never got past the surface level of Dom. Either because he didn't trust to share it with anyone, or he didn't trust to share it with me.

"Sorry, Iz, I'll see you tomorrow, though." Dominic turned, lifted his arm in a wave, parted the heavy velvet curtains, and let them sway shut behind him.

"Asshole," I said under my breath, but it still brought out a chuckle from behind me.

I turned on my heel to face Max. All I wanted at this point was to get out of this damp dress, out of my waterlogged heels, and into the warmth of sweats and a bed with a glass of red wine. But I had none of those things. Well, my sweats were buried in some suitcase, waiting to be unearthed. The bed was one of my parents' guestrooms, but the wine could be plucked from my parents' cellar. One out of three wasn't bad.

"You look like you could use a drink." Max sat an empty wineglass he'd buffed on the marble bar top.

"Do I look that haggard?" I hoped he didn't answer honestly.

"I don't think you could look haggard if you tried. Just . . . maybe lonely." When I looked up at him, his eyes were soft, not condescending.

"I think I'm still jet-lagged," I said as I walked over to the bar, pulled out a stool, and slid in.

"If this is what you look like jet-lagged, I can't wait to see you refreshed." Max grinned as he pulled a bottle off the rack and worked the cork. My eyes followed how his arm flexed as he held the bottle in one hand and twisted with the other.

"Is this how you get women to order more drinks?" I watched as a deep red wine filled the glass in front of me.

He shrugged. "The club has a two-drink limit." He placed a stopper in the bottle and said, "Besides, the women who come to this bar aren't here for my attention, so I don't need to flirt with them."

"But you are flirting? Right now?" I reached for the wineglass and slid it across the counter. I swirled the inky liquid and took a deep inhale. Tobacco, chocolate, and spices. This was a good red.

"If I were flirting right now," his eyes scanned down the front of me as he said, "I'd tell you I can't wait to get my sweatshirt back so I can see what rubbing against your chest smells like and that I'm not going to look away as you slip it off because I know it's still cold in here."

My eyes flew open wide, and my face warmed from the

first sip of the red wine and Max's comments. My tongue reached out to taste the wine on my lips, and Max's eyes followed the movement. Jesus.

"Is this how you talk to all of your employees?" I asked.

He grinned. "Just when I feel like they're stuck in their head too much."

I stared into my wineglass as I twirled the stem between my fingers. Apparently, my identity crisis had been clearly playing out all over my face.

"So," I cleared my throat and sat up straighter, "how does someone like you end up working at a place like this?"

"Now that sounds like a cheesy pickup line." Max had gone back to polishing glasses, and I wondered how someone's hands could be so big.

I chuckled. "I'm serious. This place"—I looked around the lounge—"is unique. Why here?"

"Well, I'm working through my sommelier certification and needed a bit of a less chaotic place to work so I could focus on studying but still make good money. I've known your brother for years, so when I heard about this place, I reached out."

"Why haven't we met before?" I asked, curious about the fact that he seemed to be so close to my brother.

"I think you were somewhere between Portugal and Rome when I was graduating high school with Dom, so we wouldn't have really run into each other," Max said.

I groaned into my glass. "And *that* makes me feel ancient." I rolled my eyes and tipped my glass to drain the last sip.

"Sorry, but seven years older does not put you into the ancient category," Max said as he headed toward the end of the bar. "Come on, I'll show you where you can store your stuff."

Behind the bar was a hidden door painted the same deep emerald as the lounge, with molding to match. A small seam gave it away when Max pushed against it. Through the door was a small hallway with a set of lockers and three doors.

Max pointed to each locker as he said, "You can snag one of those lockers to keep your things in. This room is where we keep the extra towels and bar stuff. That's the bathroom, and here's the office."

He led me to the last door, the office, and bumped open the door with his hip. Inside was *tiny*. A desk along the right side held a small computer and a shit ton of paperwork. They'd somehow fit a small couch, a tall filing cabinet, and a lamp on the opposite wall. Hanging on the walls were various posters and signs for compliance and Max's sommelier certificates. My eyes skirted over them. He'd made it to Certified Sommelier, and, by the looks of the textbooks on the desk, he was actively studying for his Advanced exam.

I knew, from chatting up with plenty of sommeliers while I was in France, that making it to the Advanced and then Master level was *hard*. Max might be the youngest one to do it.

"Since Dominic got you in the system earlier, you should just be able to clock in yourself tomorrow. I'll pull it up and show you how it works." Max sat down in the soft leather chair and opened up a few screens on the computer to show me the basics. I resisted the distraction of how good his arms looked in his black t-shirt and how I could smell his shampoo being this close to him from my spot on the edge of the desk.

"Most of your training, really," Max said as he swiveled in his chair, "comes down to being comfortable with two things."

I leaned back a bit, wanting to give Max some space, and looked down at Max as he held a finger up.

"One, the drink menu." Max continued to hold up a finger as he talked. "I'll send you home with packets about the wine and our cocktails so you can familiarize yourself with everything. Our members have *big* wallets, so sometimes they like to be fancy with what they order. But remember, if anyone has a reservation upstairs, they have an automatic two-drink limit."

"Two-drink limit. Got it." I hoped the limit wouldn't impact my tips, but I was crossing my fingers for this rich clientele to tip generously no matter what.

It's not like I necessarily *needed* the money, I still had my inheritance, but I had been getting this strong urge to make something on my own. I didn't know what yet, but the fact that I'd been handed everything in my life wasn't good for my confidence. I was ready to prove I could make something for myself, even if I had no clue what that was supposed to be yet.

Max put up a second finger. "And two, the open sexuality of this club." I stopped my daydreaming, and my eyes flicked over to Max. He grinned lazily. "If you were that uncomfortable seeing me without my shirt on out there, just wait until you walk through your section and notice one of our members getting finger banged under the table."

Max nodded in silent confirmation to my raised eyebrows and wide eyes. "Or when you go to make your rounds to check the upstairs lounge area and see some guy getting his dick sucked."

My cheeks warmed. "I thought all that stuff happened once people made a reservation inside the private rooms? Those things just *go on* out there?" I asked.

"The general agreed-upon rule is there is no actual intercourse out in the semi-private spaces, but our members are welcome to warm up however they like, wherever they like." Max shrugged like he was used to it by now.

"And the lounge upstairs is in my section too? I thought I would just stick to the main lounge." I wasn't a prude by any means. I'd skinny-dipped with strangers in the Baltic Sea. I'd even given a blow job in a train bathroom on my way to Milan. But this was work. Would it feel different to be constantly exposed to such proclivity?

"You won't serve in the traditional sense upstairs." Max dug through the pile of paperwork.

"There are semi-private lounges that members can use while they wait for their private room to be ready. We like to stock each lounge with sparkling water, glasses, and light snacks." He handed me a binder full of sheets from the menu with long descriptions. Apparently, this was my homework. "So it'll be up to you to make sure the lounges are turned over. Jules will give you the reservation sheet at the start of your shift each night so you know when you'll need to be up there."

"Okay, so memorize the drink menu, and don't freak out about the foreplay, got it." I held the binder to my chest.

Max smiled up at me. "See?" He tapped my knee with his knuckles. "You're gonna do great."

I hadn't meant to jerk off to the memory of Dominic's sister's hard nipples, but nevertheless, it had happened. I'd gotten one look at Isabella standing like a literal wet dream, chest heaving in her sheer dress, and knew I'd be filing the material for later. Isabella was one of those girls whom other people liked to watch. Not just because she was beautiful, but because she was interesting. I'd only met her once before, well, in person, and now seeing her in my domain did something to my insides.

God, I needed to get laid. And as much as it hurt my heart, and my dick, to say, it shouldn't be my friend's sister who breaks my dry spell.

It had officially been 117 days since I'd gotten laid. It had been 117 days since my ex, Ana, had decided dating a bartender wouldn't work for her long-term. We'd been lying in bed at my apartment after having some pretty solid shower sex when she'd broken up with me. Who breaks up with someone less than twenty minutes after they come inside you?

"I guess I didn't really think the sommelier thing was going to last this long," she had said. "I thought you'd have gotten a real job by now." She was lying in between my sheets, her long hair wet on the pillows.

My hand had stopped making small circles on her shoulder, and my breath caught in my throat. Every word felt like a punch. "It's a real job, Ana," I had responded, trying to keep the defensiveness out of my voice.

I recalled the pride I felt when I had landed the position at the Prism Society. Dominic hadn't even hesitated before bringing me on board when I offhandedly mentioned it one night when we were grabbing dinner. His offer had saved me from having to do another shift at Corkbuzz. The experience I was getting in that upscale wine bar was good, but if I had to watch one more person do a line of coke off the stainless steel kitchen table, I would have lost my mind.

Ana sat up, clutching the sheet to her chest. "You promised nights together. Instead, I lie for you to my family. Hide where you really work. It's like *I'm* the only one making sacrifices."

That was a thing that Ana did. It'd been a point of contention in our relationship on more than one occasion. She cared a lot about how she presented herself to the world and, therefore, what others took away from that presentation. And if I wasn't adding to the well-curated version of her life, then I was out.

"You told me you didn't have a problem with me

working at the Prism Society. You were even at the charity event with me last summer." I slid out of bed and pulled on some sweats. My skin was still hot from the shower, and I felt heated to my core.

"And I fully support sex positivity! You just *give* your money to those causes, Max. You don't actually *work* there." Ana looked at me like I was stupid for not getting it. This is what people like Ana did. When you're the daughter of an investment banker and successful PR agent, you know how important your image can be to people. It wasn't solely her fault. She'd grown up with parents who were masters at the art of spin.

I glanced down at my old worn-out sneakers, peeking from under the bed, the blue plaid sheets my mom had picked up for me at a big box store, the Ikea lamp standing in the corner—all were a silent testament to the two worlds I straddled. In one, I was the "Fancy Boy" as my sisters liked to call me, the one who had outgrown my modest upbringing. In the other, I was blue-collar Max, the enigma these people had let into their world, but who clearly didn't fit in. A luxurious world where even my dreams felt second-rate.

My voice was thick with emotion. "I've been working there for a *year*, Ana. Pushing myself for this certification, and you thought I'd just . . . quit?"

She sighed, the bedsheet still wrapped around her. "I thought you'd see it wasn't for you. Maybe join my dad in finance or something stable." Her voice was getting shrill in the way it does when she's trying to plead her case.

But there it was. The expectation. The same one that

made my sisters call me Fancy Boy and had my mom raise eyebrows at my choice of workplace. But Ana and her circle? To them, I was always playing catch up. No trust fund, no ritzy holiday homes, just ambition and dreams, and a lot of crossing my fingers, hoping it would all work out.

I caught sight of the cheap, store-bought wine rack, a gift from my mom, standing proudly amidst my collection of expensive wines. A symbol of the balancing act I performed daily between two worlds. What Ana didn't fully realize is that training to be an Advanced Sommelier felt stable to me. I was raised by a schoolteacher and transit manager and lived in a small house with five other people. Living in my own apartment, by myself, in Queens felt like I'd won the lottery.

This was the line I walked on a daily basis. My sisters called me Fancy Boy because of whom I hung out with, and my mom definitely didn't understand the club environment I worked in. But with Ana, my friends, and even Dominic, I always felt like I fell short. I didn't have a trust fund or a vacation home. I didn't use a car service or get my suits custom-tailored.

But I wasn't embarrassed by my dream. I worked my ass off to get as far as I'd gotten. The pass rate of the next phase of my sommelier certification was only 25 percent, so I was already half expecting to fail anyway. But isn't that the beauty of relationships? You choose to have someone around who supports you even when the odds are stacked against you, even when it feels ridiculous to have the dream and even more ridiculous to think you'll achieve it.

I whispered, more to himself than to Ana, "I thought

love was about supporting each other's dreams, not waiting for them to give it up." I ran my hands down my face as I let my eyes take in Ana in a whole new light. Her face relaxed and her eyes squinted, revealing she thought I was about to give in. Disagree and commit. Isn't that what all the relationship coaches tell you to do?

With a deep sigh, I said what needed to be said. "I'm not ready to give up on this dream. And, honestly, if I did, I don't think I would give it up for you." I started picking up her scattered clothes around the room and tossing them all in a bag.

Her mouth fell open as she watched me buzz around the room. She shook her head as if pushing out what I'd said from her memory. She sat up and walked on her knees over to the edge of the bed, letting the sheet fall to the bed. Ana cleared her throat and when she spoke, gone was the shrill tone, and in its place was what I knew to be Ana trying to use sex to get her way.

"Baby, I don't need to leave now. I can pack my things up over the next few days." Her skin was still pink from the hot shower, and her nipples hardened from the exposed air. Water droplets from her hair trickled down between her breasts.

She placed her hands on my bare chest and looked up at me with what I called her "Blow Job Eyes." She'd make this face whenever she knew she'd made a mistake. Instead of saying sorry, she'd get on her knees. Now that I think of it, I've *never* heard her own up to a mistake. Ana gave *a lot* of blow jobs.

And my treacherous dick knew it. As Ana ran her hands down my sides, it sprang to attention in my pants. She slipped her hand under the waistband of my sweats and gripped me, slowly pumping me back to life.

Even if Ana and I hadn't had the perfect or most supportive relationship, we had always been good at this. We could always come back together after a fight or misunderstanding and work out the details as our bodies entangled. It was our love language. And it seemed like it was our way of saying goodbye also.

And so, even though I'd be sleeping on the couch tonight and making Ana leave in the morning, I let her drag my pants down to the floor. I let her put her warm mouth on the head of my cock. And she let me grip her hair a little tighter than usual as I reached for her head and fucked her face. We both knew this would be the last time.

And that moment, when I had come down Ana's throat, was the last time I'd had sex. So it shouldn't have surprised me that tonight, standing in the shower after seeing Isabella in person for the first time in five years made me grip my own cock and come at the thought of putting those nipples in my mouth.

But I will get it out of my system tonight. Isabella and I had training together tomorrow, followed by her first shift, and then shifts together every Tuesday–Saturday night. I would need to get myself together if I expected to work in such a sexually charged environment with her. I didn't know Isabella's type, but it certainly wasn't a bartender or wannabe sommelier who couldn't figure out how to get laid in the last three months.

Not that I should be worried *at all* about what kind of men Isabella loved.

Not that someone like Isabella would even spare me a second glance. As if aware of the energy she brought to a room, she had a quiet confidence that didn't require her to be loud or critique other people's dreams. And even though I had spotted a little bit of a lost look in her eyes, I didn't expect it to last long. Isabella had always been someone who was able to get exactly what she wanted.

So when I needed to, I would take it out on my cock, but at work, I would remain focused. There was no way I was going to let another little rich girl back into my world.

As I strode into the Prism Society the next day, earlier than usual, I deliberately pushed all thoughts of Isabella to the recesses of my mind. There were more pressing matters to attend to, like the special wine shipment I was expecting that morning for a high-end client.

I checked my watch, the minute hand ticking away anxiously. The shipment was late, which was odd given the punctuality of the supplier. I waited another twenty minutes before making a call, only to be informed that due to unforeseen circumstances, the delivery wouldn't be coming in at all.

I felt a mix of frustration and panic. I had a special tasting this evening for one of our most discerning clients, and the wines selected were specific to their palate. I quickly texted Dom an update on the situation.

I then spent the next couple of hours on the phone, calling up different retailers to replenish the stock, scribbling notes, and trying to find a brand-new partner for wine and liquor.

My fingers drummed nervously on the bar's polished surface. I ran through a mental list of available suppliers, but the odds of finding the exact high-end wine I needed in such a short amount of time seemed slim. This wasn't just any client—these were influential figures in the art community, connoisseurs who had the kind of pull that could either elevate the Prism Society's reputation or dent it significantly.

I felt the weight of the evening's responsibility on my shoulders. One misstep could set the club back in terms of reputation and future collaborations. I took a deep breath and tried another number.

"Hey, Gerald. It's Max from the Prism Society. I know it's short notice, but I need . . ."

Each call resulted in the same response: apologies, explanations, but ultimately, no wine. As the clock ticked, my anxiety multiplied. I felt cornered. For all my connections and knowledge, I was drawing a blank on how to pull this off.

I closed my eyes momentarily, trying to collect my thoughts. I remembered an old contact who'd once mentioned a private collection of rare wines. It was a long shot, but at this point, any shot was worth taking.

After another round of calls leading to more dead ends,

beads of perspiration formed on my brow. The atmospheric lighting of the bar seemed suddenly oppressive, the weight of the evening's expectations bearing down on me. With a frustrated sigh, I removed my tie, then unbuttoned my shirt, shedding it along with my tight undershirt so I didn't get them dusty. Maybe, just maybe, there might be something in our own collection I had overlooked.

I glanced upward. The Prism Society had a few high-end bottles tucked away on the higher shelves, reserved for special occasions or specific clientele. Climbing the ladder might be symbolic, I mused, of the uphill battle I was currently facing.

With a deep breath, I began to ascend, hoping against hope I'd find a bottle, or even a combination of bottles, that would save the evening.

FOUR
ISABELLA

The next morning, with the clarity only a good sleep can bring, I likened my attraction to Max to my urge to touch wet paint—tempting, but certainly not wise.

No matter how soft his eyes looked when he talked to me or how his forearm seemed to call me to trace it, Max was a temptation I had to resist.

A new city, a new job, and a new Izzy.

One who was strong, independent, and not swayed by handsome bartenders who smelled like woodsmoke and dreams.

I was here for a fresh start.

Besides, I had decided at the last brunch I attended with three of my girlfriends, all now engaged, settling down wasn't for me.

Especially after Nikos.

As I stood in the space that had once been my childhood

bedroom, the silence around me was a stark contrast to the bustling life I had known. The truth was, I had always been a free spirit, a seeker of the next thrill, the next story to tell. I was the epitome of adventure, my heart pumping for new experiences and new people, especially if that new person brought along the promise of excitement. Yet deep down, I realized the adrenaline rush was a temporary fix, not the foundation of a life shared with someone I could truly call a partner.

I had always been the protagonist in my own romantic saga, weaving in and out of whirlwind escapades that promised the rush of love at first sight. Yet, the idea of love as an enduring presence, a steady flame rather than a firework, was something I'd not truly entertained. My rendezvous across the globe had been chapters of excitement, not lifelong commitments. And Nikos, with his dreams of a family life abroad, had been yet another adventure I was almost ready to embark upon.

But the quiet confession in Nikos's farewell had struck a chord. I realized it wasn't about missing him or our could-have-been life. It was about finding myself. The realization dawned that I didn't need to be swept off my feet. I needed to land. To settle not for less, but for real—for the real me to emerge and decide what my next chapter would be, for myself and no one else. I was not looking for Prince Charming. I was searching for my place in the world. The adventure would always call me, but now I sought an adventure that could lead to a homecoming, to a place and a person where my heart could finally rest.

Promises to myself now took a different shape: no more mistaking excitement for depth; no more conflating fleeting passion with enduring affection. The brush of fingers, once electrifying, now spoke of momentary pleasure, not lifelong companionship

When the conversation I had long evaded surfaced, the truth in his words was undeniable. *"Settling down isn't you, Iz,"* he'd said, not with malice but with a clarity I had shielded myself from. *"We both knew where this was headed from day one; we just let it go on a little longer than we should have."*

He was right. Not because I feared commitment but because my spirit hadn't yet found the peace needed to commit. Nikos had seen the horizon of our ending before I had, not because our love was flawed, but because our paths were always meant to diverge. His vision of the future was clear, and mine—a mosaic of experiences—was still arranging itself into a picture I could call home.

Luckily the skies outside had also cleared, and as I stepped out onto the sidewalk and slid into the waiting town car, I felt confident in my refined direction. The sun was shining, my black satin button-up didn't forecast my nipples to the world, and I was actually excited about my new job.

My confidence quickly shifted to annoyance as I took in, what was apparently going to be a routine sighting, Max high on the bar ladder, his back muscles flexing as he reached above him. Max wasn't thick and buff like someone who lived at the gym, but he *was* fit. It looked like he was the type of person who enjoyed going for a hike or a run but also enjoyed saying yes to takeout and dessert. He had the body of a man who didn't make you feel insecure about yourself. But these were details I did not need to be noticing.

"Why do you not have a shirt on?" were the first words out of my mouth.

"Hi, good morning." Max's face did this stupid lopsided grin making one single dimple pop up on his cheek.

"It's not morning." I slid my phone out of the side pocket of my bag—I'd given my Celine time to dry out and had switched to my black Prada—and tapped the screen. "It's 1:53 in the afternoon."

"It's the first time I've seen you today, and it feels weird to tell you good afternoon when I haven't gotten to tell you good morning." Max sat the wine bottle on the bar top and then turned to grip the ladder to make another journey up to the top.

"What are you doing anyways?" I had to ask the question to justify why I stayed rooted to my spot, eyes cascading up as Max climbed the rungs. God, his ass looked good in those pants.

"I was expecting a shipment today for a private tasting I'm doing tonight but it never showed. I wondered if the Château Margaux would be a good substitute for what I had originally planned," Max said as he reached the top.

"But I also wonder if I should go with the Château Cheval Blanc." He seemed to be speaking to himself at this point.

Max twisted and reached for another bottle from the very top. "Or perhaps the Romanée-Conti." He examined the bottle and brought both down to the bar top before turning and heading right back up the ladder. "Or I could go with the Penfolds Grange from Barossa or the Screaming Eagle Cabernet Sauvignon from Napa."

I could spot the panic in his eyes all the way from down here. Even if I had to trail my eyes past his wide chest first. "Okay," I said as I sat my bag down on the counter loud enough to zap him out of his panicked trance. "What would help you make your decision?"

"Honestly, the best way to decide is to sample them." Max glanced over to a high-tech device sitting on the corner of the bar. "I've got a Coravin here. It lets us pour wine without removing the cork, preserving the rest of the bottle."

I raised an eyebrow. "Fancy. Will it affect the taste?"

Max chuckled. "Trust the process. It'll be just as if we uncorked them."

He carefully picked up each bottle and wiped away the dust, revealing the glistening glass beneath. "You know, most people buy these bottles for the name and to showcase them in their homes. Few actually drink them."

"You're awfully chatty when you're nervous," I remarked, my tone teasing.

Max flashed his lopsided grin again. "And you're still ogling me." He reached down and pulled on his undershirt that was draped over a nearby chair. "Better?"

I pretended to ponder. "Marginally."

With that, Max began the sampling process. My gaze was drawn to the muscles in his hands and forearms as he fixed the Coravin atop the first bottle, the Château Margaux. He pressed the device down, and a thin stream of wine poured into one of the glasses.

As he moved on to each bottle, he offered a tidbit of information. "Château Cheval Blanc is known for its elegance—a perfect blend of Cabernet Franc and Merlot. The Domaine de la Romanée-Conti? It's one of the best Pinot Noirs in the world. It embodies the essence of Burgundy."

Pouring from the Penfolds Grange bottle, he continued, "Australia's pride. A rich and powerful wine that speaks volumes of the Barossa Valley."

Lastly, as he poured the Screaming Eagle Cabernet Sauvignon, he added with a note of respect in his voice, "A cult classic. If you're looking for the pinnacle of what Napa Valley can produce, this is it."

I swirled the first wine in my glass, admiring its deep crimson hue and inhaling its complex bouquet. "Well, let's find your replacement, Wine Guru."

I couldn't stop the moan that escaped my mouth if I had been promised a million dollars to *not* do it. The taste of the wine on my tongue melted me. I closed my eyes and held the flavor in my mouth to savor it.

"It's okay if you swallow," Max said from the other side of the bar. My eyes flew open as a blush crept up my cheeks at the tone of his voice. He was leaning against the back of the bar, wineglass swirling in his hand and a smirk on his face.

"I'm almost scared to try the others," I said. "That one is *so* good."

"I'm glad you like it." Max smiled. "For this next one,

close your eyes. Swirl the glass and smell the wine before you taste it."

I nodded, an obedient student. Max slid a glass over to me and our fingertips grazed as I reached for the stem. I closed my eyes as I felt the brush of his thumb against my pinky. I lightly swirled the glass and lifted it to my nose to absorb the aroma.

When I closed my eyes and swirled the Château Margaux, I was immediately enveloped in a complex bouquet. The predominant scent was that of ripe blackberries and cherries intertwined with subtle undertones of violets. As I continued to inhale, layers of cedar, tobacco, and a hint of graphite came forward, rounded out by a whisper of vanilla from the oak aging.

It made me feel warm and relaxed, and I melted into my seat. Max's voice was low and calm from across the bar. He leaned in toward me, watching my every reaction. "Now," he said, his voice slow and steady, "tilt the glass back just a little. I want just the tip of your tongue to get the first taste."

My heart was pounding in my chest as I lifted the rim of the glass to my lips. The cool edge pressed against my bottom lip as I tipped it up. The warm liquid hit the tip of my tongue, and I could detect the fruit and woodsy flavors.

"Now," Max continued, his voice taking on a suggestive lilt, "let the wine flow across your palate. Roll it around, letting it touch all parts of your mouth."

I followed his instructions, allowing the wine to dance over my tongue, tasting the subtleties in every corner of my mouth.

"Breathe in gently with your mouth open. It helps to aerate the wine, letting you experience the deeper flavors and undertones," Max instructed. I did as he said, inhaling softly, which intensified the taste and brought out more nuanced flavors.

I opened my eyes to find Max observing me intently, a teasing smirk on his lips. "Good, now swallow. And after you do, press your tongue to the roof of your mouth. You'll get the wine's full finish that way."

As I did, I caught hints of dark chocolate and soft spice, finishing with a gentle tannic grip that lingered delightfully. The wine was truly exquisite.

Max leaned forward, placing his elbows on the bar, his face inches from mine. "And? How was it?"

"It was . . . intense," I admitted, my voice huskier than I intended. The close proximity and the intimate lesson were clearly affecting me.

Movement caught my attention from the corner of my eye, and I sat up straight at the edge of the bar. Dominic walked through the lobby and stood at the end of the bar.

The silence following Dominic's entrance was heavy, filled with the unspoken tension that always seemed to buzz around forbidden things. His gaze was locked onto Max and me, an unreadable expression etched across his face. Max's smile faltered, the closeness of our laughter-filled moment now a stark contrast to the stiffness that replaced it.

Dominic's voice broke through the stillness, his words carrying a weight that anchored me back to reality. "You guys know you shouldn't fuck, right?" His words weren't harsh but were tinged with the concern of crossing invisible lines.

"Jesus Christ, Dom!" The protest erupted from me before I could temper it, while Max managed a strangled cough, the sound a perfect echo of the awkwardness now hanging between us.

Dom raised his hands defensively, a clear sign he wanted to ease the tension he'd inadvertently caused. "I'm just saying. This place . . . it can mess with your head, and I don't want to see you guys getting hurt or making things weird for everyone else. So please, just don't go there."

My heart pounded a rhythm of panic and denial. "Oh my god, Dom. He's your age, for heaven's sake. I'm not going to fuck him." The words, meant to sound decisive, came out more like a plea, even to my own ears.

A look passed between the three of us, a silent acknowledgment of the complicated dynamics at play. We lingered in that awkward space, the air thick with the things left unsaid, each of us processing the unexpected interruption to the afternoon's flow.

Trying to break the tense moment, Max cleared his throat and motioned toward the boxes of wine he had selected for the evening. "I'll start setting up," he said, his voice steady but tinged with the effort of regaining composure. "We've got a big night ahead of us." Max busied himself with the wine again, a futile attempt to smother the tension. I could sense the change in his demeanor, the ease we shared moments ago now replaced by a careful distance.

I nodded, my earlier defiance slowly crumbling into

contemplation. Was I really as transparent as Dom suggested? With a deep breath, I pushed off the bar and turned my attention to the task at hand, the preparation for the evening's tasting event—a convenient distraction from the complexities of what lay unspoken between us. It was clear now that whatever was unfolding couldn't be contained within the walls of the Prism Society, nor could it be as easily dismissed as I had hoped.

FIVE

MAX

"*O*bviously, *I'm* not *going to fuck him.*"

The words Isabella had said earlier played on repeat in my mind as I watched her work. Even as Isabella's eyes found mine from across the lounge as my eyes scanned the room. Even as she caught me checking her ass out as she bent behind the bar to grab a new tray.

It's not like I expected Isabella to *actually* fuck me, but the finality in the way she'd delivered that fact to Dominic when he awkwardly caught us in a *moment* was enough to bruise my ego. But I knew I shouldn't let it get to my head. This was a *good* thing. My upstairs *and* downstairs brain needed to get the picture that she was off-limits.

Women like Isabella were expected to make all the right moves in life. The right career, the right partner, the right private school for their children, and the right luxury New York City property to raise them in. None of that could come together if they looked too far outside their circles.

But there's something about the way that I felt like Isabella did things differently. Or at least *wanted* to.

Isabella, the trust fund baby of a world-renowned sex therapist, author, and speaker. And that was just her mother. Her father came from a long line of money from his own family, so together, they were a multimillion-dollar powerhouse of a family. I couldn't let myself be convinced that Isabella liked taking in strays as much as her brother did.

I should at least be thankful that, unlike Ana, Isabella wouldn't string me along for two years waiting for me to turn into something I wasn't. She set the precedent early, and that, at least, deserved some respect.

I knew befriending the rich kid at summer camp would open me up to a world I'd never experienced before. But I hadn't anticipated I'd feel like such an outcast even all these years later. Dominic and I had known each other since we were fourteen. We'd been randomly assigned bunkmates in a cabin at a camp for boys.

My parents sent me there because there was no one else to watch me during the summer while my parents worked. I wasn't sure why Dom's parents sent him there, but I was grateful. With Dom's menacing glare, quiet attitude, and "don't fuck with me" face, no one messed with him—or me —all summer.

For some reason, Dominic had kept inviting me to things even after summer camp had wrapped. It took me a while to fully let it sink in that me and Dom were actually friends. That in a city where class was clearly divided throughout the boroughs, this teenage boy didn't care. Dom hadn't cared that my dad had to pick up night shifts to be able to afford my soccer uniforms or that my parents only had the one home where me and my three sisters grew up.

By the time I had met Dom, Isabella had already moved out. At that point, she was probably somewhere between Barcelona and Lisbon, and it would be a long while before I'd meet her in person. She'd swept into town to celebrate her mom's birthday, and there was so much energy around her that I got sucked in. I'd watched her from the sidelines as Dominic and I prepped the pool, and Isabella had helped the florists place their centerpieces on the outdoor tables. She'd been wearing a dark red summer dress dotted with tiny white and yellow flowers. Her feet were bare, and an ankle bracelet with dangling golden butterflies glistened in the sun on her tan skin.

But even though the memory had aged over time, I remembered how I felt when I first laid eyes on her, listened to her speak, and heard her laugh.

To say I'd been instantly infatuated was an understatement. But I knew the bro code, and I held strong and fast to those rules for fear of losing the friendship and connections Dom brought me. A poor kid from Brooklyn didn't grow up to be a Master Sommelier without the influence of the wealthy.

It didn't matter if her brown eyes twinkled in the chandelier light or her face heated when I'd told her about some of the member activities that went on in the lounge areas. It didn't matter that I'd like her on her knees in front of me doing some of those activities.

When I'd seen her for the first time after all these years, that same electric feeling zapped through my belly. I hadn't been able to keep my eyes off her then, and I couldn't figure out how to do it now either. It didn't help that Isabella was somehow even *more* attractive now than she was back then.

Even back when I'd barely known her, there was a pull, an intrigue about Isabella that caught my attention. But time, the sun, and life experiences had shaped Isabella into someone I really wanted to get to know now.

"Hey." Isabella's voice brought me back from wherever my mind and dick had traveled off to. "I think your private-tasting clients are here. Do you need anything?"

"Yeah, you," I said.

Isabella turned to face me. "What?"

"I mean, I could use your help. With them. Just switching out glasses and making sure they're all topped up while I explain things. I set up a tasting station over there in the corner at the high-top marble table." I pointed over to a round table set back in a small alcove.

"Oh, yeah, of course, whatever you need," Isabella said. "I'll bring them over."

I watched as she walked away and greeted the two couples who were here for the tasting, guiding them over to the table.

"Obviously, I'm not going to fuck him."

"Obviously, I'm not going to fuck him."

"Obviously, I'm not going to fuck him."

I repeated it like a mantra, mostly to keep my aching dick at bay.

I didn't need one of my best friend's sisters to know how badly I'd like to bend her over in that back office.

Or how badly I'd like to trace the fading tan lines I'd spotted on her shoulders.

I thought I had gotten Isabella out of my system this morning in the shower, but being around her at this club was stirring up weird feelings inside me. That's just what this place did to you.

A place Dominic and his friend Liam had created for sexual exploration and positivity. A place where it was expected that you, as the employee, keep your own turn-ons at bay even as members were in various states of pleasure all around me. At the end of the bar, a couple was making out. In a wide lounge chair angled slightly away from the bar sat another couple, and I saw a flash of upper thigh as the woman leaned forward. An older gentleman sitting between two women was getting a rubdown in a booth.

I grabbed a fresh bar towel and headed over to the table to greet my guests. My demeanor was a stark contrast to my relaxed, flirty self at the bar. Now, in front of the guests, I tried to exude confidence and control. My eyes, however, flicked toward Isabella, locking eyes with her for a split second before acknowledging the guests.

"Mr. and Mrs. DeLorenzo, Mr. and Mrs. Whitfield, welcome to the Prism Society," I greeted, extending a hand to each of the guests. Their hands were accepted with firm handshakes and nods of acknowledgment.

"Isabella will be assisting me this evening," I said with a note of finality as if expecting no objections. Izzy squared her shoulders, giving a polite nod to the two couples. The DeLorenzos, prominent figures in the art community, had a reputation for being exacting in their tastes. The Whitfields, though younger, were rising stars in the world of art curation.

As the couples settled around the marble-topped table, I directed my attention to Izzy. "Isabella," I began, my tone imperious yet not unkind, "please ensure each guest has a clean glass in front of them."

"Of course." Isabella swiftly moved to distribute the wineglasses, her movements precise and efficient. I watched her every move, nodding slightly when she was done. "Thank you. Now, the first wine we will be tasting this evening . . ."

I launched into an intricate description of the first wine, discussing its origin, the notes to anticipate, and the correct way to taste it. I felt Isabella's eyes on me as she observed me work.

At intervals, I would give Izzy commands, some overt and others more subtle. "Isabella, the decanter," or "A touch more for Mrs. Whitfield, please." Each time, she responded promptly, and I would show my approval with a small touch of my hand on her lower back. I didn't know what game we were playing, but I sure as hell loved it.

The evening flowed smoothly, with Izzy and me working seamlessly together. The couples seemed thoroughly engrossed in the experience, hanging on to my every word and frequently engaging Isabella with questions about the wines.

As the tasting concluded, I turned to Isabella, my voice

low so only she could hear. "You did well, Isabella," I murmured, my eyes intense.

Isabella smiled, a flush creeping up her cheeks. "Thank you," she whispered back.

Her wide eyes glancing down in shyness at my feet did something to me. For as strong and confident as the woman before me was, there was something inside her that seemed to be begging for direction. I wasn't sure how much longer I could hold onto my control around her.

SIX
ISABELLA

It had been a week and a half since I started working at the Prism Society, and each shift peeled back another layer of the city's nocturnal charisma. It was a different New York than the one bathed in sunlight, with its own rhythm and secrets—one I was becoming part of in ways I never expected.

However, if there was one skill I had perfected over my years as both a New Yorker and a globe-trotter, it was the uncanny ability to suss out the best hole-in-the-wall eateries. The grungier the façade, the more tantalizing the food.

That's why I found myself audibly groaning as I picked up the plastic sack, which was emitting a strong garlic smell, off the sidewalk in front of the side door at 3 a.m. After my first few shifts at the Prism Society, I had clocked out and headed home as the last member left. Max had never asked me to stay behind, and he seemed content to close down all by himself.

But as I lay in bed, night after night, still awake at four in the morning, I decided to try something different tonight. I was always starving when I got home and had pent-up energy from hustling around the club all night that I needed to get out of my system. Even busting out my yoga mat at 4:15 this morning hadn't helped put me to sleep.

So tonight, after a week and a half of leaving as soon as the lights came on, I was mixing it up. There's no way Max would turn down dinner that smelled this good. I heaped giant scoops of garlic chicken, sauteed vegetables, and rice on paper plates I'd found in the back office. I slipped off my wedges and carried the plates out into the lounge, where I expected to find Max.

As I rounded the corner, the melancholic chords of Something Corporate's "Konstantine" echoed through the lounge. Max was standing there, clipboard in one hand and a bottle of wine in the other, passionately belting out the lyrics with his eyes closed.

"It's to Jimmy Eat World and those nights in my car . . ."

Caught off guard, I snorted out a laugh, the plates wobbling dangerously in my hands.

Max's eyes snapped open, the bottle of wine almost slipping from his grasp as he twirled around. He wore a comically horrified expression as he caught sight of me, trying to catch his breath.

"Holy shit! I thought you left!" he exclaimed, clutching a hand to his chest.

I couldn't help but smirk. "Honestly, didn't think you'd

be the 'emo-kid-at-heart' type. Your scream-singing to Something Corporate was pretty spot-on."

He reddened slightly, trying to regain his composure. "It helps with the inventory checks. Sort of a stress release, you know? And, for your information, 'emo-kid-at-heart' happens to be a very accurate description. But I didn't expect *you* to know that song," Max replied.

"What, did you expect me to only know the music they play at Pacha?" I asked, eyebrows raised.

Max held his arms up in defense, a kitchen towel dangling from one hand, but said nothing.

Smirking, I held up the plates, the strong aroma filling the air. "I come bearing food from places with questionable exteriors and unparalleled culinary prowess. Care to join?" I asked.

His eyes lit up, looking grateful for the food, and Max nodded. "Hell, with a sales pitch like that, how could I refuse?"

"So," I started, as I gently blew on a steaming piece of garlic chicken, "I've been meaning to ask. Did you ever think you'd end up working at a sex club?"

Max chuckled as he scooped some food on his fork. "Definitely not. Mostly because what I had in my head as a 'sex club' was a whole heck of a lot dirtier than here."

"And stickier," I added.

A laugh, deep and infectious, came from Max and it made me smile. "Yes, definitely stickier. It was a bit of an adjustment at first, for sure. My mom and sisters really don't understand it. But once you hear the purpose of this place from your brother or Liam, something changes."

"Yeah, it's weird feeling *proud* of my brother for owning a sex club. But you're right . . . there's something different about this place," I said.

"They're wanting to expand, you know," Max said between a bite of chicken, "to other clubs."

I raised my eyebrows in question. "Really? Hmm. Okay, I have another question for you."

"Shoot, I'm all ears," Max said.

"Are you setting out to be the youngest Advanced Sommelier in the world?" I asked.

Max looked up at me as he leaned against the back of the bar with his plate in his hand. "Do you know much about the sommelier programs?"

I shrugged. "I've chatted with enough sommeliers all over Europe. I know it's crazy hard to do and there aren't that many young people who make it through the highest levels."

Something odd flickered in Max's eyes before he answered. "Yeah, it is crazy hard. I think there might be a young guy from Japan who made it to the Master level, but I'd be the next youngest for sure. But that test has a massive fail rate so who knows." He glanced down at his plate, mixing some rice in with the sauce.

"Well, maybe I can help you study, you know, like flash-cards or something," I said. "You did really well at the tasting last week. I don't think our guests would have guessed that you were panicking just a couple of hours before they got here."

"You were a big help with that, you know," Max said. "Your brother did say that the Whitfields specifically called to rave about it and asked if we were going to host more." He let out a huge breath.

"You seem overwhelmed," I commented.

"It's just a lot of details I'll need to work out on top of everything else. I have this idea of partnering with lesser-known growers across the globe." Max's face lit up as he spoke. "I know we have great ones in our vendor list already, but they're established and doing well. There are a lot of growers out there that haven't been discovered yet or been given a chance because they're so small. I want to introduce our guests who have *really* deep pockets to new sources."

I smiled. "You have a good heart, Max."

He shrugged. "I just know what it feels like for someone to take a chance on you, and I know how important it is to have someone believe in you. Especially when most people expect you to fail."

My eyes turned soft as they held Max's. There was something under the surface of this man I was itching to figure out.

"But doing that," Max continued, "means a lot more events that I just don't have the bandwidth to organize right now."

My face lit up. "Well . . . I *love* planning events! Can I help you? Let me help! We could do cute invitations. Oh, they could be designed like little tasting menus where people could pencil in their RSVP. Oh, and I can get some chocolates from this cute little dessert place over by my parents'. People could use it as a palate cleanser."

I was bursting with ideas for this event I hadn't even been invited to, let alone asked to help with, but Max was smiling when he said, "Yeah, of course, you can help. I'd really appreciate that."

"Sorry for the overzealousness." I bit my lip nervously, slightly embarrassed at my high energy around the event. "My parents used to have me be their little party planner whenever they'd have friends over. I'd make it into this huge ordeal with hand-drawn menus and invitations and I'd decorate the living room or set the dining room to match the theme." I found myself lost in thought at how my parents indulged me. "It was a lot of fun."

"Well, I could use all the help I could get, so please feel free to take over," Max said as he grabbed our empty plates and tossed them in the trash, pulling up the drawstrings of the bag to toss it. "I might know a thing or two about tannins and up-and-coming growers, but I know *nothing* about event planning.

"Events like these," Max said with a weary smile, "they need a personal touch, something to make them memorable. A theme that ties it all together."

I tapped a finger against my lips, already visualizing the possibilities. "How about a 'Journey through the Vines' theme? We could take our guests on a sensory trip to different vineyards with each tasting." My mind raced with details—invitations designed like vintage postcards, table settings that mirrored the rustic charm of a vineyard, maybe even a bit of live music to set the ambiance.

Max's smile broadened as he leaned on the bar, clearly intrigued by the concept. "I love that. It's perfect—elegant but still relaxed. And the vineyard vibe is totally on-brand for us."

"Great! I can curate a selection of chocolates that pair well with each wine," I continued, my enthusiasm bubbling over. "I know a great local chocolatier. That way we can keep the whole experience authentic and boutique."

He nodded, his eyes shining with gratitude. "You're a lifesaver, Isabella. This is why you're perfect for this."

Flattered by the trust he was placing in me, I couldn't help but blush. "I just want to create an experience that feels intimate, even if it's in the middle of New York City. Maybe some string lights, gentle music—nothing too loud, just . . . something that enhances the wine."

Max tossed the trash bag into the bin and wiped down the bar one last time. "A month, then," he said, looking at me with a nod that sealed our informal agreement. "We can iron out the specifics over the next few days, but I trust your vision, Isabella."

A rush of warmth spread through me at his words. "Then it's set, Boss," I said as I gave him a mini salute.

As I busied myself collecting the last of the glasses, I felt a new sense of purpose. I had always loved organizing these little gatherings for my parents' friends, transforming their spaces into themed wonderlands. But this was different—this was mine to lead, and the prospect was both thrilling and a touch daunting.

Max rinsed the glasses, his movements methodical, as Panic at the Disco continued to play in the background. By four in the morning, the weight of the day settled into my bones, but the excitement for what was to come kept the fatigue at bay. Finding Max buried in his wine notes in the back office, I knew we were both gearing up for a busy month ahead, but with a shared goal now in sight.

"I'm gonna head out if that's okay," I said as I tapped my knuckles on the doorframe. Max's hair was in disarray, and he had glasses pushed up on the bridge of his nose. The top few buttons of his collared shirt were unbuttoned, and his sleeves were rolled up, exposing his forearms. These were all details I should not have noticed.

Max smiled up at me. "Good night, thanks for the dinner. Tomorrow's shift might be a little crazier since it's a weekend, so get some good sleep."

"Sure thing, Boss," I said over my shoulder as I walked back down the hall, and I heard Max chuckle from behind me.

Max had undersold just how wild a Saturday night at the Prism Society was. It was as if all of New York's wealthy and horny came together in one place to let out their frustrations they'd let build up all week.

So far, I had made over seven hundred dollars in tips,

seen three pairs of tits, and walked in on one blow job being given in a lounge upstairs. And it wasn't even ten o'clock. But I was also working my magic on hyping up Max's event. I was busy schmoozing members to get them to verbally commit to joining the tasting next month. I knew how much the hands-on practice would help Max with his exam and I desperately wanted to make the event incredible.

I also desperately needed to find more comfortable shoes. I thought I was a pro at being on my feet in designer footwear. I was one to not sacrifice style for comfort and knew the way my legs looked in a nice heel. But the shifts this week and the busy back and forth I was making tonight from the lounge to the bar and back again were killing me.

But if I took my shoes off now, they wouldn't go back on my feet, so I took a deep breath, ignored the throbbing in the balls of my feet, and put a smile on my face. I might have to make a fashion faux pas and switch to *comfort* footwear next week. The thought made me nauseous.

"How's your first couple of weeks going, sis?" Dominic's voice stole my attention away from my achy feet. I was pleased he and Liam kept their appearances in the club to busy nights and big events. I really had no interest in seeing my brother waltzing around a sex club.

I let out a breath. "It's good, my feet hurt, but the tips are good."

Dom leaned against the bar, his gaze thoughtful as he watched me rearrange the cocktail menus. "Izzy, about this wine-tasting event next month . . ." He paused, choosing his words carefully. "I've been thinking it might be time to take event planning off Max's plate, especially with his sommelier exam coming up."

My heart skipped a beat, sensing where this was going. "Really?"

He nodded. "Yeah, and I was thinking, if this event goes well—by which I mean, it draws a good crowd, gets positive feedback, and brings in some new memberships—then maybe we could make event planning an official part of your job here."

The stakes had never been clearer, and a thrill of excitement coursed through me. The idea of having a more concrete role in shaping the experience at the Prism Society, especially in a way that played to my strengths and passions, was both daunting and exhilarating.

Dom continued, a hint of a smile on his face. "I've seen how you are with people, Izzy. You have a knack for this. And I trust you to bring something special to the table. So, what do you say? Think you can make this wine tasting a night to remember?"

Fired up, I locked eyes with Dom. "You got it, Dom. I'll make this event killer, promise."

He grinned, a rare sight from him, his confidence in me a tangible thing. "I know you will. And you'll have the entire atrium upstairs at your disposal. I can't wait to see what you do with the space."

The challenge was set, and I was ready to rise to it. This event wasn't just an opportunity to showcase my event-planning skills. It was a chance to carve out a new role for myself within the Prism Society, one that could potentially shape my future. The thought filled me with a mix of nerves and anticipation, but I was determined to succeed. After all, with the support of Dom, Max, and the rest of the team, how could I fail?

I smiled at Dom, a bit of nostalgia filling my head. Seven years didn't seem like a huge age gap for siblings, but when it meant you moved out of the house before your younger sibling could even drive, it felt like a gaping timeline. I was so ready to leave the city that I didn't even think twice before hopping on the plane. I'm not sure if I even said bye to Dominic before I'd left.

And since I'd been gone he'd grown into a whole ass adult. Well, as much as a twenty-eight-year-old man can really be. But I *was* proud of him. He'd had an idea for something and made it come to life, no questions asked.

"Hey, I haven't seen Liam yet. Does he ever come around?" I asked. I'd met Liam only once before and it was via Facetime. I'd called Dominic when I'd made the decision to move back home and had practically begged him for a job or at least a reference for one. He and Liam had been in the club when I called, and Dom had offered me a spot at the Prism Society with zero hesitation.

"Yeah, he's here somewhere, probably trying to sneak away to a room with Emma," Dominic said.

I had heard Dom mention Emma a few times before; he seemed to have a fun little friend group that all helped bring the club to life in some way. Emma had designed this place and so, even though I hadn't met her, I knew she would love me—my taste was impeccable.

"You talking shit about me?" I turned to see Liam and a *stunning* brunette at his side. Liam clapped Dom on the back and smiled at me. "We finally meet in the flesh."

"Liam! Hi, thank you so much for letting me be a part of this." I leaned in to hug Liam, his broad shoulders tight under my grasp.

"Of course, we'll do whatever for the family. Iz, this is Emma, the mastermind behind all of this," Liam said with a huge smile on his face, his arms fanned out wide.

Emma smiled softly, leaning in to hug me. "It's so great to meet you. Dom's told us all about you."

My eyes flicked over to Dom. "Oh, there's not a lot to tell, just an old haggard sister with nothing going on in my life."

Dom gave me a curious look but said nothing. Because there was no arguing with that sentiment. I was standing in front of, what felt like, *babies*, who had way more direction and progress in life than I did.

"Well, we're really happy you're here," Emma said, breaking my inner pity party, "and Dom told me about the event upstairs. Let me know if you need any help with the setup or design, I'm here if you need me."

I smiled at Emma. I knew I would love her. "Thank you, I'll let you know for sure." I waved goodbye to the group as I checked in with a few tables I felt were ready to slip me some more cash and watched as my brother and his friends made their way through the lounge greeting members.

They were like the Fantastic Four of the sex club scene, and as wild as that sounded, it was even crazier that I was envious of it. My girlfriends were busy picking out the best country club location for their bridal showers and adding dishes to their registry list while I was brainstorming ideas for orthopedic high heels.

"Sorry, but you're gonna have to deal with my stinky feet," I said as I *finally* had the chance to take off my heels once the front doors of the club clicked shut and Max turned the lock.

Dominic and Liam had come to make their rounds, chat up VIP members, and check on the staff, but they had left hours ago. Maureen and Jules had closed down their stations and said good night as the last member was leaving. Now, it was just Max and me.

I put one hand on Max's shoulder and reached down to slide off a heel. I winced and audibly groaned as my foot became free from the leather confines, red lines marking up the sides of my arch. I stood on one foot for a while, my barefoot suspended in the air, flexing my toes. I was anxious to place my foot on the carpet, afraid of how putting my weight back on it would feel.

Max looked down at me in question, holding me up with his body weight. I sighed and started to lower my foot to the ground, squinting my eyes in anticipation of the pain. If years of stumbling around cobblestone streets in five-inch heels hadn't taken a toll on my feet, the broken ankle from a cliff dive in Belize sure sealed the deal.

But, tonight, my foot never touched the ground.

Instead, it swung up in the air, my shoe clattering to the floor as Max scooped me up. A yelp escaped my mouth as Max carried me through the velvet curtains and into the lounge. His arms felt strong beneath me, and I felt his hands curl around my waist and under my knees. His chest was so warm, and he smelled like whiskey smoke and oranges.

He walked me through the lounge like I weighed nothing. I brought my arms up around his neck to steady myself even though something told me there was no chance of me falling.

Max sat me down gently in one of the cushioned lounge chairs and I immediately missed his warmth. He scooted another over so I could use it as a footrest, lifted my legs, and placed them on the second chair, sliding off my other shoe for me. I winced slightly at the relief of pressure.

"Thank you," I said. "I'll wear better shoes next time, Boss."

"That sounds like a good plan. I'm sure your feet will thank you," Max said. "By the way," he said, glancing down at my feet, "your feet don't smell."

I chuckled and reached down to rub the balls of my feet.

"What's funny?" Max asked.

"Oh, nothing, just remembering about this guy I met in Prague. He . . . had a foot fetish." I shivered at the memory. It had *really* creeped me out. "We worked together at this little café, and I went back to his apartment one night after working a shift wearing Chuck Taylors all night."

Max started walking around the lounge, picking up crumbled napkins, highball glasses, and abandoned cocktail straws. The lights from the overhead chandelier still showed down on the lounge, and a mix of expensive perfumes from members clung to the air. I could swear I could sniff out Clive Christian's No. 1.

"I cannot picture you wearing Chucks to save my life," Max said from across the bar.

"It was part of the uniform," I continued. "Anyways, he slipped off my shoes and smelled my feet, but like, in a way that it seemed like he liked it? And, oh god, I can't believe I'm telling you this." I winced at the memory.

"Come on, it can't be that bad," Max said.

"He . . . he started sucking on my toes." I buried my face in my hands at the memory.

Max threw his head back and laughed. "I'm sorry, your feet are cute and all, but I just don't picture myself wanting to put those toes in my mouth," Max said.

"Hey, don't yuck someone's yum, but yeah." I laughed. "It was . . . an experience. I ended up getting the heck out of his apartment and quit the next day. I couldn't bear to face him again."

"Note to self: don't suck on Isabella's toes, or she'll quit," Max said.

"Yeah, something like that," I said. "Okay, I think I'm going to brave standing on my feet. I actually have a surprise for you."

Max held up his hand to stop me.

"What do you need?" he asked. "I'll go grab it, or we'll be waiting here all night for you to get back." I rolled my eyes but sighed and slunk back into the chair.

"Just grab my bag from the locker," I said. "Be gentle with her, though!"

Max came out seconds later, cradling my purse like it was a national treasure. He set it on my lap, and I reached inside to grab what I'd been working on. I pulled out a stack of blue-lined cards, straightening them in between my hands.

"I figured if you're going to be staying late, you might as well get some studying in." I sunk back down in the lounge chair, lifting my feet back up and flexing my toes. I started rifling through the index cards, looking for a challenging question to fire off at Max.

"You made me study cards?" Max asked.

I shrugged. "Yeah, I went through some of your homework and jotted down some questions I thought seemed hard. I don't have a ton yet, but I'll keep adding to the stack. Okay, ready?"

Max's face had an odd look as he stood at the end of the bar with a handful of glasses ready to clean, but he nodded.

"Okay, 'Noble Rot.'" I read off one side of my flashcards. "Sounds like the title of a Victorian-era mystery novel."

Max snorted as he walked behind the bar and started putting the glasses in the sink, "Close, but it's actually a beneficial fungus for wine grapes. Makes for some of the best dessert wines."

"Wine and fungus." I scrunched up my nose as I flipped to the next card. "Now that's a romantic pairing."

"Okay, what's the primary difference between the Champagne Method and the Charmat Method of sparkling wine production?" I asked, flipping over the flashcard to spoil the answer for myself.

Max paused washing before answering, "The Champagne Method involves secondary fermentation in the bottle, while the Charmat Method does it in large tanks. I think."

I nodded, signaling he'd gotten it correct. I kept flipping through the stack of cards and Max kept getting them all right. He was way more ready than he was giving himself credit for.

"Okay, here's a hard one: What role does sulfur dioxide play in winemaking?" I asked.

"It acts as a preservative and prevents oxidation," he answered.

"Ding, ding ding! You got it. You're gonna crush this, Max," I said as I flipped through the deck of cards to find another hard one.

"Thanks," Max said quietly with his back now turned to me. Was there something cautious in that "thanks"? Was there hesitation underneath the surface?

"I mean, you knew what I meant when I butchered the word *Brettanomyces* so I think you're going to do just fine," I said.

Max chuckled. "Thanks for the vote of confidence, Isabella." His gaze lingered on me for a moment longer than necessary, sparking an unexpected warmth inside me.

Looking to shift the atmosphere from this unexpected moment of intimacy, I jumped to a topic that had been swirling in my mind. "Speaking of getting together, Jules keeps inviting me to go on a double date with her and her partner, but something tells me I might be a little out of their age bracket of double-date fun."

"Why do you do that?" Max set down the wineglass and leaned on the counter.

"Do what?" I asked, setting down the flash cards.

"Lump yourself in this geriatric bucket like you can't have fun anymore," Max said.

I lingered on Max's face before I answered, noticing the furrow between his brows and the intense stare behind his brown eyes. "I don't know, I kinda *feel* geriatric. I'm actually considering buying orthopedic shoes for goodness' sake." I lifted my feet and wiggled my toes.

"Well, that's just a smart decision considering your job; it has nothing to do with your age," Max said.

My laughter held a tinge of self-deprecation. "I don't know, it's just . . . I'm starting to think I should be further along in life given my age. I'm feeling a bit . . . left behind, I suppose."

Max's response had a sharper edge to it, teasing but probing. "So this job is what, just a placeholder? Something to pass the time with us bar-lurkers until your real life begins?"

"That's not it," I said quickly, a rush of heat coloring my cheeks. "You have this big goal, this dream, and every step you take is in pursuit of it. I'm just here—treading water, not sure which direction to swim in."

"And you're just waiting?" Max curled an eyebrow. "Hoping for some grand epiphany or for someone to make up your mind for you?"

I exhaled slowly, feeling the weight of his gaze. There was an intensity in his eyes that I hadn't noticed before. "I suppose so. I mean, no one wants to be indecisive, right? But I'm scared of choosing the wrong path and wasting time. I'm just . . . looking for a sign or something."

The space between us filled with my confessions, and for a moment, we both just existed within it. I felt vulnerable, my admissions hanging in the air like delicate glasswork, ready to shatter.

"Did you always know you wanted to be a sommelier?" I redirected the conversation away from the precipice of my uncertainties, focusing on Max in an attempt to tether myself back to the ground.

Max chuckled before he said, "No, I didn't even know what a sommelier was until I met your brother. Growing up in Jackson Heights didn't necessarily expose me to the finer things in life. It was at a dinner your parents hosted where I actually met my first sommelier. From there, I was hooked. I love the idea of guiding someone to have an experience they might not have considered."

I envied how sure Max was about his passion. He saw something that interested him, and he *just knew*. I quieted as my mind flipped through all my past jobs and small bursts of passion projects. Waitressing, hostel admin, writing, even that time I thought I would love being an au pair, or the time I tried to teach yoga to tourists. They all breezed through my mind as fun memories, but nothing lit me up.

The dim lighting of the lounge created a quiet ambiance, punctuated only by the soft clink of glasses as Max cleaned up. Candlelight flickered, reflecting off the mercury glass vases and casting shadows on the wall.

"So, who would you take?" Max's voice, a deep lull from across the room, pulled me out of my reverie.

"What?" I replied, blinking a few times, my brain still stuck in overthinking mode.

"On the double date. If you had to choose, who would you bring along?" His brown eyes met mine, searching.

"Oh," I paused, biting my lower lip in thought. "That's, um, a detail I've overlooked. There's, well, no one really."

A teasing smile tugged at the corner of Max's lips. "I'm right here, you know."

"You?" I raised an eyebrow, a playful smirk forming. "Offering to be my knight in shining armor and save me from the horror of showing up dateless?"

Max leaned on the bar, his voice dropping an octave. "It wouldn't be a favor, Isabella. I'd genuinely enjoy taking you out."

"Sure," I scoffed, feigning nonchalance. But as I moved to collect my belongings, I felt the intensity of his gaze. A warmth crept up my neck, not entirely unpleasant.

A fleeting thought crossed my mind: Was it so bad if someone like Max was interested in me? Lately, it felt as if time was running out, each ticktock of the clock a reminder of my advancing age. Yet, I knew better. Delving into something with Max? It was inviting chaos. I'd learned that lesson before.

My phone buzzed, signaling a message. It was my driver, waiting around the corner. I exhaled in relief. Tonight, I craved the comfort of my childhood home, the luxury of a hot bath, and the solace of being wrapped in the familiarity of my past.

"I'll see you, Max," I murmured, heading toward the velvet curtains that hid the front door.

As I left, I couldn't help but glance back once, catching the lingering look in his eyes.

"Isabella! You have a delivery!" My mom's voice woke me from my slumber the next morning, and I groaned into my pillowcase. I had never looked forward to Mondays before, but considering now they were one of my only two days off from work, I loved them.

I tried to trick my brain into being lulled back to sleep, but it didn't work. Another oddity that came from being in your thirties was the inability to sleep in. I slipped on a sweatshirt and padded out to meet my mother in the kitchen. My parents' home was one of my favorite places on earth, even if they'd converted my bedroom to a craft room as soon as I'd left.

I was lucky enough to call their five-story townhome in Gramercy Park my childhood home. I'd held many sleepovers here, snuck booze out of their basement cellar, and even stained the carpet permanently in my bedroom from a straightener I'd accidentally left on all day. I made my way down from the third floor to meet my mother in the kitchen.

Gloria Esposito was a powerhouse of a woman packed in a tiny body. Her thick, Italian accent sometimes muddied my words, and her crisp gray hair sat in a perfect bob. My unruly morning curls looked like a lion's mane next to my mother's hair. I eyed the small box on the counter, forgetting what I'd ordered.

Another retinol cream? Perhaps a cooling eye mask to tame my new undereye circles? I slid a knife under the flap and grinned at what lay shrink-wrapped inside. The invitations for Max's wine-tasting event were waiting for me. I squealed as I picked them up and turned them over in my hands, reading every word on the cardstock for the millionth time.

I had gone all-out with the wine and chocolate theme, deciding on *The Enchanted Vineyard: An Odyssey of Wine & Chocolate* as the overall theme of the event. The invitations were a beautiful creamy chocolate color with metallic white accents. I was planning on having a courier hand-deliver the invitations to the club's VIP members, each with a small box of chocolates.

I was meeting with the chocolatier today to set the menu of treats so Max could pair them each with a glass of wine. I hoped he could flex his wine muscles with this event and that it could give him some more confidence that he would pass his exam. I felt this weird hesitation from Max when it came to his certification. Almost like he was embarrassed by his goal, that it wasn't enough. I hoped this event would show him how cool his job could be.

"Oh, those are beautiful, dear. Are those for the club?" my mom asked over my shoulder, and she peered into the box. Given my mom's profession and my parents' overall progressive beliefs, Gloria knew all about the happenings at the Prism Society. It was an unspoken family rule that we didn't share too many details of what went on, and our parents could absolutely under no circumstances ever visit, but besides that, there was zero judgment.

"Yeah, for Max's wine-tasting event; he asked me to help plan it." I put the invitations back in the box, wanting to keep them clean.

"You were always so good at events, Izzy, I bet it's going to be incredible." My parents were two of the most supportive people I'd ever met. Heck, they didn't hesitate when their thirty-something-year-old daughter came crawling back home after declaring she would "never live in the city, ever again." Even if they had turned my old room into a guest room.

There were no limits to what my parents would do for both me and Dom, but it was up to us to actually try. It was up to us to set our mind on something and go forth with it confidently. Dominic had never had a problem with that part, but me, now that was another story. I gladly took the cappuccino my mother made and headed back upstairs to look a bit more presentable for the chocolatier.

After a chocolate marathon, I had my picks. Merlot-soaked

cherry chocolates topped the list for their punchy flavor, a nod to the robust reds we'd be serving. The lemon-infused white chocolates were a hit too, light and zesty, just right for the lighter wines. I picked them because they either made my taste buds sing or because they were too interesting to pass up.

I ended up choosing this chocolatier because it was a spot I'd walked by a thousand times on my way to prep school, always stopping to drool over the chocolates being drizzled and dipped right behind the windowpane. Their craft had always fascinated me, and now, it was a part of our event.

Riding a sugar high, I couldn't wait to loop Max in. I rummaged through my onboarding papers to find his number, thinking he'd get a kick out of my chocolate-fueled enthusiasm. A quick text later, I leaned back, satisfied with the day's work and eager for what was next.

> Isabella: Wanna taste some goodies I picked out for your event?

A few minutes later, my phone buzzed in my hand.

> Max: Not that I don't want to immediately say 'yes' to whoever this is, I want to confirm first. This is Isabella, right?

> Isabella: Oh my god, yes, it's Izzy.

> Max: Just making sure. It's not every day I get texts from strangers asking me to taste their goodies.

> Isabella: I DID NOT say 'my goodies'. I said SOME goodies. As in chocolates. I just picked out the menu for your event. I figured you might want some time to think about the wines you'll want to pair with them.

> Max: The menu? Already? Okay, yeah, I'll be there soon. You're still at your family's place in Gramercy Park, right?

A slight flutter of nervousness tickled my stomach at his question. Of course, he'd been to the house before. He and Dom were close after all.

> Isabella: Yeah, that's the one. Can't wait to show you what I've got.

His confirmation set a flurry of preparations in motion on my end. As I laid out the chocolates and napkins, a mix of anticipation and second thoughts danced in my head. The idea to pre-select the chocolates seemed good in theory, and I even had a list of potential wine pairings as a backup. Still, a thread of anxiety wove through my excitement, leaving me second-guessing my initiative.

I busied myself as I waited, setting out the chocolates and little napkins, and anxiously tapped my nails on the counter-top. I jumped when the buzz of their doorbell vibrated through the walls.

Seeing *Casual Max* shouldn't have made the little flutters in my belly go off, but it did. The way he handsomely *existed* in jeans and a plain t-shirt was a crime. I tugged open the arched wooden door, smiling at Max through the glass panes.

"Hey," I said as I stepped aside to let him up the steps.

"Hey," Max replied, raising his eyebrows quickly.

"Uh, everything's upstairs," I said as I turned to lead Max up to the kitchen. There was awkwardness in the air, but I didn't know why.

"Great," Max replied from behind me.

"Um, okay, so." I clapped my hands together in mock cheerfulness and turned to Max. "I don't know what you want to see first. I have the invitation here." I placed my hand on the stack of cardstock in front of me. "And the chocolates laid out here." I pointed to the ornate chocolates lining the edge of the counter.

Max took a deep breath and picked up the invitation. I watched silently as he read the words embossed on the front. "Fancy," he said.

I held my breath as his gaze skirted over the chocolates, leaning forward to read the descriptions that sat in front of each. His eyes squinted and his eyebrows furrowed. Something was wrong.

"You hate it, don't you?" I asked in a whisper.

Max sighed before answering. "It's not that I hate it. It's just . . ." He finally looked up at me. "These are *very* specific palettes to pair with. I mean, a raspberry and rose filling?"

"Right, okay, well, I also," I said as I pulled out my notes, "mapped out some potential pairings that you could use with some of them. I'm no sommelier, but I *love* wine with chocolate, so I just thought about what I might like."

I turned the list over to Max so he could see what I'd put together. I'd thought of everything. I wanted this event to be a huge success for him. A chance for him to show off his knowledge and take people on a tasting experience. Heck, *I* couldn't wait to try the pairings, so the clientele at the club would love them.

"Ornellaia, Masseto . . . Penfolds." Max read the list of growers of the wines on the list out loud. "These are some of the most well-known growers, Isabella."

I didn't say anything as I tried to think back and process his meaning.

"I specifically told you that's not what I wanted my events to be about," Max continued. "These growers get a shit ton of press and orders every single day. They aren't hurting. The purpose of these events with our rich-ass members is to show them something *new*. To give a smaller establishment a chance to get put on the map."

"If you had looped me in first," he continued, his voice sounding tired, "I could've given input on some of these choices. On how I wanted this to be . . . presented."

Max let out a long, weary breath, his eyes still locked on the list of renowned wine labels before him. The room seemed to hold its breath with him, the thick tension palpable between the ornate chocolates and the gleaming invitations that lay untouched on the counter.

I felt a sudden tightness in my chest, my own excitement over the preparations melting away into a pool of anxiety. I'd been so wrapped up in wanting to impress that I had missed the heart of what he was trying to do.

"I . . . I'm sorry, Max. I thought—"

Max cut me off gently, but there was a sharpness in his voice that hadn't been there before. "You thought you were helping, I know. But this isn't just about putting on a successful event or pairing the perfect wine with chocolate."

The silence that followed was broken only by the quiet ticking of the kitchen clock. My eyes traced the lines of concern etched into Max's face, realizing for the first time how deeply his passion ran for not just wine but for the stories behind them—the unknown vintners, the hidden gems of vineyards that so rarely found their way to the spotlight.

"This is about advocacy, Izzy," Max said softly, his voice a blend of frustration and earnestness. "It's about using our platform to lift up those who don't have the means to do it themselves. It's about discovery, about connection. Not just the wine but the hands that toiled to make it. The small businesses, the families. That's where my passion lies. That's the direction I want to take."

I felt a flush of shame wash over me. All my attempts at perfection, at creating the "ultimate event," now seemed superficial in contrast to Max's genuine ambition.

I swallowed hard, my heart pounding with a mixture of regret and a new understanding. "I . . . I missed the mark. I get it. You shared that with me, and I didn't realize that—"

"Do I want more?" Max finished for me, his gaze dropping away from mine. "Yeah, most people don't. They see the sommelier title and they think it's all about sniffing, swirling, and sipping the most expensive bottles I can get my hands on."

I took a step closer, my voice a quiet whisper now. "Tell me, then. Teach me, Max. I want to understand. I want to help make this right."

For a moment, we just stood there, the air between us thick with the weight of unspoken thoughts and realizations. Then, slowly, Max's expression softened, and something like forgiveness flickered in his eyes.

Max's enthusiasm was palpable as he leaned closer, his excitement breaking through in a smile. "We start with the wine," he explained, his tone turning earnest. "There's this vineyard I've had in mind for a while now, Linden Hollow. I've followed their journey for years, admired their dedication to sustainable practices and the unique way they craft their wines. I think showcasing their products at our event could really highlight what they're about."

Genuine passion sparkled in his eyes as he spoke about the vineyard. It was clear this was more than a choice of convenience. Max saw a kinship in their mission, a shared goal that went beyond wine and chocolates. "I was thinking," he continued, his gaze meeting mine, "are you up for a road trip there? It could be a great opportunity to really understand their philosophy, pick out the perfect pairings for the chocolates you've selected."

Heading to the vineyard with Max sounded like a blast. I was all-in for getting a firsthand look at how they made their wine, especially since we'd be matching it up with some delicious chocolates. I got the sense we were teaming up for something bigger than wine or chocolate—it was about shining a light on a place that was doing cool stuff with their grapes. "Count me in," I said, thrilled Max was bringing me into this part of the project. I was all geared up to dive into the vineyard scene, eager to soak in the sprawling fields and the stories they harbored.

EIGHT
MAX

I zipped out of Isabella's place with a plan in motion, taking the tunnels through the city to make sure my car was prepped for our little adventure. While she got herself ready, I swung by the store, picking up an arsenal of road trip essentials—snacks that ranged from the healthy to the decidedly not-so-much. It was all about balance, after all. Tossing bags of chips, fruit, and a couple of indulgent treats into the backseat, I made my way through the dense New York City traffic back to Isabella.

As I pulled my car up to the curb, her front door opened, and I had to actively lessen the joy that spread over my face at the sight of her. Isabella walked down the front steps, a tote bag full of our fancy chocolates in hand, and sunglasses on her face. The sun was shining, and her hair was a mass of unruly curls, but the *sundress*.

Were women aware of what they looked like in sundresses? Did they know when the sunlight catches the fabric the right way, you can see the outline of their hips? Did they know how many times we'd imagine sliding the hem of that dress up to discover what was underneath? How we wanted to bunch up the fabric in our fists?

I shook my head as I walked around to the side of the car to open my door. I pasted a friendly smile on my face, hoping like hell I could hide the lust I felt in my eyes.

"Can we start today over, Boss?" Isabella asked quietly, handing him a to-go cup of coffee. Goddamn, her calling me boss, even though she did it to be funny, sent blood straight down to my dick.

I cleared my throat, took the mug, and nodded, walking back to the driver's side before sliding in.

"Before you get too bossy about the inevitable *car rules* you probably have," she said as she settled in the passenger seat, "I brought snacks and made us a playlist."

"I don't have car rules," I said as I finally looked her in the eyes.

Isabella squinted at me, angling down her chin slightly. "As bossy as you are, you definitely have car rules."

"I don't—no feet on the dash," I said as she went to rest her feet, "have car rules," I finished as I buckled my seat belt.

"See! You can't even help yourself." She chuckled, but she kept her feet on the dash.

"It's just not safe, Isabella. If someone were to hit us, both of your legs would break on the impact. I don't consider that a *rule* if I'm just trying to keep your legs in one piece."

"You *would* want to keep my legs in one piece, wouldn't

you?" Isabella joked, but this time she slid her feet back down to the floorboard.

I didn't try to hide my smirk when she glanced over at me this time. I said nothing, but enough passed through my glance that she turned away. I flicked on the turn signal and pulled away from the curb. Today was about to test us both.

"Okay, Ms. Brag About the Playlist, what've you got for us?" I asked as we made our way out of the city. The traffic was surprisingly light today and before long we'd be out of the congested part and onto the wider highway.

Isabella laughed and bounced in her seat, pulling out her phone and connecting it to the car's Bluetooth. She tapped the screen a couple of times before I heard the first song come through the speaker and I groaned.

"If *you* get to torture me with 2000s emo punk music every night then *you* get to listen to 2000s pop all day today," she said as she grinned wide. The lyrics to "Toxic" blared through the speaker.

I shook my head but smiled as Isabella belted out the lyrics next to me. Unbeknownst to her, I knew every word to every 2000s pop song. I'd grown up in a house full of older sisters who were ruthless in their girlhood.

So when "Case of the Ex" by Mýa came on and I belted out the bridge I laughed at the absolute shock on Isabella's face.

"Were you a DJ in another life or something?" she asked, turning down the music a bit.

I laughed. "No, just partially raised by three bossy older

sisters. This playlist is basically the soundtrack to my childhood."

"Okay, so Britney or Christina?" Isabella asked, turning in her seat a bit to look at me.

"Ah, ah, you don't put two queens against each other. Christina's voice, especially on that *Mulan* soundtrack, was unbeatable. But, I absolutely believe the theory that they made Britney baby her voice so she'd sound different. I think she can sing just as well."

"Okay, *who* are you?" Isabella asked in disbelief as she shook her head and scrolled to select the next song.

We ended up getting through a bunch of *NSYNC, TLC, Mariah Carey, and even some Aaliyah before I pulled off the highway at our exit. The car bounced along the pothole-filled off-ramp. A small sign let us know the winery was a mile and a half to the left.

Our tires crunched on the gravel as we turned onto the windy road leading to the vineyard. A large stone sign announced our arrival at Linden Hollow Vineyards. The drive up to the property was flanked by rows and rows of grape vines, currently lush and green for the season.

In the heart of the acreage sat a stone chateau, reminiscent of classic French wineries. Ivy crept up the walls and large, wooden barrels lined the porch, no doubt filled to the brim with wines. Kitschy signs and grape décor hung above the door, welcoming guests inside. I hoped we'd be able to find something suitable for the event here. Rooting for the underdog was one thing, but trying to convince a wine lover like Isabella, who was accustomed to specific tastes, was another.

I took a deep breath as I turned the large brass knob and stepped inside the lobby, a bell ringing as the door swung open. I guided Isabella inside, my hand hovering above her lower back.

"Welcome, folks! Come on in, are you here for a tasting?" An older woman stood behind the counter spanning the entire length of the room. She wore an apron over her striped button-up, her hair in a messy bun at the top of her head.

"Hi!" Isabella greeted her enthusiastically. "Yes, we're here to hopefully fall in love with some wines. We have an event coming up that my boss here is *kinda* freaking out about." She whispered the last part, cupping my hand over the side of her mouth like I couldn't hear her.

She followed me up to the counter to read through the menu of what wines they had available. Isabella filled the woman in on the upcoming event and what types of wines we were looking for. She surprised him when she reached into her purse and pulled out a small box of chocolates.

"I brought the lemon-infused white chocolate that will pair with the Chardonnay and the spiced milk chocolate caramel that will pair with the Syrah. That way we can know if they'll work perfectly," she said.

"You had these chocolates in your purse the whole time and you made me snack on gummy worms on the drive down?" I teased.

"Somehow, I think you'll live," she said.

The woman behind the counter, Kerry, started pulling

bottles for them to sample. "A little wine will calm any lovers' quarrel with the first sip," she said with a smirk.

I kept quiet, waiting for Isabella to correct her, but she just smiled. I wanted to slide my hand around her lower back and had to physically stop myself from doing it.

They had a few options for each wine I wanted to replace, so now we just had to cross our fingers they'd be good enough for the event. Kerry got us set up with some samples of our preferred wines but threw in some additional options for fun.

She created a spread with glasses, chocolates, and some palate-cleansing crackers and set us up on the back patio. The wrought iron table and chairs overlooked the hills of the vineyard, and it was truly stunning.

"Even though you forced me to come here, this is really beautiful," Isabella said as she picked up the first glass of wine to sample.

I chuckled. "I don't remember *forcing* you, but I am glad you came." We locked eyes for a second and I smiled. "Now, what does your refined palate think of this wine?"

I picked up the Chardonnay, swirled the liquid, noting the legs, took a deep inhale, and held the glass up to the light before taking a tiny sip. Isabella mimicked my movements before taking a small sip herself.

"It's . . . buttery. Almost like toast." She took another sip. "It's thicker than normal but really good."

I smiled. "Well, the 'toast' taste is likely because it underwent malolactic fermentation and was aged in toasted oak barrels. The malic acid, naturally found in grape must, is converted to softer lactic acid by bacteria. This process not only softens the wine's acidity but also introduces flavors reminiscent of butter or cream."

"Show-off." Isabella teased.

"I'm sorry, it probably sounds like I'm mansplaining wine to you, but this does actually help a ton for me to be ready for the exam," I said.

"It doesn't come across as condescending, I promise. I can tell you're really just a wine nerd, that's all," Isabella said, smiling.

We sampled the next Chardonnay, both immediately preferring the first, before trying them both again with the chocolates.

"You truly prefer this one?" I asked as I sipped the Chardonnay we both seemed to prefer.

"Yes, truly, and yes, I think other rich-ass people will too," she said, bringing up my description of our members earlier.

I winced and said, "I'm sorry about that comment."

"It's fine." She shrugged. "Most of those rich-ass people care more about the label anyways."

"That's what I'm worried about with this event," I confessed, reaching for the Syrah so we could taste it next. "I'm afraid they'll judge the wine if they don't recognize the vineyard."

"Then don't tell them. Have that be a part of the event. Have them speculate where they think it originates from and surprise them at the end. They might be more bought that way," she said.

"That's brilliant, Isabella. Get them in love with the wine for the taste then maybe they'll care about getting it in front of more people." I could feel the excitement building for the event now, not just nerves.

I poured us each a sample of the next wine and we clinked glasses. It only took seven sips, four nibbles on the caramel, and long moments of quiet pondering for me to decide on the second Syrah as the winner.

I felt immediate relief once I'd settled on the wines to complement two of the chocolates. I had some ideas for which wines could pair well with the others, but those vineyards were more like a plane ride away, so I'd order a few bottles so we could taste them here.

"Okay, so I feel like I totally rained on your event-planning parade," I said as we both cleansed our palates with some oyster crackers. "How's everything else coming together?"

I didn't miss how Isabella's face lit up as she walked me through some of the setup she and Emma had planned for upstairs. I was dizzy thinking about all the details she was already mapping out. From floral to signage to hand-delivered invitations. She was going to make this event magical.

"You seem like you really love this part. The event planning. Dom talked to you about having it be part of your official job description, right?" I asked.

Isabella shrugged. "Yeah, he did. I think that's also why I got so carried away. I really wanted to impress him—and you."

"From what I've seen, you more than have what it takes to excel," I said.

"Maybe," she replied.

Down to our last wine, we took a walk through the vine-yards. The summer sun beat down hot on us as we made our way across the lawn. Rows and rows of grape vines wrapped around thick wire trellises. The expanse of the rolling hills made me feel like I was in another world instead of being outside of the concrete jungle of New York.

"You know that whatever you want to do with your career, or whatever, doesn't have to be earth-shattering," I said. "I didn't mean to force you to turn something you like doing for fun into a job." Isabella had been quiet for a while, perhaps lost in thought.

"No, it's not that." She placed her hand on my forearm as she spoke. I loved that she kept finding ways to touch me as she opened up. "I just . . . everyone else in my life seems to have always known exactly where they want to live, what they want to do, who they want to be with, and I . . . just don't."

I stopped walking and turned to face Isabella. "No one says that you have to. Now or ever."

Her face was soft when she said, "Sometimes I just wish someone would tell me what to do. That someone would just take the pressure of making the decision off my plate for me."

I smiled down at her. "I wouldn't have pegged you for someone who wanted to be told what to do."

"I don't know, it sounds nice sometimes," she said.

Her hand was still on my elbow, my skin felt hot under her

fingertips. Her neck and cheeks were flushed a bit from the wine, and I wondered what her lips tasted like. I bet the warmth of the tannins could still be tasted on her tongue. Isabella tilted her chin up slightly; it was so subtle I could've missed it.

I leaned my head down slowly and kept leaning down when she didn't stop me. I could see her teeth behind the part of her lips and, god, I bet her mouth was warm. My eyes scanned hers for permission, but her own gaze was locked on my mouth.

"Do you mind taking our picture?" The drunken request came from a girl who was already staggering in her heels on the lawn. Her friends all huddled up together against the grapes as a backdrop. The moment was sucked up in a vortex and thrown across the world.

"Oh, of course!" Isabella let out a breath, reached out for the outstretched phone, and turned away. She helped arrange the group of giddy girls and started snapping a few photos.

I stepped back a bit. I was *that close* to kissing her. And she had been *that close* to letting me.

NINE
ISABELLA

My pulse quickened with a mix of nerves and excitement as the elevator doors parted, revealing the bustling third floor of the Prism Society. The last time I had been here, the rain had cast a solemn mood, but today, sunlight flooded through the large atrium, infusing the space with a sense of possibility.

Three days had passed since the *almost* kiss with Max happened in the vineyard. My eyes had been locked on the fullness of his lips as he leaned down and down and down. And like an alarm clock going off way too early, the demand of a drunk girl had zapped us out of it. I'd spent the last three days wondering what he would've tasted like. How he liked to kiss.

Clearing my head, my eyes scanned over the vast room that lay before me like a painter's canvas, bathed in the warmth of the sunbeams filtering down from the clear blue sky above, visible through the geometric dance of the atrium's glass panels. Today, that same sky lent an almost ethereal quality to the room, a stark contrast to the stormy gray that had greeted me before.

With the wine-tasting event drawing closer each day—two weeks and six days to go—the pressure was mounting for me to bring my vision to life. In a move born of both desperation and inspiration, I had reached out to Emma, who had a talent for turning the mundane into the sublime. Emma's skills in design had already transformed the club into a beacon of luxury, and I was counting on it to conjure that same magic for Max's event.

Emma's footsteps indicated her arrival, her heels clicking a confident rhythm on the marble. "Izzy!" she called out, her face alight with the thrill of a new project. "Ready to create something unforgettable?"

"Thank you so much for your offer." I sighed, already overwhelmed. "I was already beginning to drown in decisions. What color should the tablecloths be? What's the right music? What about table settings?" I rattled off a few of the items that were spinning around in my mind.

I calmed as Emma rested a warm hand on my shoulder. "I've got you. There's no reason you have to figure this out alone. We're family here at the Prism Society. You're one of us now." Emma winked at me as she circled the space, pulling up a sketch on her iPad.

I couldn't help the envy that laced my gut when I looked at Emma. Someone who was so young yet so *sure*. She had her dream career, a booming luxury interior design business, her dream partner, the *very* handsome Liam, and great friendships.

"So tell me what you're thinking," Emma said, interrupting my thoughts. "What's the vibe?"

I took a deep breath, and my apprehensions slightly eased. "I'm thinking of deep hues, velvety tones, and an ambiance that invites guests to lose themselves in the wine and chocolate experience."

Emma, looking down at her iPad, nodded enthusiastically. "I love that. Maybe we can bring in some moody flowers to go with your *Enchanted* theme."

"Yes," I said, my voice raised in excitement. "What if it's, like, a secret garden-type experience? Each tasting could be set to a different vibe in little corners around the room. Is that too much?" I worried that my big ideas wouldn't be able to come to life and that I was asking too much from Emma.

"'Too much' is not a phrase we use here at the Prism Society, Iz," Emma said, "Too much is my *favorite* way to do things."

I helped Emma map out the zones for each of our tasting experiences. There would be purple orchids and moss for the port tasting, pink peonies and ivy for the Chardonnay, cream roses to go with the Champagne, orange ranunculus and cinnamon sticks for the Syrah, and finally, deep red roses and eucalyptus for the Cabernet Sauvignon.

This event was going to be next level. I already had a list of floral pieces to order, tablecloths to reserve, and lighting to figure out. Emma offered her team up to create any sort of signage or wall backdrops for the event.

We could have small wooden signage directing guests to the next tasting, leading them further into the secret garden of flavors. Emma gave me the idea of lighting the pathways with floor lanterns and hanging string lights from the atrium windows to add a magical feel.

"Ah, there she is." Jessie burst through the door with her portfolio of set design ideas clutched tightly under her arm. I turned as Emma tugged her best friend, Jessie, into a hug. Emma had brought Jessie in to help with building some of the elements for the event. Max had filled me in on the drama that had unfolded with the design firm Emma and Jessie had worked at. It turns out not everyone is super cool with the whole sex club vibe.

Emma had taken the leap and started her own firm and hired Jessie as a contractor here and there. Jessie, with her ridiculous woodworking skills had gotten to stay at Spectra, but I got the vibe that wasn't going to last for much longer. I'd picked up on some *vibe* between Jessie and Dom whenever they were in the same room together, but no one had shared any insight, so I let it be.

While they worked, laughter bubbled up from down the hall, drifting from the partially open door of the back office. I had peeked inside to see Max, Liam, and Dom, a trio of easy camaraderie, each with a beer in hand, their banter as light as the foam on their drinks. The sight of them, so at ease and content in each other's company, filled me with a quiet joy. It was a reminder of the friendships that thrived within the walls of the Prism Society.

As the afternoon light softened, we spread Jessie's

sketches across the table, engrossed in a world of creativity as we discussed incorporating whimsical elements to bring our secret garden theme to life. We envisioned hanging lights to mimic the delicate twinkle of stars and pathways lined with soft, glowing lanterns, inviting guests to wander and explore.

The atmosphere in the club was electric, charged with creativity and the hustle of preparation. Jules, the front desk manager known for her charm and efficiency, breezed in to offer her support. She assured us she'd handle any overflow of reservations brought on by the event, seamlessly integrating herself into the whirlwind of activity.

My primary hope was for Max to see and love the world we were creating. I wanted this event to be more than a showcase of exquisite wines. I aimed for it to be a reflection of Max's journey and his sommelier expertise. It was essential for me that Max saw this space as a true testament to his hard work and dedication to the craft of wine.

Amidst the flurry of preparations, I couldn't help the flutter in my belly surrounding the stakes of Max's upcoming sommelier exam. Passing would not only elevate the Prism Society's wine program, making it a standout feature of the club, but it would also cement our status within the elite circle of wine connoisseurs. The prospect of bringing in more business, especially with members who were here for the wine *and* what the sultry club offered, was exciting. With Max's test a month away, the pressure was like a simmering pot of water.

With each detail for the event falling into place, my vision became more vivid and more real. And when the day's work was done, as the others headed out, Max pulled me aside. He'd received a notification: tomorrow, the special selection of wines for the event would be delivered.

"Think you could help me with a wine tasting tomorrow?" he asked, a hopeful note in his voice. "Could use your palate and your expertise."

My face broke into a wide, genuine smile. "I'd love to," I said. And with that, the promise of tomorrow's tasting lingered in the air, a tantalizing preview of the magic we were about to create.

Friday afternoon held a quiet hush over the Prism Society, the kind that settles over a stage when the audience has yet to arrive. The club was closed to the public, but within its walls, anticipation was being uncorked, its bouquet ready to fill the room.

Max had transformed one of the plush, curved booths in the lounge into a private tasting tableau. The seating, which normally embraced groups in the revelry of the night, now held a more intimate arrangement. It was set with precision and care, with each glass sparkling under the subdued glow of the wall sconces, their light dimmed to a warm, inviting hue.

The table was draped in a charcoal velvet cloth that caught the light, its surface a study in understated elegance. Atop it, the array of crystal stemware was laid out like instruments awaiting the conductor's hand, each glass promising a different timbre and tone of the wines they were soon to hold.

I stepped into the space, a smile spreading across my face as I took in the scene. Max had thought of everything. He'd created a tiny tasting experience just for us. The chocolates I'd picked laid out on a platter in the middle of the table, and two small flickering candles sat in mercury glasses, the shadowed light casting shapes on the table.

The air was cooler here, the light danced in flickers across the glasses, and the table seemingly shaded away from the hanging chandeliers. Here, in this hallowed space of comfort and luxury, the outside world felt leagues away. The lounge was a sanctuary, its ambiance a gentle embrace.

I walked over to the booth, my fingers grazing the back of the velvet upholstery. I thought we'd throw back a couple of ounces of wine like we had at the vineyard to make our final selections to go with the rest of the chocolates. But Max had created an experience for us instead.

Max, with a bottle already in hand, greeted me with an easy smile, his excitement barely contained. "Ready to taste some magic?" he asked, his eyes shining with the same fervor I felt bubbling inside me.

I nodded, my anticipation palpable. "I can't believe you did all this," I replied, taking my seat and allowing myself to be fully absorbed by the moment.

"I wanted to practice creating more of an experience with this tasting, to prepare for the event. Will you judge me if I go full-on sommelier tonight?" Max asked with a bit of a blush.

"By all means, wow me with all your nerdy knowledge, Mr. Sommelier," I said as I slid further into the booth.

Max's grin widened at my challenge, a playful glint in his eye as he assumed the role of the evening's guide into the world of fine wines. He uncorked the first bottle, a ceremony in itself, the subtle pop a prelude to the evening's symphony.

"As we embark on this journey," Max began, pouring a ruby liquid that seemed to capture the fading daylight in its depths, "we'll explore not just the taste, but the story of each wine. How it speaks of its origin, the earth where the grapes were lovingly cultivated."

I leaned forward, my elbows on the table, my chin resting on my interlocked fingers. "Tell me its secrets," I teased, watching the wine swirl in my glass, creating a small vortex of aroma and anticipation.

Max played along, adopting a mock-serious tone. "This first contender hails from a vineyard where the fog lingers like a whisper of ancient tales. It's a Pinot Noir, with whispers of cherry and a hint of spice. It should play well with the dark chocolate, don't you think?"

The wine was cool on my lips, the flavor blooming on my palate as I took my first sip. I closed my eyes, savoring the layers as they unfolded. "Mmm, it's like the first crisp night of fall," I mused.

Max chuckled as he said, "I love how you describe what you're tasting."

He watched me with appreciation as I described the experience, my enthusiasm stoking his own. With a flourish that demonstrated his increasing comfort in his role, he presented the next bottle, a Champagne, with the light catching its graceful curves. "Now, let's elevate the experience," he announced, his voice a mix of reverence and excitement. "A little sparkle to cleanse our palates."

He expertly popped the cork, the sound a festive exclamation point in the lounge's quiet. The Champagne fizzed to life as Max poured it into our flutes, the bubbles racing to the surface like tiny dancers in a rush to perform.

The wine was a vivacious contrast to the Pinot Noir, with each sip full of effervescence and hints of green apple and toasted brioche. "It's like a celebration in a glass," I remarked, the corners of my mouth rising with delight as the bubbles tingled on my tongue.

Max nodded, his eyes reflecting the golden hues of the drink. "Exactly. It's meant to invigorate the senses, to prepare us for the next act of our tasting journey."

Our eyes met over the rim of their glasses, a silent toast to the moment.

"Will it be weird if I ask you to come sit by me?" I asked as I reached out, my hand brushing Max's as I passed back the bottle. The contact was brief but electric, a current that seemed to flow through both of us, leaving a lingering warmth. "Or will that break some sommelier rule?"

Max's smile broadened, a soft light glinting in his eyes as he inched even closer, erasing the scant space that had remained between us. His presence was a tangible warmth, a magnetic pull I found myself powerless to resist. Every brush of his clothing against mine, every shared breath, proved our very heartbeats were syncing in that moment.

"Your turn to impress me," Max said, popping the cork of the Cabernet Sauvignon. "Describe this one."

I took a slow sip, my gaze never leaving Max's. "Bold," I started, each word deliberate, "with an unapologetic intensity. It doesn't ask for your attention, it demands it. Just like someone I know."

"Bold and demanding, huh?" he echoed, his voice laced with an undeniable intrigue that sparked a flutter in my chest. His gaze lingered on mine, deep and searching, as if he was trying to read the unspoken words dancing behind my eyes. "Sounds familiar, but I'm curious to hear more about this . . . intensity."

The atmosphere was thick with an unspoken promise, a silent acknowledgment of the connection unfurling between us. The outside world seemed to fade away, leaving the two of us in our bubble of shared glances and whispered words. The wine, rich and complex on my tongue, was no match for the complexity of emotions swirling within me.

We were down to our last wine, but I didn't want the night to end. I liked how I felt around Max. Like I didn't have to pretend to have it all together for once. I could sit here for hours, sipping wine and flirting.

As I reached for the lone piece of chocolate, our hands brushed, sending a jolt of electricity through me. Max's eyes, usually so confident and focused, held a softness, a vulnerability I hadn't seen before. It was as if, in this secluded space, we were allowing ourselves to drop the façades, to truly see and be seen.

"What about the port? The one that pairs with the dark

chocolate and sea salt." I eyed the lone chocolate left on the platter. The only one without a chunk bitten out of it.

"The problem is, ports are notoriously harder to select," Max said. "Smaller vineyards typically don't attempt to make them so we might have to go with something more well-known."

"Well," I started, my voice teasing the edges of a playful scheme, "we could always raid my parents' cellar."

There was a look on Max's face that I couldn't quite pin down. But the corners of his mouth lifted in a smile, and I knew he was in.

TEN

ISABELLA

I didn't know why it felt like I was sneaking a boy in as I brought Max through the front door of my childhood home. But I pressed a finger to my lips for him to be quiet as the latch clicked shut.

I reached for his hand to guide him up the dark stairs since I knew every floorboard by heart, especially the extra creaky ones. His palm was warm and wrapped around mine, expertly intertwining his fingers through my own. Max's hands found my waist as they reached the landing, and I passed my hand over the wall looking for the light switch.

I didn't miss the squeeze of his hands or how large they felt wrapped around me. Finally, I found the switch and slid the dimmer up a tad, enough to light our path to the arched door that led down to the cellar.

"Are you sure this is okay?" Max's voice came out in a whisper over my shoulder.

"Definitely. They won't mind if we drink *all* of their

wine, but if we wake up my mother, we'll have hell to pay," I replied.

Another squeeze at my hips in response and I almost leaned back into him to feel more of his touch. Somewhere between the lounge and my parents' foyer, we had escalated our flirtatious banter to flirtatious touching. I wasn't mad about it one bit.

I guided us through a tucked-away door hidden at the back of our butler's pantry. A skinny set of stairs led down to a temperature-controlled room where my parents stored their favorite wines. They weren't wine snobs by any means, but my parents held memberships in various wine clubs around the world, which meant a fully stocked wine cellar at all times.

The room was long, with shelves on three sides, a stunning arched brick ceiling, and a large table in the middle. An iron chandelier hung from the ceiling, casting the cedar wood in a beautiful glow.

"Wow, this is quite the collection," Max whispered, even though it was no longer necessary, as he looked up at the shelves stacked high with bottles.

"Yeah, I don't think my parents have as many people over these days, so they don't go through the bottles fast enough," I said.

"Well, I guess we'll have to take some off their hands," Max said, winking.

"All the ports are in this section." I turned and pointed to an angled section of the cellar, small, but stocked floor to ceiling with various ports.

Max walked over, eyes wide, as he took it all in. I leaned against another shelf, watching him. I eyed him as he picked up bottles, read the label, put some back, and circled back to others. "You're taking this very seriously, Boss."

Max turned to me, placing another bottle back on the shelf, with an odd glint in his eye. His lip turned up in a slight grin as he said, "Well, you picked out a fine chocolate for this wine, so it has to match it in quality, yes?"

In the tight space of the cellar, I had to look up to meet his eyes. They were eyes worth staring into, getting lost in, lingering on. The golden-brown flecks glimmered in the cedar-colored light of the cellar. I felt drunk just from the sight of him.

Max turned to face me, put his hands back on the sides of my hips, and grazed his thumbs over the edges of my hip bones through the fabric of my dress.

"You and these dresses . . ." Max murmured.

"Is there an end to that sentence?" I asked, eyebrows raised in a challenge.

"Yeah, they make me want to fuck you in them," Max said without hesitation.

I sucked in a breath at his confession, heat pooling in my belly, and raised my eyebrows. Our eyes darted across each other's faces, each scanning for a sign of what was next. Max inclined his head, a silent question. All I could do was give him a smirk.

"If I asked you to take off your panties, would you do it?" Max asked.

"What?" I asked, eyes blinking.

"Can I do this with you? Can I be like this with you, right now?" Max asked as he placed his hand on my cheek, his eyes never leaving mine.

I didn't fully understand what he meant, but I could only hope where it would lead and so I nodded.

"Say it, Isabella. Tell me yes or no. If you say no, I'll pick a wine and head home, no questions asked." Max's breath was heavier now, the room felt warmer.

"And if I say yes?" I asked.

"Then I'm going to tell you exactly what you need to do so I can fuck you *and* you're going to listen," he replied.

God, my heart was going to beat out of my chest. "Then, yes."

"That's my girl," Max said slowly. "Now slide your panties off those gorgeous hips and hand them to me." Max lifted his hands off my waist and took one step back.

I took a deep breath, slid my hands up the fabric of my billowy dress, hooked my fingers around the band of my panties, and started tugging them down. I let them fall past my knees and kept my eyes on Max as I felt them pool at my feet.

Max held out his hand, waiting.

I stepped my heeled feet out of each leg of my panties and scooped up the yellow lace fabric. I held them in my hand before reaching out to give them to Max.

He cupped his hand beneath mine, waiting. I dropped the fabric into his open palm and watched with wide eyes as he slid them into his pocket. Max took a step closer to me and found his spot back at my hips. He squeezed roughly and slid his hands to my backside to grip my ass over the fabric of my dress.

His eyes were dark, and he groaned as he squeezed hard enough to bring me to my tiptoes.

"Do you know the first time I saw you, you were wearing a dress like this one?" Max said in my ear, inhaling deeply.

I wracked my brain for the time he was talking about but came up blank. "No," I whispered.

"It was your mother's birthday," Max said. "You flew into town just for it. You were wearing this red dress and whenever the sunlight would catch the fabric I could see the outline of these hips," he said as he moved his hands down my sides, "and you would turn and I'd see the curve of this ass," he cupped me again, scooping me up.

My legs dangled on either side of his waist and with only the thin fabric of my dress in between them I felt his hardness pressed against me. I nearly moaned at the friction. Max walked forward, to the edge of the table in the center of the room. This table was normally meant for unloading new boxes of wine and the marble felt cool as I was placed on top of it.

Max brought a hand up my side slowly. He left goose-bumps in his wake as he rounded my shoulders and across my chest. His large palm rested on my throat as his fingers reached up to grab my chin gently.

"I'm going to check in with you one more time, Isabella," he said as he locked eyes with me. "Is this okay?"

This time I didn't hesitate. "Yes," I said. My body craved his. Needed him. Wanted him.

"I knew you would be a fast learner," Max said as he smirked. In a flash, his hand left my chin and gripped the back of my head, hair twisted in his grasp. He tilted my head up to his as he crashed his mouth to mine.

The kiss wasn't slow, it wasn't soft, and it wasn't gracious. It claimed me. It marked me. It devoured me.

His mouth was hot as it opened up against mine. Max pressed my head into him as if he could get me to climb into his skin. I moaned against his mouth as his tongue found mine in a frenzy. He hardened his tongue as it flicked against mine and I wondered what that tongue would feel like in other places.

If this was the kiss he would've given me at the winery, I'm ninety-nine percent certain we would've been kicked out. I opened my mouth and let him fully invade my space. He tasted like berries and chocolate.

I leaned my head back as his mouth trailed down my neck to my collarbone and into the skin between my breasts. Max rubbed my breasts from the outside of my dress, pushing them up as he inhaled deeply.

"Every inch of you is so fucking gorgeous," Max said as he ran his tongue up my sternum.

I leaned up a bit so I could slide my shoulders out of my sleeves. I wiggled out of the fabric and let it settle at my waist. Max didn't wait for me to unhook my lace bralette before he pushed the fabric down, allowing my breasts to spill over the edge of the fabric.

He paused for the briefest of moments as he took in the sight of me. My breath was quick, my chest rising rapidly, as I watched him take in my hardened nipples and the soft swell of my breasts. My eyes scanned his face, waiting for any sign of hesitation. All I saw was hunger.

Max's palms were on me, rubbing and tugging at my nipples then lapping up the pain with his mouth. I found myself grinding into his waist as he stood, still fully clothed at the edge of the table.

"It's always the good girls, isn't it?" Max asked as he watched my eyes darken as he rolled my nipple in between his fingers. "The ones who like it to hurt."

I reached for his waistband, wanting desperately to feel his skin against mine. Max chuckled in my ear. "I didn't tell you that you could touch yet, baby girl."

"Please," I said, not caring what came out of my mouth. I needed him.

"Already begging for my cock, huh?" Max asked as he pushed the fabric of my dress up toward my waist. The cool air landed on my thighs, and I shivered. "Let's see if you're even ready for me."

I heard Max suck in a breath and for a second I froze. What if I wasn't what he expected? What he wanted? My thighs were full and thin stretch marks ran across my upper thighs. I swallowed deeply and started to bring my knees in ready to call it. He didn't have to do this.

Max's hands were at my knees in an instant, pushing them out wider. "Did I tell you to close your legs?" he asked. "I want to get a good look at you before I devour you."

His promise made me shiver and I was afraid I might just come from his dirty talk. I watched his face as he took me in.

His eyes flared as he caught sight of me. With my arousal sticky on my inner thighs, I knew he could see how turned on I was right now. His face turned into a smirk, and I couldn't help the moan that escaped my throat as he pushed a finger inside me.

"You were already warmed up for me, baby girl. I'm so sorry I couldn't wait," Max said. "God, you're so wet. So soft. Imagine what you're going to feel like wrapped around my cock."

I leaned back, my elbows on the hard table as Max pushed another finger inside me. I was already trembling.

"Okay, baby girl, listen to me," Max spoke seriously as he fingered me. "I know you're close. So when I lean down and lick your swollen clit, you're going to come for me, okay? Can you do that?"

My voice was shaky as I said, "Yes."

Max hummed his approval as he pumped his fingers inside. I held my dress up as I watched Max lean down, his brown hair tickling my belly. And as soon as his warm mouth landed on my clit, his mouth creating a suction that brought my back off the table, I exploded. My limbs went numb and the breath was stolen out of my chest as I pulsed around his fingers and on his face.

"You did such a good job, baby," Max said from above me. He pulled his fingers out from inside me and his other hand reached to yank off his shirt before he unbuttoned his jeans. Once I heard the metal zipper slide down, I leaned up on my elbows. I needed to see him.

He pulled himself out, stroking himself a couple of

times. *God, he was thick.* A protruding vein marked the entire side of him and seemed to pulse.

"I have an IUD, by the way. I haven't been with anyone in . . . well, it's been a while," I said.

Max smiled at me. "I was tested after my last breakup, I'm clean."

I nodded, our eyes locking. His fingers traced my middle slowly, creating aftershocks of my orgasm throughout my body. But I needed more.

"You're going to take my cock like a good girl now," Max said. "I'm sorry, but I don't want to be easy tonight."

"Don't be," I replied. And before the last word left my lips, Max pressed himself to my entrance and shoved himself inside me. It took the breath from my chest. My mouth fell open, and the sound was stolen from my throat.

He was impossibly thick. He stretched me wide as he settled himself all the way in with one thrust. Max barely let me catch my breath before he gripped my hips and started thoroughly fucking me.

"Fuck, you take me so well, Isabella," Max said through gritted teeth as he pounded into me. "You look so beautiful swallowing my cock up with your pussy."

I had never heard dirty talk like this. I was afraid Max could whisper a line and I'd come on command. Because I wanted to. I wanted to come for him over and over again.

His praises were my reward and I'd chase them until I was sore. I'd do anything to keep hearing his rough voice command me. The sounds of our bodies moving filled the room and I leaned forward to watch him slide into me.

"Do you like watching me fuck you?" Max asked, his hand finding the back of my head again and gripping tightly. "I hope you do because I'm not sure I can ever leave this pussy."

I filed that statement for later even though I knew not to analyze the things men say during sex.

Instead, I let a low moan leave my body as he reached new corners of me. Max released the grip on my hair but kept exploring my body. With one hand holding my lower back up so he could drive himself into me, his other hand trailed up my belly, tweaked my nipples, and squeezed my throat.

He was everywhere all at once and all I wanted was more.

"You're going to come for me again, baby. I need to feel you strangle my cock," Max said. "I think I might know just how you like it. And if I'm right, god help me."

Max lowered me back down to the table and slowed the movements of his hips slightly. With one hand, he danced his fingers around my clit, circling and tugging roughly. With the other hand, he reached up for my throat and squeezed.

As Max slowly drilled his cock deeper and deeper, I felt the buzz building deep in my belly. With one pinch to my clit and a sharp squeeze at my neck, I felt myself go completely numb. My vision blurred at the edges as my orgasm jolted through my body, my scream cut off by the hand around my throat.

Warm liquid spread between my thighs as I gasped for breath when Max finally let go. The aftershocks of my orgasm weaved through my body as Max set his sights on his own. His large hands found their place on my thighs as he pounded into me.

"Come inside me," I whispered from below, and I could tell by the dark look on his face and the stillness of his hips that Max also liked being told what to do. His body stilled as a deep, low groan tumbled out from between his lips. After a few moments, he leaned down and placed gentle kisses on my chest. Each one felt like a quiet thank you.

"Um, there's a bathroom right outside the cellar if you want to . . ." I said as Max started to slide out.

He smiled at me as he said, "Okay, be right back."

Max was back before I could fully catch my breath, my chest still splotchy and heaving. He gently wiped between my legs and thighs, creating shivers up my legs as he grazed my sensitive places. He had shoved himself back in his pants, but the top still lay open and wide, his shirt still off.

God, he was something to look at. His chest was wide and fit, with softness in just the right places. His skin glistened with a sheen of sweat, and his eyes intently focused on me. Once he was finished cleaning me, he gently set my legs down and helped me sit up. He adjusted my bralette and brought the sleeves of my dress back up, straightening the fabric at my shoulders. He kept my panties in his pocket.

With every move, his eyes bore into me, seemingly memorizing every pore of my skin, every mole that marked me.

"That was . . ." he began.

"Yeah, that definitely was . . ." I could finally breathe

normally, but the pounding in my chest wouldn't go away. "We didn't even get to sample a port," I added.

Max threw his head back and laughed. "You're right, we didn't. Are you still up for it?" he asked.

I nodded.

He turned back toward the angled shelf stocked full of options as he zipped and buttoned his jeans. He ran his hand through his hair as he hunted for the perfect bottle before selecting one from the shelf.

"A nice Taylor Fladgate twenty-year-old Tawny Port should do the job. It'll be sweeter than any of the chocolates you picked out, which will help pull the rich flavor profiles out," he said, holding the bottle and examining the label.

"Sounds great, Boss," I said as I slid off the table.

Max caught my wrist and spun me around as his mouth found mine. "You're going to be the death of me, aren't you?" he asked with his lips hovered over mine.

"I don't know what you're talking about," I said with a smirk.

In reality, I wasn't quite sure what to expect after tonight. Was this a one-time thing? Would we still keep up our flirting? I hadn't realized how much I missed the kind of attention he had been giving me, so I wasn't ready for it to go away. I grabbed some glasses from a small shelf and led us back up the narrow staircase.

After snagging the chocolates off the kitchen counter, I led us toward the back of the townhouse. My parents' backyard was a slender slice of cobblestone heaven and the thought of fresh air on my face was exactly what I needed right about now.

The garden was overgrown in a way that invited butterflies and honeybees to the space, and twinkle lights strung from the edge of the home to the corners of the patio.

Wrought iron furniture sat in zones through the space, and stepping stones created walkways through the yard. I decided to post up at the wooden table that sat under a pergola of purple wisteria. The sweet pea smell from the flowers came through when the breeze ruffled the blooms.

"This place feels like an actual secret garden," Max said, looking around. "I can see where you got your inspiration for the event's theme."

"Yeah, it's one of my favorite parts about this house. The garden has really filled in since I've been gone," I said.

"Are you glad to be back?" Max asked as he poured some port into our glasses, and I unboxed the chocolates.

I tilted my head from side to side. "Yes and no. It's hard to explain."

"Try me," Max said.

I dug out the dark chocolates for us to sample as Max opened up the slim port bottle and filled our glasses with a small sample.

"You know when I was traveling, there was this constant sense of movement and discovery, and every decision I made was my own. There were no guide rails. But after years of that, I craved some kind of anchor, a sense of place and direction. I thought coming back to the city, being surrounded by these familiar walls, and living under my parents' roof again would offer me that. A moment where someone might just hand me a roadmap or even gently nudge me down a path."

"... But?" Max asked, urging me on.

I chuckled. "But . . . that's not really how life works, is it? No one is just going to start telling me what to do. I'm gonna have to actually figure it out myself."

"I know that whatever you figure out is going to be amazing. You've got to just stop overthinking it so much. Just let go and see what happens," he said.

"Yeah, maybe," I said as I bit into the chocolate and took a small sip of the port. My eyes closed as the flavors exploded in my mouth. It was dreamy.

I didn't know what would come next between me and Max. Or if I'd just royally fucked up our friendship or working relationship. I didn't know if or when Dom would find out or if it would ever happen again. But, oh, did I want it to happen again.

Instead, I let this gorgeous man in front of me lull me with his nerdy knowledge of the flavor profiles and grape origins as the lights twinkled above and soreness in between my legs reminded me of what we'd just done.

ELEVEN

ISABELLA

I stared at my buzzing phone, a headache forming at the base of my skull and a callus forming at the base of my right heel. The brightness from the screen momentarily blinded me, and I squinted at the name *Natalia - Bora Bora Babe*. The nickname I'd given my best friend during my extended island vacation had stuck.

I snorted. *Spill the tea,* indeed. The only thing I longed to spill at the moment was my entire body into a hot bath. Between all my late shifts at the Prism Society, stressing about the upcoming event, and, oh god, last night.

Max.

There was tea to spill there. Not that I was ready to divulge what was going on between us. Not that anything *was* going on between us. After we'd sampled the port with the chocolate and Max had made his final decision for the wine list, I'd claimed to be tired and ushered him out of my parents' front door.

Then, I'd laid in bed for hours, replaying every single second that had passed between us down in the cellar. The way he'd taken charge as soon as he knew what I'd crave. How he knew *exactly* how and where to touch me. How he spoke to me.

I let out a deep sigh and groaned as I rolled over. My thighs were tender from where Max had gripped them last night. But even with a headache, sex soreness, and massive overthinking anxiety, I wouldn't turn down getting together with Nat.

I had missed her these last few weeks. I couldn't wait to hug her sun-kissed shoulders and hear all about her time in Bora Bora. I held my phone up to my face so I could unlock my screen and fired off a text.

> Isabella: Yesssss, can you meet today? I could be at Buvette in an hour.

I got an enthusiastic slew of emojis from Nat, and the plan was in place. Before pressing the lock button on my phone, I saw I had another text waiting for me. I tapped the green bubble with the red alert and couldn't help the smile that spread across my face.

Max: Good morning, beautiful. Remember to drink extra water today. See you later at work.

Max. Well, there goes my plan to pretend like nothing

happened between us. There goes my assumption that he regrets last night. Like it or not, the *thing* between me and Max was definitely going to need to be figured out.

But for now, all I had to do was get myself out of this bed and into the shower. If only I could float over to the hot water instead of having to use my feet.

Exactly fifty-three minutes later, I pulled open the glass-paned door of the cozy and charming French-inspired café that Nat and I loved. My stomach growled as soon as I smelled the fresh bread and coffee wafting through the small dining lounge.

As my eyes wandered the vintage furnishings of Buvette, I remembered the first time Nat and I had stumbled upon it during our prep-school days. Nat had been the one to discover it after ditching a particularly boring art history class, and I, always the diligent student, had been coerced into joining her. The two of us had spent hours here, giggling over hot croissants and plotting our future globe-trotting adventures.

Luckily, Nat knew I would need the caffeine and fuel. I smiled at the French press of rich coffee and a plate of croissants already waiting for me at a back corner table where Nat was sitting. Natalia and I had practically been joined at the hip since prep school.

I remembered my first day roaming the echoing halls, feeling like a fish out of water. Even though it had been Nat's first year as well, she somehow looked like she belonged the second she walked through the doors. Her attitude was fearless, and my energy was different. Nat, with her sun-streaked hair always pulled back in a messy bun, her uniform skirt a tad shorter than the rest, and her mischievous green eyes, had me hooked from day one.

By the end of our first week, we'd pinky-promised never to leave each other's sides. And over the years, we'd kept that promise. We had navigated boy drama, academic challenges, and the school's strict dress codes.

Nat had introduced me to the thrill of adventure, dragging me on impromptu trips to secret spots around the city, sneaking into concerts, and even making the drive out to Penn State just to make out with some boys. Nat was my person. It was Nat who gave me the confidence to purchase that one-way ticket almost ten years ago that kickstarted my travel adventures.

I slid into the booth next to Nat and snuggled into her side, craving the warmth of her skin. Nat threw her arms around me and squeezed tightly, kissing the top of my head. After our hug, Nat scooted back to lean against the wall as she turned to face me. I slid my ankle under my knee and picked up my coffee cup.

"Being back in the city looks good on you, Iz," Nat said as she sipped her coffee.

"Being back in the city makes me feel my age. These blocks were a lot easier to walk a decade ago," I said.

Nat laughed, the sound light and free. "You always exaggerate. And please, I've seen your step tracker. You walk miles daily."

"I'm actually surprised to see you back already. Last I saw, it looked like you and what's-his-name were having a lot of fun." I smirked.

Nat winked. "Oh, he was tempting, but New York has its hold on me. But . . . I wanted to tell you first—I'm actually back for good. My parents wanted me to take over the family business."

"Holy shit, Nat, that's huge!" I responded. "What area are you taking over?"

The Beaumonts were a huge figure in New York City. What started as a textile and spice trading company back in the 1800s has since ballooned into an entire holdings company that deals with real estate, antiquities, non-profits, spas, and wellness centers.

"I'll be overseeing the health and wellness side. I know there's a lot I could bring to spice it up from everything we learned while traveling." Nat shrugged. "Who knows what area we end up exploring next?"

"This makes my heart so happy, Nat," I said. I tore off a piece of buttery croissant and popped it in my mouth. "I'm so glad you're back. Oh! And since you're here, you *have* to come to this event I'm helping with in a couple of weeks."

I filled Nat in on all the details about the Prism Society and the wine-tasting event I was putting together for Max. I kept what had gone down last night to myself.

"Is he hot?" Nat asked in the middle of me explaining the chocolate taste test Max and I had done to prepare for the event.

"Who?" I asked.

"Max. The dashing, young sommelier." Nat clarified.

"Oh, uh . . ." I stared up at the ceiling like I had to think about it. "I mean, one might say he is attractive."

"Oh, 'one might say,' huh?" Nat teased, bumping my shoulder. It reminded me of all our times abroad when we would huddle close in a sticky booth at whatever pub we could find and scan the crowd for available guys.

Nat had always been such a good wingwoman for me, reminding me to go after what I wanted, to claim it, and take it. I had missed her energy.

"You were always *so* good at putting together amazing events, Iz. Remember when you threw that stunning summer solstice party in Greece?" I smiled at the memory. The travel guides had sent out a photographer to use for their next magazine. I hadn't thought it had been a big deal, but they were still using the photos from that event, even now.

"I can't wait to see it all come together," Natalia said, sipping her coffee.

"So I guess you should also know that . . ." I hesitated, trying to figure out exactly how to describe what the Prism Society was like. "The club is . . . adult."

"Like a strip club?" Nat asked as she brought her coffee cup to her lips.

"No, not like that at all," I said. "More like a place for people to explore their . . . fantasies. They have different rooms upstairs that members can reserve and use . . . however they want."

"Oh, spicy!" Nat said quietly. "What kind of rooms?"

I should have known I could count on Nat to be curious instead of judgmental. I smiled and said, "I don't really know,

I haven't actually been in them. But I hear there's a sensory deprivation room, one that has a lot of *accessories*, one that has multiple beds. . . . It's very posh though."

Nat shivered with excitement. "Well, maybe you'll just have to take some PTO just so you can spend some time in the spicy part of the club."

I shook my head. "Honestly, letting loose in a club *my brother* works in gives me the heebie-jeebies. He would have to be, like, out of the country or something."

I continued, "But . . . maybe *you* could host a retreat at the Prism Society, blending in your 'specialties.' I can just see the tagline: 'Discover your desires and find your center.'"

"As long as I have you to plan it, girl, I'm in for whatever," Nat added and laughed. "Okay, well, unfortunately, I have to run. I have an actual *board meeting* to attend."

"Oh, she's so fancy!" I teased. "See you soon, love."

I could smell Nat's vanilla rose shampoo when she reached in for a hug and I squeezed extra hard before letting go. Something settled in me with Natalia around. It's like she could ground me with just a simple catch up and it refueled me. Good friends were like that, and I was lucky to have her.

I felt a newfound sense of confidence with the upcoming event knowing Natalia would be there by my side to help with any crisis. Not that I *needed* the reassurance that moving back to the city was the right choice (okay, so *I did* need it) but having Nat here was the validation I needed that I was exactly where I belonged.

TWELVE
ISABELLA

With my fingers smudged with hints of chalk from sketching out seating arrangements and the earthy smell of fresh flowers enveloping me, I carefully adjusted the placement of the last wineglass on the port-tasting table. The evening was finally upon us, and the fluttering in my stomach was unmistakable. I was eager, anxious, and everything in between for two significant reasons.

This event marked my first foray into planning and hosting a high-profile occasion in what felt like forever. Not only did I desperately want it to unfold seamlessly for the club's sake, but I also had a personal stake in its success for Max. I yearned for it to draw in more interest toward the club's wine offerings, showcasing the depth and passion he brought to the table.

More than that, I had set myself a goal: if tonight resulted in at least ten new member sign-ups, it would solidify my place in taking the reins of event organization at the club. Such an outcome would not only be a testament to the evening's success but also a thrilling leap forward in my career, one that felt both daunting and incredibly exhilarating.

Then, there was Max. Those deep, thoughtful looks caught me off guard every time he glanced my way and filled me with a warmth I wasn't expecting to feel in such a professional setting. It wasn't just his looks that made my stomach flutter. It was the fleeting touches, the way his fingers would occasionally brush against my lower back as he passed by, igniting a cascade of tingles that raced along my nerves. These small, innocuous interactions stirred a tumult of emotions within me, blending anticipation with a kind of nervous excitement I couldn't quite pin down.

Every casual touch and shared glance seemed to blur the lines between professional collaboration and something much more personal—something I wasn't sure I was ready to explore, yet found myself drawn to nonetheless. It was as if, amidst the stress and bustle of event preparations, we were dancing around the edges of a deeper connection, leaving me to wonder about the possibilities that lay beyond the professional façade we maintained.

We definitely hadn't ignored that we'd slept together, but we hadn't exactly had enough time to figure out the details of it either. So, for now, it was our little secret, flashbacks of it shared through heated glances from across the room as we worked.

It had turned a switch on in Max, though, one that I was obsessed with figuring out more. Ever since our time in the cellar, Max had become hell-bent on making sure I was taking care of myself. He'd refill my water during shifts, silently setting a fresh glass on the bar top for me. He brought my snacks and ordered food while I worked away on the third floor setting up for the event. By the time the day of the event came, I barely had time to stop to pee, so I was extra grateful for his odd attention.

As I chugged a fresh glass of water I watched as Natalia meticulously draped the last of the table linens, her practiced eye ensuring perfection. Having my best friend Natalia by my side was a godsend. She had been just as busy the last two weeks so having her here today felt extra special.

Despite taking on her family's business, Nat was happy to help out, and it put a smile on my face. Years of attending fancy parties had sharpened Nat's designer eye for detail, which could be seen in her work that day. We worked in a fluid tandem, utilizing the muscle memory we'd built from decades of friendship.

Every inch of the room was a masterpiece—a verdant secret garden, hidden away from the bustling city outside. Velvety moss, cascading purple orchids, and twinkling string lights illuminated each tasting zone with an enchanted glow.

The Pinot Noir's pink peonies mingled with ivy, while Champagne's cream roses invited each guest to explore further. A dash of cinnamon sticks surrounded by vibrant orange ranunculus beckoned for the Syrah lovers. An elegant setting of deep red roses paired with eucalyptus marked the Cabernet Sauvignon corner—fit for royalty.

Floor lanterns lit a path through this paradise of taste, and I hoped our guests would be swept up in the flavor and beauty of it all. I was proud of what I'd helped create. It had scratched an itch and lit a fire in me that I didn't know I'd had.

"Isabella," Max's voice interrupted my thoughts. I turned, seeing him standing at the entrance of the atrium. His normally confident demeanor was replaced by nervousness, his fingers playing with the cuffs of his tailored suit. He stepped closer, and his eyes widened in awe as they surveyed the transformed space. "This is . . . breathtaking."

"Thank you," I said softly, feeling my heart swell with pride. "Let me walk you through it so you know the flow."

Guiding him, I began at the port station, explaining the choice of orchids and moss, how it played with the richness of the wine, and the sweet depth of the accompanying chocolates. We moved seamlessly from one zone to the next, with me detailing the thought behind every element.

"You really outdid yourself, Isabella. The layers, the attention to detail," Max mused, pausing at the Champagne table to admire the cream roses. "Every station perfectly complements the wine it hosts."

I laughed lightly, brushing a stray curl behind my ear. "That was the idea. And you better be ready to wow everyone with your impeccable wine knowledge."

Max smirked, his playful side returning. "Challenge

accepted. Though I think my sommelier skills have met their match with your event planning."

Our eyes locked for a moment, the world around them blurring. My heart raced, but I broke the gaze, my cheeks coloring. "Well, you better be ready. We're a team tonight."

Max stepped closer, a teasing glint in his eyes. "Always, when I'm with you." He brushed a thumb over my cheek, sending shivers down my spine. "Thank you, Isabella. This means more than you can imagine."

"Well, you know," I replied, trying to keep my voice steady, "always here to save the day."

My chuckles echoed in the atrium as guests filtered in, marking the beginning of a magical night. I took a deep breath, smoothed the fabric of my black dress, and watched as the event began.

As the night progressed, Max slipped seamlessly into his role, guiding guests through the intricacies of each wine. I observed from a distance, admiring the way he swirled the wine in its glass, allowing it to breathe, before explaining its distinct aroma and taste profile.

Max's enthusiasm for wine transformed the tasting into an intimate gathering of old friends. His knowledge about the vineyards, the soil, and the vintage years made the pairings come alive, enhancing the experience with each sip. Guests were visibly moved, murmuring their approval, particularly enamored with the Syrah and caramel chocolate pairing.

As the room buzzed with energy, the chemistry between Max and me became a silent conversation. His casual touches and proud glances sent waves of excitement through me, which Natalia noticed and couldn't help but tease, "There's more than wine and chocolate chemistry here, Iz."

Trying to maintain focus on the event proved challenging as the night unfurled into a blend of animated discussions and laughter. Max's skillful presentations, like describing the Champagne's interaction with white chocolate truffles, captivated everyone. His ability to engage and educate created a magical atmosphere, underscored by the soft glow of string lights and the melody of clinking glasses.

The event showcased our combined efforts and positioned Max as a sought-after sommelier for private tastings. Watching him, his passion so evident, filled me with a deep sense of pride and connection to the work we were doing together.

Natalia's words, acknowledging the unique vibe of the place, echoed my sentiments. It was indeed a night to remember, a testament to the harmony between meticulous planning and genuine passion.

"There's so much potential here," Nat said, coming up to stand next to me. "You know, with the new departments I'll be overseeing, I've been thinking about the concept of self-love and indulgence. What if we introduced an aspect of this kind of luxury, this kind of exploration into the family business? There's nothing quite like self-care, right?"

I raised an eyebrow, intrigued. "Are you suggesting what I think you're suggesting?"

Nat smirked. "A little wine, a little relaxation, and

perhaps . . . a touch of the risqué? It could be an entirely new way of approaching wellness."

I chuckled. "You always did have an adventurous spirit. But I love the idea. A unique blend of sophistication, relaxation, and exploration. It's bold."

"I'd want to work with you, though. To make it happen." Natalia turned to face me, her eyes serious.

"Nat, I'm just a cocktail waitress, so you're going to need to talk to Dom and Max about that move." I took a small sip of wine, the warm red liquid coating my tongue.

"You and I both know that's not true. I mean, come on, look at what you did with this whole event. You always knew how to take a theme and run with it." Nat smiled.

"I'd have to talk to the guys. And I don't know the first thing about finding a place and all the logistics about opening a club like this and—"

"Leave *those* details to me." Nat put a hand on my shoulder. "Just tell me you'll help with the overall vibe and theme of the place. And of course, getting him," she cocked her head over to Max, "to come on board. Something tells me we'd get a lot of new clientele just from having the promise of Max and wine."

I chuckled. "This is crazy, Nat, you know that, right?"

"And what about it?" Nat tilted her wineglass up, draining it, before making her rounds around the room.

I didn't want to encroach on my brother's entire business model, but the concept of helping Nat create something like this *was* exciting. And I couldn't help but think it'd be a lot easier to try out the *spicy* side of the club if my brother wasn't roaming the halls.

It was impossible to not daydream about the activities going on upstairs as Max and I worked the lounge downstairs. But this was my brother's space and the last thing I wanted to do was cross some unspoken boundary. But if Nat led her own space . . . now that would definitely let down some walls for me.

Not that I had anyone to take upstairs. But that was kind of the point, right? Sexual exploration for the sake of exploration is what the club promised.

"What are you daydreaming about over here?" Max's voice cut through my thoughts and my cheeks warmed instantly. I hadn't been thinking about spending time behind one of those oxblood doors with a stranger just now. I'd been thinking about what that would be like with *Max*.

"Uh, nothing, just, uh, about to get started cleaning up," I stammered out my response, unable to make eye contact with him. Guests were filing out now, heading downstairs.

Max chuckled at my nervousness. "Well, I just wanted to say thank you. Truly. For everything tonight. And everything you did to prepare for it."

I regained my composure enough to say, "Of course. You're welcome. It was a lot of fun."

"You know, if you ever get tired of working with me in the lounge, you should definitely go into event planning," Max said. "You really crushed it tonight, Isabella."

I chuckled. "You know there's been a lot of career opportunities talked about tonight. I guess we'll just have to see."

I cleared my head while I started cleaning up the space, tossing wine bottles in the recycling bin and shaking off tablecloths. I should most definitely *not* be daydreaming about my boss-slash-younger brother's friend.

Even if the opportunity with Nat turned into something real, there was no promise that Max would want to work there. I couldn't let myself get distracted by how easy it felt to be around him. Or how his stupid smile made a tiny little flutter in my ribs.

THIRTEEN
MAX

You know how they always say *it just takes one connection to change the rest of your life*? Well, the saying goes something like that. But it's true. The domino effect of happenings following the wine-tasting event still made my head spin.

My private event calendar was filling up. I had known Isabella was being particular about whom we invited to the tasting, and now I knew why. So far, I had been requested for a girls' night in the penthouse suite of 432 Park Avenue, an anniversary dinner in a private room at Per Se, and an intimate company retreat at the Soho House.

I'd also caught wind of a potential *new* club Isabella's friend Natalia wanted to talk about running, and rumor had it she wanted *me* to be a big part of it. The idea of juggling all of that, plus shifts at the Prism Society *and* finishing my last bit of studying before my exam date in just a couple of short weeks, stressed me the hell out.

While the idea of all of these opportunities excited me, I definitely felt like I was in the grind. The beginning stages of creating my career and life. I didn't know if Isabella was the kind of person to stick around through all of that. She had her own name that opened doors; she certainly didn't need to wait around while I built mine. But when she let me take charge the other night, something had eased in me.

Something I hadn't experienced with Ana. Whenever I was with Ana, even intimately, I got the impression I had to constantly prove myself. That I had should feel honored she was even giving me her attention even as I slid inside her. But not with Isabella. The absolute need I saw reflected back in her eyes drove me wild. I'd do anything to see it again.

This morning, Dominic had texted me to come in earlier than normal today to chat about upcoming projects. I couldn't help but cross my fingers that things were moving forward with Natalia's idea. Even though I already had a thousand things on my plate, getting to lead the opening of a new club excited me. I just hoped I could juggle it all.

As soon as I walked through the velvet curtains of the club, I headed upstairs to the third floor. Seeing the atrium open and empty again after seeing it become such a magical space a few short nights ago was odd. Natalia, Isabella, and I had stayed behind to tear down the event and decompress with our own bottle or two.

The gals had danced around the atrium to Green Day as they boxed up the florals and tossed the linens in the dry-cleaning bag. Nat had been whispering about something to Isabella all night, and I hadn't hidden the smile on my face when Isabella's eyes kept catching me across the room. Her cheeks would blush every time.

I was used to the quiet whispers followed by silly giggles that ensued when girls got together. I'd lived my whole life being surrounded by it. I couldn't help but smile at how easily Isabella would fit in with my rowdy sisters at a Sunday dinner at my mom's house.

I needed to clear my head of my daydreams about Isabella before I walked into a meeting with her *brother*. I cleared my throat and tapped my knuckles on the doorframe of Dom's office. He and Liam sat together, scrutinizing some paperwork.

"Hey man, come on in," Dominic said from behind his desk.

I had been amazed at what Dom and Liam had decided to create together when I first heard about their idea. Dom had always been quiet and calculating. He kept to himself and made his own moves in private. One day, you'd look up, and he was ten steps further than he had been the last time you noticed.

It was an immediate yes when they asked me to come on board, especially with the leeway they gave me to study. While working in a sex club was never on my bucket list, the environment of the Prism Society was anything but slimy. I'd grown accustomed to the nonjudgemental atmosphere of the club and absolutely saw the lure of it all.

Emma, Liam's girlfriend, had poured her heart and soul into this space to turn it into something magical. Something sensual but luxurious. They were working hard at creating a space, a community, that valued sex positivity and exploration, and I was happy to be a part of that. Even if my mom shushed me every time I dared talk about work.

"I heard the event went really well. Congratulations, Max," Liam said.

"Yeah, thanks, man. Isabella really helped put all that together honestly, I just showed up." I slid my hands in my pockets and leaned against a large bookshelf.

"I'm just going to cut to the chase," Dominic said. "We have a proposition for you."

"Okay, what's up?" I asked, my curiosity piqued. Dom was never one to mince words or waste time on small talk.

"I know you met Natalia Beaumont the other night. Well, she's been a family friend for a long time. Anyways, she came to us the other day with an idea for a new club." Dominic turned the stack of papers around so I could see.

"There's a club whose owners have been wanting to sell," Dominic continued. "It needs a refresh, a little bit of a rebrand, so to speak, but it's got good bones. We're thinking we could have it re-opened in just a couple of months."

I peered down at the paperwork. The building in question was called *The Mirage Guild*. It was an old building in Greenwich tucked behind a tavern. The owners owned both the tavern and the large space behind it but were ready to retire and close up shop. Dominic and Liam knew it was prime real estate, and it made sense that they wanted to snatch it up.

"Oh, I think I've seen this space. You can only get to the club from behind a bookshelf in the tavern, right?" I asked.

"Yeah, exactly," Liam said, "It's got loads of hidden rooms and hallways. It's a really cool space." His face already held excitement about what they could turn it into.

"We're thinking of making it more of a wine bar instead of a tavern," Dominic said, bringing them back to the point. "With you managing it. If you want."

I paused. "Are you serious?"

"You've done great here. I trust you. It just makes sense," Dominic said plainly like there was no room for doubt.

"I . . . I mean, that sounds incredible." I found my voice, grappling with the sudden shift in my future. "Managing a whole wine bar? I'd be honored."

Dominic nodded, as if he had expected no other response. "We've seen what you can do, Max. We wouldn't offer this if we didn't believe you were the right person for the job."

Liam chimed in, a grin spreading across his face. "And just think of the pairings you could create with a place of your own. This could really put the Mirage Guild on the map, especially with the unique selections you've been championing."

Dominic leaned forward, clasping his hands together on the desk. "We've got Natalia on board for the club side of things, and she's ecstatic about working with you. Plus, Isabella's officially our event coordinator now. Her success with the wine and chocolate night was undeniable. We're looking to replicate that magic on a regular basis."

My heart skipped at the mention of Isabella. Working closely with her? That was an unexpected bonus.

"So, what about the transition period?" I asked, my mind already racing through logistics. "I've got my sommelier exam in a couple of weeks, and then there's the day-to-day here at the Prism Society."

"We've thought about that," Dominic replied. "The Mirage Guild won't be ready to open for another four to six months. That gives you plenty of time to study for your exam and start planning the launch. We'll look for your replacement here in the meantime, someone to handle the bar while you focus on both your studies and the Guild."

"And don't worry about being stretched too thin," Liam added. "We want this transition to be smooth for everyone, especially for our members. Natalia's idea is to create a seamless experience between the Prism Society and the Mirage Guild, elevating our wine program to new heights. Your role will be pivotal in achieving that."

Dominic's eyes met mine, serious yet reassuring. "This isn't just a new job, Max. It's an opportunity to shape something from the ground up, to make it your own. You have our full support and trust. We know you'll make us proud."

Gratitude washed over me. "Thank you," I managed, my voice thick with emotion. "I won't let you down."

Leaving Dominic's office, I fully grasped the magnitude of the journey ahead. The change wasn't merely a job switch —it marked the beginning of a new chapter in my career, one that could shape my life's direction. And with Isabella by my side, both professionally and personally, I felt ready to take on whatever challenges came our way. My to-do list had indeed grown, but so had my excitement for the future.

As I made my way downstairs, my updated to-do list ran through my mind. Now, all I had to worry about was finding two new bartenders, studying for my exam, working my current shifts, prepping for my private events, and finding ways to keep working with Isabella.

Isabella, who was currently dangerously teetering off one rung of the bar ladder in impossibly high-heeled shoes. As I rounded the last step, I could see her long, tan legs from across the lounge. She had one foot out and one arm reaching high above her head.

"What the hell, Isabella?" I rushed over to the ladder and, without hesitation, gripped her waist so she could right herself. The heat of her skin through the waistband of her skirt beckoned my fingers to the flesh underneath the hem of her top. She was warm and soft, and I wanted to explore more of her.

I'd thought of nothing else but the feel of her underneath me every night since the wine cellar. I heard her soft moans in my sleep and would wake up to a rock-solid hard-on, and remembering the way her throat felt underneath my hand was the only thing I thought of as I jerked myself.

"What are you even doing up here? And in these shoes? Are you insane?" My questions came out in a fury.

"These shoes are perfectly acceptable, thank you very much," she said as she reached the shelf and slid a wine bottle into an empty slot. "I was just putting the leftover wine from the event back up; otherwise, it would sit behind the bar for days."

"Well, I appreciate your tidiness, but you could've asked

me to do that," I said. I hadn't let go of her waist, and I wouldn't until she was safely back on solid ground.

Finally, Isabella started making her descent. When she had less than three rungs left to go, I lost my patience and lifted her up off the ladder and set her back on the ground. I held onto her for a moment longer as she swayed.

"That ladder goes up a lot higher than it looks," Isabella said as she blew a stray curl out of her face, her cheeks red.

I chuckled. "Yeah, it really does."

"Well, thank you for coming to my rescue, beast," Isabella said as she tapped my chest and stepped out of my grasp. I missed the feel of her between my hands.

"Beast? Is that what you just said?" I caught the phrase a second later.

Isabella sucked in her lips, clearly not meaning for me to hear. She sighed and said, "It's what you looked like the first day I met you. I walked in, and you were on this ladder. And in my head, I thought you looked like Beast from Beauty and the Beast. But, like, a smutty version."

"A smutty version?" I chuckled and followed Isabella through the lounge as she set up the tables.

"Yeah, 'cause you didn't have a shirt on. And you look like . . . that . . ." Isabella waved an arm in my direction.

"Oh, my heavens, is Miss Isabella Esposito giving me a compliment?" I teased.

"Take it however you want, Max," she said.

"Beast. Take it however you want . . . *Beast*." I locked eyes with Isabella before adding, "Maybe I will."

I found joy in the fact that even as her cheeks flushed, she didn't take her eyes off mine.

"Have you heard the news? About the new club?" I needed to change the subject before I walked over to her and *actually* did what I wanted to do.

Isabella released a breath. "Yes, when Nat gets an idea for something, there's no stopping her. I think she went and talked to the owners of Mirage, like, the day after your event."

"Our event," I corrected before diving in with what was on my mind. "I heard you've been dubbed the official Event Maestro for the Mirage Guild," I said, eager to confirm the rumors of her new title.

"Yeah, something like that," she replied nonchalantly, adjusting the chairs around the marble-topped tables. "Just helping out with promotions at the moment; it's not a full-blown career or anything."

"But it could be, couldn't it?" I ventured, placing the mercury glass vases filled with cream roses on the tables. "The success of the wine and chocolate night wasn't just a fluke. It's opened a lot of doors, hasn't it? Seems like you've got a real knack for this."

"Trying to get rid of me?" Isabella teased, and my brows scrunched up.

"The opposite, actually." I stopped my movements and smiled over at her. "I'd love to see more of you at Mirage."

Isabella stared back at me as she let my words sink in, a little bit of that heat simmering in her eyes.

I should've seen the storm clouds gathering over my day from the moment the morning started on a sour note. First, it was a nick on my knee in the shower, then came the shattered body oil bottle. I should've taken the hint then. The coffee shop's oat milk drought should've been my second warning, and the accidental dousing of my limited-edition blouse in cold brew was a siren call I blatantly ignored.

Expecting the Prism Society to be my sanctuary as usual, I craved the dimly lit peace it always offered. But tonight, my haven was breached by a digital missive that threw me off-kilter. My usually stowed-away phone remained on the bar, buzzing with a reminder of a past best left forgotten.

Perhaps it was the universe and the stupid retrograde that told me to leave it out. If I hadn't, then the sensation that currently lined my gut would have at least been pushed off until later. The feeling that I couldn't quite put my finger on.

Was it disbelief?

Shock?

Irritation?

Dis-shock-ation, perhaps.

It shouldn't bother me. It really shouldn't. But the way he had *worded* it.

The message was from Nikos. Nikos, who had convinced me that stability and roots were for other people, not for us, the adventurers. Nikos, whom I somehow, against my better judgment, envisioned a future with. And now, he had the audacity to share his engagement and impending fatherhood with me, as if it were some consolation prize for our failed romance.

> Nikos: Issa, I wanted you to be the first to know that Clara and I are engaged. She's expecting, actually, I'm going to be a dad! If this hadn't come about maybe you and I could've found our way back to each other. I've been thinking about how we left things. I miss you.

The impact of his words spiraled me into an introspective abyss I wasn't prepared to explore mid-shift. I masked my turmoil with a practiced smile, but the evening's tips and snippets of trivial arguments couldn't distract me from my own storm brewing within.

Who the hell sends an engagement *and* baby announcement in the same message with their *I miss you* confession?

Someone pathological. And so with the buzz of the message, the reality of it on my screen, and the icky feeling in my gut, I had started my shift.

Max could tell *something* was off, but he also seemed to have a sixth sense about it and was giving me space. I was afraid I'd burst into tears and scream if he asked me what was wrong. And so I swallowed my emotions, closed my phone, held my head high, and plastered a friendly smile on my face.

Even the tips coming in that night were affected by the retrograde and whatever else was in the air. I could overhear tidbits of senseless arguments from couples as I walked through the lounge, refilling sparkling waters.

My current state of dress, a hasty replacement for my ruined blouse, was just another layer to my growing discomfort. I longed for the simplicity of a wine bath and the quiet of solitude, away from the unending reminder of my perceived failures.

I was grappling with a whirlwind of wants: love without confinement, a career filled with passion, a stable yet thrilling life. The paradox of my desires left me feeling adrift, questioning if a balance between these extremes was even attainable.

I was tired. And not just from the evening. I was tired of constantly feeling like I was playing catch-up in my own life. I was tired of second-guessing every choice I made. It's not that I believed something better was around the corner, it was that I didn't actually know what I wanted.

Nikos's message, a trigger to my spiraling self-reflection, underscored a deeper longing within me—a desire for direction, for someone to navigate the murky waters of my future for me. Yet, admitting such a wish felt like a betrayal to the fiercely independent façade I upheld.

The fact that I even craved that made me angry. At myself. At societal expectations. I walked behind the bar to drop off a tray of dirty glasses along with a few full-to-the-brim wasted cocktails. Because I'd jotted the order down wrong, or delivered it to the wrong table, distraction taking over.

"Hey," Max said as he was remaking three cocktails for me, "I don't know what's up with you tonight, but is it something you can compartmentalize? All these mess ups don't really bode well for me."

"For you?" I asked sharply. "Of, course, Boss, my apologies." I set the new drinks on my tray and turned on my heel before Max could respond, his face softening at the last second.

Getting through the next few hours of this shift was going to be hell for me. I had to school my face to neutrality as I watched couples snuggling and heading upstairs to their private rooms. I grinned like a psychopath as I heard another couple bickering in a velvet booth. The same one me and Max had started our tasting the night that led to the wine cellar.

Finally, with seven messed up orders, but thankfully with only one customer making a comment, I turned the lights up in the lounge and walked to the back. I wouldn't be sticking around tonight. I didn't want to see Max. While I wish I could turn off my anger and confusion and fall into our normal flirty banter, I knew I didn't have it in me. I wanted to be shoulders deep in a hot bath with a glass of wine in my hand, crossing my fingers that a good sleep would chase all these feelings away.

The weight of my phone sitting next to my bag brought back both Nikos's message to the forefront of my mind and that weird pit in my stomach. He had some audacity to message me that he missed me when he had a *human baby* on the way.

Holding up the screen, I saw a slew of messages sent from friends I shared with Nikos. A bunch of shocked emoticons and exclamation marks filled my screen. A few offers for me to call and vent if I needed to and one Venmo payment for drinks in case I needed to drown my sorrows in cocktails.

I tossed the phone a little roughly to the bottom of my bag and it hit the metal edge of the locker with a bang. I wanted to yank my tote out of the small locker but, even in this state, I couldn't do that to my dear Prada.

I walked past the small office where Max was starting closing duties, the heat building up in my chest. I should apologize. But so should he. Sleeping tonight would be made a thousand times easier if I tried to make peace with him before I left. I tapped my knuckles on the door, a neutral expression on my face.

"I'm sorry about what I said out there," he said before I could even open my mouth. "We all have bad days. No one is going to die over getting the wrong cocktail. I'm sorry for making it a bigger deal."

I could already feel some of the tension leave my shoulders. A man that took accountability for his role in a disagreement? What a concept.

"You were right, though, I was having a bad day, and I should've compartmentalized better before coming to work. I'm sorry for all the mix-ups." I was already turning to head out, ready to be done with the day.

"Tell me what happened," Max said. His voice made me stop. Maybe talking about it *would* help. Normally, I'd call Nat, but I'd bored her so many times with Nikos drama I was sure my bestie was over hearing about it.

With a deep sigh, I stepped back in through the doorway and started spilling my guts.

In a moment of vulnerability, I found myself divulging my tangled thoughts to Max. The safe space of the club's back office became the confessional for my insecurities and doubts, a rare moment of raw honesty in my carefully curated world.

As I unraveled my story, revealing the depth of my self-doubt and the shadows of a relationship that had once seemed my compass, Max's simple interjection, "So what?" struck a chord. His challenge to the societal script I felt pressured to follow sparked a glimmer of defiance within me.

His empathy and understanding, paired with his refusal to see me as anything less than capable, offered a moment of clarity amidst the chaos. In Max's eyes, I was not a woman out of time or options, but someone on the precipice of discovering her true desires and potential.

I had only planned on glossing over the details of Nikos, just enough to explain the impact of the text tonight, but I found myself going through every messy aspect of our relationship. I walked him through all our petty fights and Nikos's reason for ending things. I walked Max through all my insecurities and lack of direction and confusion about what I was supposed to do in life.

"Oh, and don't worry," I said, "I *also* still live at my parents' house. I mean, what thirty-five-year-old still lives in their childhood home? My room isn't even still there! I'm in a freaking guestroom and I—"

"So what?" Max's voice cut through my rambling.

"What do you mean 'so what'?" I asked. "I'm *thirty-five* without a solid career, relationship, home, or anything else for that matter."

"And what, you're supposed to? Says who?" Max asked.

I sighed. "It's different for us, you know. Women? Guys can spend all their twenties and thirties dicking around, having fun, trying new things, and by the time they're ready to settle down, they're still handsome and can bag some hot, young chick who's ready to pop out babies. *We* have to lock that down early."

As I ranted, Max listened intently. He let me ramble and pace and talk over myself. He kept his eyes on me as I paced the floor and nodded and furrowed his eyebrows as I walked through all my anxieties.

"So at this point," I continued, "I've missed the boat on being the young, hot chick for some guy *and* I don't have anything in my own life figured out." I didn't expect Max, or any guy for that matter, to understand my position. It was different for them. It always would be. But, god, even spelling it out like this made it all feel worse somehow.

"I didn't picture you as 'some guy' material," Max said, "I've kind of always thought of you as *the girl*. The one the right guy would be lucky to have. Just because you've kept company with guys who didn't get that doesn't change the fact."

"And what? *You* think you're that guy?" I asked before I could stop myself. I wanted to take it all back and swallow the words. That's not what I meant. I was under no delusion that Max thought of me in any sort of future way at all.

"Isabella. Sit down." Max's voice was firm and left no room for question.

I stopped my pacing. My mouth was slightly open as I locked eyes with Max. He was sitting in the desk chair, leaned back, knees spread out wide. He was taking up the space he knew he could.

God, this man was gorgeous. I let myself take in all of him. His dark navy slacks were raised to show his striped socks, his long legs were bulky in the thighs, and I wondered for a brief moment what they would feel like for me to sit on them.

My eyes made their way up the rest of his body. Cataloging the shiny cuff links at his wrists, the large watch on his left arm, and the way his sleeves were pushed up to his elbows. I found his face again.

"Isabella, let me take your mind off things. Sit down," Max said, his voice clear and calm as he inclined his chin toward the sofa.

A million things were buzzing through my mind right

now. But they all quieted as I slowly backed up against the small sofa. I didn't quite understand why my body wanted to immediately listen to him, but I let it guide me. My body sank into the cushion and as I lifted my gaze back up to meet Max's all of the overthinking and the criticizing chatter in my mind disappeared.

I heard the sternness in my voice, and I almost apologized for it. That was until I saw something flash across her face. It was like something clicked in her mind and settled into place. She was taken aback, but not by what I'd said. She was taken aback by how it made her want to *listen.*

Isabella didn't take her wide eyes off mine as she lowered to sit on the couch. I loved what she looked like from this angle. Chin tilted up, throat exposed, brown eyes wide, full mouth parted.

It was a delicious sight.

I wish someone would just tell me what to do.

I'd heard her say it plenty of times, and I'd wondered if it would work in a different context. Isabella wasn't someone who *actually* wanted to be told what to do with her life, but in this way . . . maybe. I shouldn't be surprised. It was always girls like Isabella who liked to be told what to do in the bedroom. And the truth was, I thought it might help her let go and stop overthinking.

When she'd come into the club tonight, I'd immediately known something was off. The normally confident and care-free Isabella was anxious and annoyed. Something had rattled her. And now I knew. She'd spilled out her anxieties and fears as she'd paced the office floor, and I'd soaked up every word.

It was funny how we both felt inadequate. Her, a trust fund girl with every resource at her disposal, and me, a kid of working-class parents who had no clue about the world I was in every day. I had wondered if I could help her. I wanted to shut off her brain so she could just be for a bit.

And so I would play that part.

I stood above her as she sat. Rooted to my spot, just watching her for a bit. Letting her wait out my next move. I straightened my tie and slowly walked over to her. I made it to the couch in two strides. This office was almost painfully small.

I reached forward and tucked a stray curl behind her ear, her hair coarse on my fingers. My thumb lingered down her soft cheeks, over her jaw, and rubbed across her bottom lip. Her skin was chapped from where she'd been chewing on her bottom lip all evening. Her chest rose, and god, I wanted to strip her naked so I could see all of her.

"I've always wondered what your mouth would feel like wrapped around my cock." Her response was a small flare of her eyes and a look that told me she was *begging* for me to turn off her brain.

I hadn't known heartbreak brought her home. It killed

me that there was some guy out there who had convinced Isabella she was anything less than worthy of the world. I made it a point to never pity the insanely wealthy, but I could begin to see the pain of being directionless in Isabella. To have access to do *anything* in the world and still not be called to anything. I have to imagine that feels incredibly empty.

Well, allow me to shut that off for her.

I checked my watch. "We have less than twenty minutes before the evening cleaning crew comes in to start their nightly routine." I wrapped my hand around her chin and tugged slightly. "And before that happens, I'm going to come down your throat."

I heard the sharp intake of her breath and watched as her eyes flicked over to the open office door, and still, she said nothing.

"I'm not going to close the door. You're going to take my cock out and lick it," I said, looking down at her. Her eyes were so wide and full of lust. I couldn't tell if she was about to tell me to fuck off or actually suck my cock. She swallowed loudly.

I smiled down at her as she moved her hands to undo my belt, her fingers graceful on my buckle. The sound of my zipper sliding down ricocheted off the concrete walls. Right now, we were alone until the cleaning crew came through. They liked to start upstairs, but they used this hallway to enter the building. Soon, the back door would bang open and the chatter of the crew would break our little bubble. But for now, Isabella was all mine.

I sucked in a breath as I felt her fingers wrap around my

cock. All of my blood had rushed straight to it the second she'd sat down on the couch, following my first demand. Her fingers didn't meet as she wrapped her slender hand around me.

"That's it. Grip it," I said, and I smiled as she obeyed. "Stick your tongue out." She did, and I rubbed myself all over her tongue. She was no doubt tasting the salty liquid already on my tip.

"Good girl." I hummed my approval from above, and Isabella relaxed a bit below me. So she wanted to be praised as much as she wanted to be directed? Got it.

"Eyes up here," I said, and she listened, looking up at me. "Now, open your mouth wide."

And goddammit, Isabella listened. I slid my wet cock past her lips and into the warmth of her mouth. I wasn't going to last long. I placed a hand on the back of her head and gripped her hair, guiding her down on me.

"Fuck, you take me so good." I felt her murmur against me. The vibrations sent a shiver down my legs. The sound of my cock sliding in and out of her mouth filled the office. The noise was filthy and crass, and I wanted to bottle it up to listen to it for the rest of my life. If someone came down the hall now, there was no doubt they would hear.

I was breaking about a million rules at this moment. I couldn't decide which was worse: disobeying the bro code or the inevitable sexual harassment laws on the line. But my cock felt at home in between Isabella's lips, and I wanted to come down her throat so badly I wouldn't stop even if Dominic called my name.

I pulled Isabella's hair back a bit more, to get it out of her face, and like the good girl she was, she kept her eyes up and locked on mine.

"Next time, I'm going to take my time with you, but for now, you're going to let me fuck your face and come down your throat, okay?" I felt her nod slightly, never pulling back. I slid myself out of her mouth. "Catch your breath for me."

Her lips were swollen, her cheeks flushed, and god, I could've come from the sight of that alone. I waited as long as I could for her to catch her breath and get ready for me before I said, "Open."

And she did. I gripped the back of her head as I shoved my cock in her mouth and pumped myself inside of her. Tears pricked at her eyes, but she kept her focus.

"Oh fuck, baby, you're so goddamn beautiful." I couldn't help the words that tumbled out of my mouth, and I hoped this felt as freeing for Isabella as it did for me. She relaxed her mouth a bit more and gave me the space I needed to get a little deeper.

She kept one hand wrapped around me, but the other she threaded up and reached for my tie. She tugged on the fabric, bunching in between her hands to steady herself. I remember the feeling when we were down in the cellar. Like I wanted her to climb into my skin.

I watched her every movement, creating a snapshot in my mind for the next time I needed to jerk off. Isabella was every man's wet dream, and I wasn't sure why she, of all people, didn't see that. Fuck Nikos. But also, thank you, Nikos, for sending her back home. *To me.*

With my orgasm building in my belly, I was about to explode. I slowed as I found my release, and my cock pulsed inside her mouth. "Take it all, Isabella, I want you to swallow every last bit of me."

And she did. I felt her throat flex as my cock sat in her mouth. I never wanted to leave. This was where I belonged. Inside her. I finally pulled myself out of her mouth and tucked myself back into my pants, pulling up the zipper and tucking in my shirt. I knelt down in front of Isabella as she sat on the edge of the couch, catching her breath. Her chest was flushed, and her lips were swollen.

I grazed her bottom lip with my thumb again. "You did such a good job, I'm so proud of you." I reached behind me for a bottle of water, twisted the cap off, and handed it to her. "Here, drink this, you need to rehydrate."

She brought the bottle to her lips and started drinking. She was such a good listener. I would need to make sure to stop and get her some food before I dropped her off at home. Isabella chugged half the bottle before pulling it away from her mouth and catching her breath.

"Shit, you're not sick are you, Iz?" Dominic's voice caught us both off guard as we looked over to where he stood in the doorway. He must have stayed late tonight to work upstairs. "You look all feverish or something."

Isabella smiled at her brother. "Nope, not sick, just couldn't breathe there for a minute. I'm good now."

I grinned down at my feet as I stood. Yeah, she couldn't breathe all right. Because one of his best friends just had his cock shoved down his sister's throat.

"All right, I'm heading out finally," Dominic said as he made his way down the hall and out the side door. "See you guys later," he said through a yawn.

Isabella flicked her eyes up to me with a knowing look, fighting back a smile. We had most certainly broken past some invisible line in the sand tonight. There was no undoing that.

I held my hand out for her to take, and she did, smoothing her skirt on the way up.

"Um, I'm ready to get home. I'm going to call my driver," she said as she reached down for her phone tucked away in my bag.

"I'm taking you home, Isabella," I said. "We'll stop and get you something to eat, then I'll drop you off at your parents'."

She nodded and let me guide her out of the office, my hand on the small of her back. I waited as she put her high heels back on and nearly scooped her up in my arms when she flinched as her feet got buckled back in.

"Bring shoes to change into tomorrow; you shouldn't be wearing those after your shift," I said.

"But they look so cute," Isabella said as she wiggled her foot out for me to see.

"They are cute, but your feet are sore, sweetie. You need comfy shoes for when you're off the floor." I kissed the top of her head as she pushed through the side door and out into the cool night air.

I lingered outside the club, the cool night air a sharp contrast to the warmth of the memories swirling inside me.

My car was parked a few strides away, and with a press of a button, the headlights blinked, signaling Isabella to its location. As she approached, I opened the passenger door for her, a small gesture, but one filled with the unspoken electricity that had charged our evening.

"I could do that myself, you know." Isabella's voice was soft, almost playful, as I leaned across her to fasten her seatbelt.

"Where's the fun in that?" The moment lingered, a mix of courtesy and intimacy, as my fingers brushed against her thigh. The door clicked shut, sealing us together for the journey back to her parents' house.

As we settled into the drive, the quiet hum of the engine accompanied my racing thoughts. Isabella intrigued me in ways I couldn't have predicted. There was a depth to our connection, a blend of vulnerability and resilience in her that called to deeper parts of myself. I used to think my attraction to her was leftover feelings from my childhood crush but getting to know her now, as a woman, felt like rediscovering her all over again.

With some years and life experiences under my belt, I found myself drawn to her in a new, more intense way. Keeping a professional distance was becoming a challenge, especially as I came to admire not just the confident air she projected but also the way her mind seemed to dance with ideas. Her blend of introspection and outward confidence fascinated me, and I was eager to see where this growing connection might lead.

Glancing her way, I noticed her thoughtful gaze, likely

piecing together the evening's revelations. "You okay?" I broke the silence, the weight of the night pressing between us.

"Yeah, just . . . thinking." Her reply was hesitant but open, a door ajar to conversations yet to be had.

As we navigated the quiet streets, the silence became a canvas for reflection. "About tonight . . . or the message?" I ventured, touching upon the unaddressed tension Nikos's message had introduced earlier.

She sighed, a mix of frustration and relief. "Both, I guess. It's strange, Nikos's life moving in a direction I once thought might include me. But now . . ." She trailed off, her voice softening. "When we broke up, he said some things that kind of hit home because maybe they are more true than I thought. I'm starting to wonder if he actually knew me better than I gave him credit for."

I listened, letting her words hang between us for a moment. Then I offered gently, "Well, all I'll say is it's completely okay to change our minds about who we are and what we seek out of life, at any point in time. Whether we envisioned a certain life for ourselves last week or have held onto a vision for years, our feelings and desires are allowed to evolve. The fact that you're yearning for something different now, compared to a few years ago, doesn't make your current desires any less valid or real."

Her gaze met mine, a silent acknowledgment passing through her eyes as she processed my words, perhaps finding in them a semblance of comfort or perhaps a new way to view her unfolding journey. The moment lingered, heavy with unspoken understanding, before she shifted, breaking the intensity with a light chuckle.

"So, speaking of unfolding journeys," Isabella began, her tone shifting toward curiosity and excitement, "how's everything coming along with the Mirage Guild? It's only a few months away from opening, right?"

"Yeah, it's getting real," I replied, feeling a mix of anticipation and nerves. "Honestly, I'm pretty nervous about the sommelier exam, but your flashcards have been a lifesaver. I don't think I'd be as prepared without them."

She smiled, pleased to have been able to help. "I'm glad they're useful. And, you're going to ace that exam, no doubt about it."

"And you, Ms. Event Coordinator extraordinaire, how are you feeling about stepping into your new role more officially?"

Isabella beamed, a sparkle of pride in her eyes. "Honestly? I'm thrilled. It feels like everything is falling into place. Getting to focus on event planning, especially at a place as unique as the Mirage Guild, is really a dream come true. I can't wait to see what we can create together."

Her excitement was infectious, and for a moment, my own concerns melted away. The Mirage Guild was not just a project. It was the beginning of a new chapter for both of us, one where our individual strengths would come together to create something unforgettable.

Sitting there, under the soft glow of the streetlights, we were on the cusp of something new, something undefined but full of potential. The earlier tensions seemed distant, overshadowed by the mutual understanding and anticipation of what was to come.

With a reluctant sigh, Isabella turned to me. "I should probably get inside. But tonight . . . thank you, Max. For listening, for understanding."

I reached for her hand, squeezing it gently. "Always, Isabella. And hey, whatever happens, we'll figure it out. Together."

She smiled, that radiant smile that had first caught my eye, and with a nod, she exited the car. I watched her until she disappeared inside, the door closing softly behind her.

Alone, I let out a breath, releasing some tension in my chest. The night had taken turns I hadn't expected, but as I drove away, my thoughts were clear. Whatever lay ahead for Isabella and me, for the Mirage Guild, I was ready. Ready to face it head-on, together.

SIXTEEN

ISABELLA

Natalia's laughter echoed through the elegant corridor of my parents' home, bringing a sense of normalcy and comfort in the midst of life's rapidly shifting sands. "Come on, Izzy, I haven't got all day!" she chided, her voice a lively contrast to the serene morning, ruffling the calm like a breeze through the leaves.

Her presence, with that oversized latte in hand—a lifeline on these early starts—and her phone abuzz with the latest on the Mirage Guild project, was a reminder of the thrilling yet daunting new chapter unfolding before us. I appeared at the door, hair and heart both in a state of disarray, the sleep barely shaken off. "You're way too chipper for—" a glance at my wristwatch cut me off, "—it's not even eight in the morning, Nat!"

Natalia, with her indefatigable spirit, pushed the latte into my hands, a gesture that spoke volumes of the early mornings yet to come. "Consider it an apology in advance for all the future early mornings," she quipped, her grin infectious despite the hour.

Taking a grateful sip, I couldn't suppress a soft moan of appreciation at the first caffeine hit of the day. "I might forgive you," I mused, locking the door behind us and falling into step with Natalia toward the waiting black town car, "given how you've mastered my coffee order."

As we made our way to the black town car waiting to whisk us away, the conversation naturally flowed to the Mirage Guild. "So, this Mirage Guild thing . . . it's really happening, huh?" I mused, the reality of it all beginning to sink in. Natalia's eyes danced with a blend of excitement and a smidge of anxiety. "Iz, it's going to be huge," she breathed out, her enthusiasm palpable. "And apparently, your boy is going to be there to shine with the wine."

I couldn't help but correct her playful assumption, "He's not 'my boy,' Nat," though my mind couldn't help but wander to the possibilities that lay ahead for Max and me in this new venture.

Nat grinned like she'd caught me in a trap. "But you knew who I was talking about," she said with a smug look on her face.

As we talked, a mix of trepidation and anticipation filled me. The Mirage Guild project represented more than a new job. It was a leap into the unknown, an opportunity to redefine my path and, perhaps, reconcile the conflicting desires within me.

It had been a whirlwind few weeks since Max and I shared that intimate moment in the office. Time seemed to compress and stretch in odd ways, leaving us both caught in a current of unspoken questions and burgeoning possibilities. When Max wasn't working his shift at the Prism Society, he was knee-deep in studying for his sommelier exam and placing wine orders for the new space.

My new title as event coordinator felt like more than a job—it felt like a calling. It was an opportunity to blend my passions and aspirations into the fabric of the Mirage Guild. Embracing this role with heart and soul, I was fully invested in creating an atmosphere filled with mystery and allure. Yet, beneath the excitement and flurry of activity, an unspoken question lingered between Max and me, unasked but always there.

What if our combined work paths created a situation too complicated for our new relationship to handle?

As Max dedicated his hours to his exam and the intricacies of the wine world, I found myself immersed in a whirlwind of planning and preparation. Reaching out to everyone within my network who might be intrigued by the sultry allure of the Mirage Guild's events, I designed themes that promised to enchant and enthrall. My days were a blur of phone calls and meetings, each one a step toward the grand vision we had for the opening night. From scouring the city for unique decorations that matched the aesthetic I wanted for events to negotiating with vendors who shared our excitement for the unconventional, every detail mattered.

I also dove deep into the world of talent scouting, seeking out performers and artists who embraced our vibe, who could bring our themed nights to life with their energy and creativity. This wasn't just about filling a space with people. It was about curating experiences that would linger in the minds of our guests, enticing them to return to the mystery time and again.

Natalia's voice pulled me back from my reverie, her excitement about the Mirage Guild infectious, but it was her next words that truly caught my attention. "You and Max are basically going to run the show, you know." Her words echoed in my mind, a reminder of the stakes at play, not just for the success of the Mirage Guild but for the delicate dance of our growing connection.

"Wait, back up a second, Nat. What do you mean, 'Max and I will run the show'?" I pressed, needing to understand the full scope of what she was suggesting.

Nat leaned back, her expression turning thoughtful as if considering how best to articulate the situation. "Okay, let me break it down for you. Dom and Liam have their hands full with the Prism Society, right? They're continuing to manage that space, to keep it thriving. But with the Mirage Guild, they're looking to take a step back, delegate more of the day-to-day and big-picture stuff."

She paused, sipping her coffee before continuing, "They approached me first, asked if I wanted to step in as manager for the Guild. But honestly, Izzy, my plate is overflowing. I'm on this path with the board, trying to bridge this gap between sultry entertainment and health and wellness. It's niche, sure, but if I nail it, I could be looking at part ownership in future clubs. It's my shot, you know?"

I nodded, her words painting a clearer picture of the chessboard we were all playing on.

"So, that's where you and Max come in," Nat said, her gaze direct and serious now. "Dom's seen what you both can do, separately and together. The chocolate and wine night wasn't just a hit. It was a revelation. You've got this creative vision, Izzy, and Max, well, his wine knowledge and charisma are unbeatable. Dom's thinking is, why not combine those strengths? Make the Mirage Guild something extraordinary under your joint supervision."

My mind raced, considering the possibilities and challenges such a role would entail. "So, Dom's really going to entrust us with that much responsibility?" I asked, the weight of the opportunity starting to sink in. It was wild how Nat stepped into roles, even part owner, with such ease, like she belonged in those rooms—which, of course, she did. I just wish I could tap into that confidence as naturally.

"Looks like it," Nat replied with a grin. "He sees potential in you, in both of you. And from what I've seen, he's not wrong. Max brings expertise; you bring innovation. Together, you'll set the Guild apart from anything else out there. And yeah, Dom's planning to have a sit-down with Max soon, lay it all out. But between you and me, I think it's a done deal."

Her words settled around me, a mixture of daunting responsibility and thrilling opportunity. This wasn't just another job—it was a chance to carve out something unique, something impactful. And to do it alongside Max, that thought alone sent a flutter of excitement through me.

But Nat's insights also hinted at the underlying complexity of working so closely with Max. Our interactions so far had been charged, a blend of professional respect and personal attraction that was as intoxicating as it was precarious. Could we navigate this new landscape without jeopardizing what was blossoming between us? That remained to be seen.

The town car slowed, halting subtly along a quaint, cobblestone street in Greenwich Village. The rich scent of sawdust, signaling fresh construction and renovation, wafted into the vehicle as we stepped out. Before us, the façade of an inviting, albeit ordinary-looking, tavern presented itself amidst the bustling village scene.

Natalia leaned in, her voice bubbling with excitement. "What do you think?"

I l took in ancient bricks, the swaying sign that spelled out "Vinifera," and the low hum of two men nearby discussing building plans. My nose was filled with a mix of smells: the earthy fragrance of wood stain and a hint of fresh paint.

I had thought the Mirage Guild grand opening would be extravagant, but then I remembered—the charm of this place lay in its secrecy and elusiveness. The Mirage Guild wasn't meant to be ostentatious. Its allure lay in its secrecy, its mystery.

I turned my gaze toward Natalia, raising an eyebrow in playful skepticism. "It's . . . subtle."

Natalia chuckled, her heels clicking assertively against the cobblestones as she led the way. "Just wait."

Inside Vinifera, the air was alive with the quiet hustle of renewal. The tavern's classic charm—dark wood panels, soft jazz tunes trickling from hidden speakers, low-hung amber lights—mingled with the energy of rejuvenation. Workers moved with purpose, their hands carefully polishing aged wood surfaces, applying fresh coats of deep, rich paint, and adjusting the newly hung lights that added a warm, modern glow.

I walked by a striking new addition near the bar's end—a floor-to-ceiling wooden and metal shelf, an artful construction designed to cradle an extensive collection of wine bottles. Its blend of rustic charm and contemporary elegance seemed to embody the spirit of Vinifera's transformation.

Nearby, a small wine cellar, its walls of glass framed in sleek black metal, caught my attention. The sight brought an unbidden blush to my cheeks, as memories of my and Max's clandestine adventure in my parents' wine cellar flickered to life. The cellar, with its inviting display of vintage and rare wines, was like a transparent treasure chest, radiating the promise of shared secrets and discoveries.

The tavern, in the midst of its transformation, felt like a bridge between the past and the future, keeping one foot in tradition while stepping confidently forward into a new era. It was in this space, between the old and the new, that I found myself reflecting on the journey I'd embarked upon—a journey of new beginnings, unexpected friendships, and a world of possibilities waiting to be uncorked.

Natalia guided me toward the back, where an immense bookshelf reached from floor to ceiling. Without hesitation, she pressed a seemingly random compilation of spines, and with a hushed creak, the bookshelf swung open, revealing the threshold to the Mirage Guild.

Stepping through, the atmosphere shifted palpably. Here, the sounds of construction and the old-world charm of the wine bar gave way to something from another world.

We stepped fully into the Mirage Guild, enveloped by a world that seamlessly wove the whimsy of a vintage circus with the plush, opulent elegance typical of a high-end lounge. The immediate view was dominated by bold, emerald greens, lavish gold accents, and sultry, velvety reds, establishing a setting that was at once inviting and thrilling.

We stood on an elevated entry, giving us a panorama of the alluring spectacle below. In the room's center, a large, circular stage commanded attention, adorned overhead by extravagant striped fabric cascading from the ceiling, creating a tent-like aura. It was as if we had stepped into a clandestine spectacle, a hidden world where the unexpected was the norm.

I descended the few steps, my hand gently gliding over the polished mahogany rail, my eyes wide and darting about, drinking in every detail. The chairs and loungers encircling the stage were low, fashioned from rich, dark wood, and upholstered with sumptuous, jewel-toned fabrics, all facing toward the stage in anticipatory arrangement, awaiting an event, a show, a reveal.

Gilded light fixtures hung low over each table, casting a

warm, intimate glow over each seating area. It was as if every seat promised its own private viewing of the impending spectacle, despite being part of a larger audience.

I whispered, still gazing around, "It's like stepping into another era. This is incredible, Nat."

The walls on either side of the circular stage boasted halls filled with doors, each distinct, yet uniformly exquisite. Some sported polished brass knobs, others intricate carvings, suggesting that behind each entryway lay a unique experience waiting to be uncovered. It whispered of mysteries and adventures yet to be embarked upon, each door a portal to a different facet of the Mirage Guild's offerings.

At the room's far end, an expansive bar stretched elegantly, immediately catching my eye. Mercury glass mirrors fractured yet somehow whole, lined the back of the bar, reflecting and refracting the warm, ambient light.

Natalia leaned in, her voice a melodic whisper, "Every detail, every piece here tells a story, Izzy. Isn't it thrilling?"

My eyes twinkled, reflecting the fractured light from the mercury glass. For a moment, my previous apprehensions seemed to melt away, absorbed by the fantastical charm of the Mirage Guild. It was a realm where we could craft stories, adventures, and experiences not just for ourselves, but for everyone who stepped into this enchanting spectacle.

There was magic here, and we were now a part of it.

"Can't you just see it coming to life?" Natalia asked as I continued to take in my fill, my eyes scanning every surface of the room.

"Yeah, actually, I can," I responded with a small smile on my face.

The stage was set up in a way that everyone in the room could see it. It was for performance. For show. Whoever ended up on that stage was going to be *seen*. I could picture some of the events they might host here. I'd been doing some reading on educational elements their members might enjoy and I found myself way more into it all than I thought I'd be.

I could plan a workshop on Shibari, or a sensual wax play, there could even be themed burlesque shows, or live erotic art performances. I felt confident I could reach out to the DeLorenzos to find artists to work with and bring them here, to the Mirage Guild.

But I didn't want to just utilize the stage. The tasting events that I'd worked with Max on were equally as intimate and sensual. Private tasting experiences could definitely be incorporated into the corners of this room.

"So the space will kind of act in two parts," Natalia said. "Back here is where the sexy things will go down." Nat shimmied her shoulders as she spoke. "And up front in the tavern is where anyone can come for a drink and listen to music. There will be a bar in this section as well, but this space is mostly for enjoying the stage and reserving a room."

"And where will Max be?" I asked the inside thought out loud.

Natalia had a sly grin on my face as she eyed me. "So *Max* will basically be the sommelier available for private events. He'll bounce around from Vinifera to the Mirage

Guild throughout the week, depending on where he's needed."

I simply nodded like it was routine information I needed, but I knew Natalia saw right through me. But for now, it still felt safest to keep what had happened to myself. For now, it was fun, and it seemed like it served as a release for both of us. It didn't need to mean anything more than that.

I took another look around the space as Natalia took measurements for a few things. New furniture would arrive next week to fill the open floor space around the stage and new lighting would be wired in shortly after that. They were putting their mark on this space, and I was happy to be a part of it.

I enjoyed the vibe of the Mirage Guild; it felt cozier and more intimate than the lounge at the Prism Society. I could see myself at home here and the thought of that both thrilled and terrified me.

"Oh, are you coming out for Jules's birthday tomorrow night?" Nat asked as we headed back through the tucked-away bookshelf and into the crew working inside Vinifera. "She's basically demanding anyone involved with the new space come out dancing so we can all hang out before things get even crazier."

"I haven't been out dancing since . . ." I said as I tilted my head up to think back.

"Marrakech. The Rose Bar." Nat reminded me. "Remember the bouncer threw that guy out because he wouldn't stop trying to get up on the bar and do the Coyote Ugly routine?"

"Oh, my god, yes." I laughed. "But yes, I will be there, I've still got some dance moves in me." I looped my arm with Nat's as we walked back out onto the sidewalk and slid into our waiting car.

Sitting outside an adult club, scheming events to plan, and daydreaming about one of my brother's best friends was certainly not how I had envisioned my life to be going at this point, but something about it all felt right.

SEVENTEEN

ISABELLA

The glow of Neon Wild bathed the Brooklyn street in flickers of pink and blue, a siren call for those seeking a reprieve from mundane days. My heartbeat echoed the thumping of the bass from inside the club, an electric excitement coursing through my veins.

I adjusted the strap of my emerald-green dress, the silk material whispering softly against my skin, offering a luxurious comfort amidst the lively clamor around me. As the slit of the dress revealed my thigh with each step, a chill reminder of vulnerability brushed against me, akin to the nagging voice that whispered of fleeting youth.

The vibrant buzz of New York City nightlife as I stepped out of the cab was a familiar siren call, yet it carried a bittersweet echo of days when such outings weren't tinged with self-consciousness. "Still got it," I murmured to myself, a half-hearted attempt to quash the small, insidious doubts that crept in at the edge of my excitement.

Stepping through the club doors brought me back to my days clubbing with Nat. The smell was always the same: a nauseating blend of perfumes and colognes mixed with the sticky stench of spilled cocktails.

I headed toward the group as I breezed past the bouncer, who hadn't even needed to see my ID. I spotted the birthday girl, Jules, shimmering under neon lights, her "26" tiara sparkling amid the kaleidoscopic glow.

Her laughter, pure and unfettered, sliced through the techno beats as she threw her arms around me. "I'm sooooo glad you made it!" Jules screamed in my ear as she hugged me.

"I wouldn't miss it." I screamed back, "Happy birthday!"

Jule shimmied away from me, grabbing a shot of pink liquid off a tray before downing it in one gulp. I made my way through the crowd over to the couple of high-top tables reserved for our group.

I squeezed Nat in a huge hug, both of us giggling at the fact we were in a dance club on a *Monday* evening. It looked like everyone from work was here, well, except for Max. I subtly scanned the club for his face as I smiled across the table at Emma and Jessie.

Liam and Emma were practically connected at the hip, his eyes never leaving her face as she talked about all the changes she was excited to make at Mirage. Her design agency had rushed their project through so it could open it on time. It turned out Jessie was responsible for crafting that beautiful cellar I had seen yesterday. They all acted like their own small family, dropping anything to help out the other. I hoped I wouldn't always feel like an outside in their group.

"The striped fabric for the tent was *amazing*," I said, leaning over toward Emma. "It makes it feel circus-y without it being cheesy. And the vintage doorknobs? Where did you find those?"

Jessie turned toward us, speaking up, "I have secret vintage shops around the city where I find my treasures." She steepled her hands together like a madwoman who would never reveal her sources.

"Well, they're amazing. You all crushed it," I said.

Another woman, whom I had never met, joined their table. She waltzed in like Barbie in a tight light pink dress and hugged Dominic tightly before squeezing Jessie and giving her a light kiss.

Jessie beamed and turned to me. "Iz, this is Reagan."

"Hi, it's great to meet you!" I had to yell across the table as the techno beats blared around them. Jules had already made it to the dance floor, dragging Maureen with her. I made another sweep of the club, looking for Max.

It's not that I *needed* him here, I just thought since everyone from work had been summoned here that, he'd already be here. Plus, the idea of seeing nerdy Max let loose in a place like this put a grin on my face. There was something about having him around that calmed me. He brought security and excitement all at the same time, and I didn't quite know what to do with those feelings.

"Looking for me?" Max's voice, a silky whisper, melted

into my senses, his words laced with a teasing undertone. My shoulders softened knowing he was here.

A playful grin stretched across my face, a flutter of anticipation lighting my eyes. Without turning, I responded, "Took you long enough."

He slid a cold, perspiring glass into my hand, his fingers lingering near mine a moment too long. "I'm sorry, dear," he murmured in my ear. "When I walked in, I saw you over here without a drink, so I stopped by the bar first to grab you one."

I turned to face him, my expression an enticing mixture of amusement and intrigue. His eyes, dark and full of depth, cradled a secret jest, inviting me into a private joke only we understood.

The moment lingered, intimate and charged, amidst the tumultuous celebration around us. It was as if everyone around us had blurred out, their chatter muffled and dim.

Max leaned in. "If I told you to take off your panties and hand them to me, would you listen." His words, a repeat of what he'd asked me in the cellar, laced through the fog in my brain and made my eyes widen.

My heart skipped, and for a moment, the blaring music, the pulsating lights, and the crowded room faded into a distant reality. It was just us enclosed in a bubble where time seemed to pause.

"What? Here?" I swallowed, darting my eyes around the table. No one was paying us an ounce of attention. All eyes were on Jules and Maureen on the dance floor, the older woman absolutely cutting it up out there.

Max stood at my side, shadowing my body with his large frame. He placed his hand at my elbow and leaned in again, "Slide your panties down and give them to me." His voice was a gentle command. One he wouldn't hold me to if I *truly* didn't want to, but the fluttering in my belly told me that maybe I did.

I glanced around again before snaking one hand up my dress through the slit at my thigh. My fingers wrapped around the thin strap of my lace thong, and I tugged. The movement was awkward and slow, but Max kept me hidden with the angle of my body. I kept one hand on my glass for balance, and finally, the fabric was nearly to my knees.

With one final look, I bent over, pretending to fix the strap of my heels as I subtly lifted each foot off the ground to step out of the fabric, bunched it up in my hands, and pushed it into Max's hands. His large palm swallowed my panties in an instant as he slid them into his pocket.

"That's my good girl," Max whispered in my ear, my hair blowing slightly as he spoke.

Fuck. Tonight was going to be interesting.

"Okay! Everyone out on the dance floor!" Jules came screaming up to their tables. "And no excuses, it's my birthday. You're legally obligated to dance."

She gripped my hand and dragged me out with her. I felt a wave of panic, suddenly *sure* everyone could tell I wasn't wearing any underwear. One glance back at the table, with pleading eyes, only resulted in Max raising his glass in the air to me and smiling.

Jules led a storm of energy, her very being seeming to

emit beams of ecstasy that painted everyone around me with a vibrant euphoria. I, hand-in-hand with her, couldn't help but be swept up in the wave of delight, my own laughter mingling with the joyous cacophony around us. The neon lights painted the dance floor in dynamic strokes of color, flickering in sync with the pulsating beats that guided our sways and shimmies.

Dancing amidst the jubilation, I felt a lightness I hadn't in ages buoy my spirits, challenging the shadow of doubt that lingered from days spent wondering if I was too old for this. Each step, twirl, and playful push from Jules seemed to whisper, "Age is just a number," but the whisper was a fighter, battling against the louder, harsher critique that often echoed in the quieter moments of my life. Here, in the whirlwind of music and laughter, I let the free and spirited Izzy take center stage, if only for the night, pushing the nagging voice to the backseat.

Jules spun around me, tiara glittering, and I couldn't contain a burst of playful energy. I danced with abandon, arms flailing melodically to the thud of the bass, body swaying in harmony with the music. We were in a world of our own, where everything that sat on our to-do lists or running through our over-anxious minds could simmer.

Looking back at our tables, I caught Max's eye. I crooked my finger and beckoned him over. I raised an eyebrow when he didn't get up. Here I was, no panties, on the dance floor. The least he could do was join me. He downed his glass and made his way through the crowd.

I threw my head back and laughed as he shimmied his way through the other dancers, his hips moving to the beat. He was in a dark t-shirt and jeans tonight, and I desperately wanted to run my hands down his forearms. I glanced at his waist, remembering what we'd done not long ago.

Leaning in, my voice barely audible above the beats, I teased, "Thought you'd be too mature for a dance floor, Boss."

Max's lips quirked into that signature half-smile, a glint of playful defiance lighting his eyes. "There's a lot you don't know about me, Isabella," he murmured, his words a melodic whisper that somehow found my ears amidst the chaos.

"Hmmm, I think that's probably true," I said.

Max's movements were fluid, a seamless transition from motion to motion that mirrored the tranquility that emanated from him. He spun me out, my world expanding into an orbit of lights and sounds, and then pulled my back, anchoring me once more. In the neon glow, boundaries blurred, and for a fleeting moment, everything was possible.

As more people joined the dance floor, bodies squeezed closer. Everyone seemed to be in their own world. Which is why I didn't mind when Max brought me close to his chest and kept me there. It's why I didn't turn away when I felt his hardness press against my backside. And it's the only excuse I had for why I didn't flinch when I felt his large hand find my thigh through the slit of my dress.

Under the cover of the dim dance floor, Max trailed his

fingers up, and up, and up. I heard him hiss in my ear as his fingers grazed the wetness waiting for him.

"*Fuck*, Isabella, what am I going to do about you?" he asked. I hoped his question was rhetorical.

He slid his fingers up and down my middle, coating the tips of them with my arousal. Our bodies kept swaying to the music, and our eyes focused in order to maintain our cover. Max held me up with one arm, letting me lean on him as we danced, but the other hand kept up its dirty work between my legs.

I wasn't sure there was an end goal in mind here, especially as Max kept lazily tracing my middle and softly circling my clit. It was as though he couldn't *not* touch me. My breath became heavy, my chest warming.

And just as I considered saying fuck it and pulling Max back down the dark hallway, he trailed his fingers down my inner thigh and removed his hand from under my dress. I turned as he slid two of his fingers into his mouth, and I thought I just might die right there on the dance floor.

We danced through more songs, and I somehow let Jules convince me to do lemon drop shots with the group. Nat and I squealed as songs from our prep school days blared through the speakers and we threw our hands in the air wildly as we bounced around the floor. Sweat was making my hair stick to my temples and my feet were aching, but I hadn't had this much fun in *ages*.

Before long, our group started to break up, Nat shouting her goodbye from the other side of the dance floor, waving wildly. Nat gave me a look that I knew to mean *you good?* I smiled reassuringly and hoped Nat hadn't caught any of Max's dance floor shenanigans from earlier.

At one point, Max left the dance floor and huddled up with Dom and Liam, while the rest of the crew kept at it on the dance floor. After Maureen, Jessie, and Reagan all called it quits, I started to feel the tightness in my hips.

My feet were sore, my hair a sweaty mess, and my ears pulsed with the beats of the music. I'd downed about three too many shots with the birthday girl, and now I was ready for the comfort of my bed.

I stumbled a bit as I let myself out of the girl's bathroom, a damp paper towel pressed to my neck. I felt cold hands wrap around my waist, gripping my hips tightly as they tried to steer me back to the dance floor.

I expected to see Max or at least Dom, but I didn't know who this was. "Come on, honey, let's go dance." The stranger's voice was slow and thick, no doubt from the vodka in his hand.

I tried to push away. "No thanks, I'm going to head out."

"Ah, come on! Just one dance. I've been watching you tonight, baby." He leaned down to my ear, and I could smell cigarettes and booze on his skin.

"There you are, you ready to go, babe?" Max's familiar voice called to me from the end of the hall. His eyes were locked on the man's grip on my hips as he made his way to me. "You can take your hands off her now."

"Ah, man, we were just gonna dance," the man's voice slurred.

"I said take your hands off her. Now." Max's voice was

crystal clear in comparison to this stranger's, and it shocked both of them. The man finally released me, raising his hands in defense. He muttered something under his breath about "crazy bitches" as he staggered away.

I released my breath, thankful for Max's presence.

"Are you okay?" He turned to me, eyes locked on my face.

I nodded. "Yeah, I'm fine, just ready to get out of here."

"I brought your slippers," Max said as he raised my Uggs in his hands. The ones I kept in my work locker to change into after a shift. "I went out to my car to grab them for you."

I threw my head back and laughed, "Wow, you have, like, a whole different kind of obsession with my feet."

"I do not," Max said.

My eyebrows lifted. "Whatever you say, Boss."

Max let me lean on him as I slipped off one heel and slid on the Ugg. There was no way I was going to put my bare foot down on this sticky club floor. I teetered a bit as I tried to swap out my other shoe, but Max had a grip on my shoulders that kept me from falling.

Finally, I held my sweaty heels in one hand and stood three inches shorter in front of Max. My Uggs felt like heaven on my feet as I shuffled my way to the exit.

Max took my purse and heels from me as I struggled to hold on to everything and then followed him out, slippers on my feet and a smile on my face. My handbag looked tiny in his hands as he made his way through the crowd, parting it so I could walk through.

The cool night air felt refreshing on my face as I walked through the doors of the club. My ears still rang as the music shut off behind us once the door snapped shut.

Max's car was waiting for us at the curb, flashers on. I smiled up at him as he opened my door, and I slid inside. He was taking care of me. Again.

Max opened his door but didn't get in. Instead, he leaned in and said, "You need carbs. I'm going to grab us some pretzels. Stay right here."

I gave him a salute. "Yes, Boss."

Max shook his head as he jogged across the street to the food cart parked outside. The lines of drunk people hadn't gotten bad yet since bars were still open. That was a perk of leaving early, I guessed. Although, I'd stayed longer than everyone but Jules and Emma.

I couldn't hold back the moan that escaped my mouth as the smell of a warm, salty pretzel filled the car when Max slid back in. I tore into the warm bread as he drove us back to my parents' house and parked on the curb so we could finish eating.

Max held out a container of cheese dip for me, his eyes reflecting the soft light from the car's interior. As I took a bite, we sat in comfortable silence, the car enveloping us in a cozy bubble amid the night's chill.

"Thank you for rescuing me earlier," I said between a bite of cheese-dipped pretzel. "And for the other thing."

"You mean when I teased your pussy while we danced?" he asked.

I nearly choked on my pretzel. "Well, when you put it like that."

"You know you can't keep stealing my panties," I said as I got back to chewing. "I'll run out one day."

His eyes had a glimmer in them as he watched me. "I'll buy you more."

"Oh," I said excitedly, "I got to see inside the Mirage Guild yesterday. The space is truly beautiful."

"Is it true that you're going to be running events there?" Max asked.

"Is it okay that I do?" I asked.

"I couldn't think of a better place for you to be, Isabella," he replied.

"And it is going to be fine? That we both work there? I mean, together?" I didn't know what I was really asking behind all my questions. The alcohol was certainly making my thoughts swirl.

"We work together now and it's fine," he countered.

"Right, but now that . . . well, you know," I said.

"Now that I always want to be inside you?" Max's voice was low, and I had the strong urge to lean across the console and taste his lips. "I think we'll be able to figure it out, Isabella."

If I had stopped drinking before the lemon drop shots, I might have felt more confident about asking Max to come inside, but for now, I needed a large glass of water and my bed. He must have seen the tiredness in my eyes because he came around the side of the car and helped me up the steps.

The pretzel certainly helped me gain a more solid footing. Carbs were always a good idea.

"Are you okay to make it inside?" he asked.

"Yeah, I can, I've made this trip far drunker than now," I said with a chuckle.

"Good night, Isabella," Max said as I stepped inside the foyer.

In the whirlwind of preparations for the Mirage Guild's grand opening a few weeks away, every moment spent with Isabella heightened my anticipation—not just for the club's launch but for every chance to see her in action. Today, the club was a beehive of activity, every corner buzzing with the final touches that would bring our vision to life. And at the heart of it all was Isabella, her presence electrifying the space with an energy that was both commanding and captivating.

Watching Isabella in her element definitely turned me on. And that was putting it lightly. The crew was gathered at the new club, the Mirage Guild, with blueprints, mood boards, and laptops spread out before them. The scent of freshly brewed coffee, freshly laid carpet, and new coats of paint lingered in the air as murmurs of discussion filled the room.

The transformation of the space had been nothing short of remarkable. Crews had diligently worked around the clock, their efforts concentrated on revitalizing rather than gutting the place entirely. This strategic approach allowed us to maintain the structural integrity of the building while infusing it with a new, vibrant spirit.

The previous, somewhat neglected, nightclub ambiance had completely disappeared and had been replaced by an elegant, circus-inspired aesthetic that managed to be both sensuous and sophisticated. Every surface gleamed with care and attention, reflecting the meticulous planning and hard work that had gone into the refurbishment. It was a stark transformation, one that had taken the space from forgotten and faded to a focal point of intrigue and allure, ready to welcome patrons into its newly imagined embrace.

And there, right in the center of the organized chaos, stood Isabella. Isabella commanded the stage with an energy I'd only seen in her when immersed in event planning. In this domain, she was confident, her usual self-doubt replaced by a commanding presence that directed every aspect of the VIP grand opening. Leaning against a polished wooden pillar, I watched her, admiring the deliberate decisions and spontaneous creativity that flowed from her with unwavering purpose.

Her voice, stronger here than in any other setting, carried throughout the club with clarity and authority, sparking excitement with every word and gesture. As she spoke, a habitual tuck of a curl behind her ear or an excited bounce on her toes revealed glimpses of the softer side I found irresistibly endearing. Watching her, it was clear: this was where

Isabella thrived, bringing visions to life with a passion that illuminated her from within.

Natalia leaned over to me, noticing my fixed gaze on Isabella. With a teasing whisper, she remarked, "Lost in thoughts, Mr. Heart-eyes?"

I smirked, my focus momentarily shifting to Natalia. "Can't help but admire talent when I see it," I replied smoothly.

Izzy happened to glance our way, catching my intense gaze. Her cheeks flushed a soft pink, but she didn't look away. I raised an eyebrow suggestively, causing Izzy to break into a soft chuckle before immersing herself back into the discussions.

Liam interjected with some logistics about the stage and talent we might have available the evening of the opening, but my thoughts were elsewhere. Watching Izzy, I was once again reminded of the layers to her—her vulnerabilities juxtaposed against her strengths, her moments of self-doubt shadowed by her unwavering confidence in her craft. And it was this tapestry of contrasts that made me fall for her even more.

I wanted nothing more than to lock everyone out of the room so I could have her attention for myself.

"Okay, I think we can showcase three separate acts on the stage. Let everyone get a feel for the vibes that Mirage can bring." Isabella was walking around the stage now, counting out steps to measure the space.

The Mirage Guild, set to open with a showcase of sensuality, had Isabella at the helm of organizing an evening unlike any other. I watched, leaning against a pillar, as she orchestrated everything with a fire and focus that seemed to light her from within. Here, away from the doubts that usually haunted her, she was unstoppable—commanding, creative, every bit the leader.

Her enthusiasm was palpable as we discussed the event's finer points, especially the drinks. "Let's make the two-drink limit work in our favor," she suggested, eager to keep the evening refined yet engaging. Her idea for specialty mocktails —a playful addition to complement the night's performances —showed her knack for blending sophistication with fun. And when she proposed creating a signature drink for the Mirage Guild, her excitement was infectious. "Purple and magical," she insisted, already visualizing the standout feature of our menu.

After wrapping up with Natalia about entrance plans, Isabella joined me at the bar, her touch sending a familiar jolt through me. Even in the midst of final preparations, our connection remained—a silent thread weaving through the buzz of activity.

As the team disbanded, leaving Isabella and me to close up, our conversation turned personal. Despite the looming exhaustion from endless double shifts, her excitement for the grand opening couldn't be dimmed. "I can't wait to see it all come together," she admitted, and I echoed her sentiment, impressed by her talent and vision.

We debated whether to open the private rooms on the night, each space a reflection of the circus theme, from the Lion's Den with its opulent twist on BDSM to the Acrobat's Loft, offering a unique vantage point above the festivities.

As the hustle of preparation settled into a quiet hush and we were left alone amid the dimming lights of the soon-to-be-bustling club, the air between Isabella and me seemed charged with a different kind of anticipation. Her indecision about the private rooms lingered in the space, a symbol of the careful balance she was trying to strike between control and freedom.

"I think giving people the choice could be part of the magic," I suggested gently, watching as her expression shifted, pondering the idea. "It's like opening up a world of possibilities for them, letting them explore on their terms. Isn't that what we're all about here?"

She paused, considering, her gaze lifting to meet mine. In that moment, the weight of our weeks of shared effort and unspoken tensions drew us closer, an unacknowledged longing threading through the practicalities of our conversation.

"You're right," she conceded with a soft smile, the tension easing from her shoulders. "It's about exploration, isn't it? Creating a space where people can discover new aspects of themselves, safely and joyfully."

Her words echoed the underlying principle that had brought us together in this project, yet now they seemed to resonate on a more personal level. The way she bit her lip in thought, the glow of the dim lights reflecting in her eyes, the warmth of her presence—it all beckoned with an intimacy that went beyond our professional collaboration.

"Exactly," I replied, moving a step closer, drawn by the warmth in her voice and the openness in her stance. "And it's not just the guests who are exploring new territories, is it?"

The question hung between us, a veiled reference to the undefined space we were navigating together. Isabella's laugh was a mix of acknowledgment and nervousness, a sound that seemed to fill the room and bridge the gap between us. "Yeah, I guess we're all a little bit in uncharted waters here, aren't we?" she mused, a hint of playfulness creeping into her voice.

The mood shifted, the professional veneer fading to reveal the underlying current of attraction and curiosity that had been building between us. It was a delicate dance, one we'd been unconsciously rehearsing since our paths first crossed, now finding its rhythm in the quiet aftermath of our collective efforts.

Our eyes locked, and for a heartbeat, the world beyond the Mirage Guild faded, leaving the two of us suspended in a moment of realization and unspoken questions. It was a crossroads, a choice between stepping back into our roles or daring to explore what lay beyond them.

"Which room would you choose first?" I asked.

"I don't know." Isabella chewed on her bottom lip.

"I would love to see you in the mirrored room," I said, letting my eyes dip down over her mouth. "It would be fun to see you from every angle."

She huffed a laugh. "I don't know about that," she replied. "That would be a lot to take in."

"Then perhaps on stage, tied up in those bands." I traced my fingertips over her shoulder and down her arm, leaving goosebumps in my wake. "I'd spread your legs out wide so I could see all of you and show you off to everyone that wanted to watch."

I smiled at the flush of red that splashed over her cheeks. I closed the distance between us and placed my fingers under her chin, tilting her head up toward me. Her lips parted and her eyes gleamed with excitement. I smiled, leaned down, and whispered in her ear. "Will you get up on the stage for me, Isabella? There's no one here. It's just you and me and right now, I really want to spread you out wide and taste you."

NINETEEN
ISABELLA

My feet felt cool as I slipped off my shoes and walked over the smooth hardwood floor to the stage. My heart was pounding in my chest, but the warmth spreading deep in my belly urged me forward.

I felt safe with Max. No matter what we were doing, he seemed to always have my safety and happiness in mind. I'd seen it that night when he helped me relax by taking charge, and I'd recognized it countless times since then. Like when he brought my slippers to the club or how he always made sure I had water and something to eat.

I could get in my head. I could get laser-focused on everything else, so much so that I wasn't my own priority. It was nice having someone look out for me like that. And when we played like this, it could feel like I was losing myself completely. It helped shut off the noise of my overthinking.

Of the little voice in my head that reminded me of everything I hadn't quite figured out yet.

I glanced back over at Max, who was now walking around from the back of the bar, as I took the three steps leading up to the top of the stage. I waited for further instructions.

"Take off your dress," Max said. He was at the stage now, ascending the steps. He slowly unbuttoned his cuffs and methodically rolled up his sleeves, making sure the fabric folded evenly at the edges. My eyes flickered at the way his forearm flexed as he moved. "Now." His voice reminded me of my directions.

My eyes flicked back up to his face at his demand. His voice was firm, but his eyes were soft. I took a deep breath and unzipped my dress at the back. I let the fabric fall from my shoulders. I slid my hands over my hips to push the rest of the dress down and let it fall to the floor.

Max froze as I stood before him. My skin seemed to glow in the dim light of the lounge. The black lace of my matching bra and panties was dark against my skin. He took a step closer and walked in a slow circle around me, eyes scanning over my body.

"You're so beautiful, Isabella," he said. "I don't think you know what you do to me."

I spun around, his comments giving me a boost of confidence, and shimmied my hips.

He responded with a low chuckle. "I'm going to help you get in the silk straps. You're going to lay back in them, and I'm going to taste you."

I sucked in a breath at his promise.

"And then," he continued, "I'm going to slide my fingers inside you, and you're going to come on my face." He stopped circling me. With his eyes locked on mine, he asked, "Do you think you can do that for me, Isabella?"

"Yes." My voice betrayed my lust, but I didn't care.

I took a deep breath, hooked my fingers into the band of my lace thong, and slid them down. I stepped one foot out and then the other, never taking my eyes off Max.

He stared at me for a while, his gaze lingering in between my thighs before saying, "I'm going to help you in the straps now."

Max took my hand and guided me over to one of the hanging aerial setups. It was part loose fabric, part constructed swing. I imagined there were countless ways to use this thing.

Max went behind the swing and held it steady as I turned and lowered myself down into the seat. My body was held at an angle but upright by two large pieces of black silk fabric. Another piece of fabric held my lower back and my thighs suspended in the air.

Max checked a couple of the straps and looped a few around my waist and thighs to secure me tightly. I hung high off the ground from a beam constructed over the stage. I couldn't get out of this device without his help. I was totally at his mercy. *And I loved it.*

Max turned to admire his handiwork. Even if I'd wanted to, there was no way for me to bring my legs together. Instead, I laid back, fully exposed for Max. He trailed his fingers over my knees and down my shins, leaving goose-bumps in their wake. He licked his lips as he took me in.

"I've been dreaming about what you taste like ever since I got a tease of you at the club," he said as his eyes scanned my body. "And I want more."

His hands gripped the insides of my thighs tightly, and I let out a breath. "Are you already wet for me, Isabella?"

"Yes," I replied. There was no denying it. I had felt it begin to pool in between my legs as soon as Max started talking about the private rooms.

"Always so eager for me," he said.

Max smiled down at me. He hiked up the fabric of his slacks and dropped down to his knees in front of me, and the sight alone almost made me come undone.

"Do you like seeing me on my knees for you?" he asked. "Do you like knowing I'd do anything to help you relax? That all I can think about is watching you squirm from underneath me?"

Max didn't give me a chance to respond as he ran his tongue up my middle. I threw my head back, *fuck this felt so good*. He hardened the tip of his tongue and used it to flick my swollen clit. His hands gripped my thighs as he dove back in for more.

I moaned as he sucked on my clit and slipped his tongue inside me. I couldn't help it when I pressed into his face. I needed *more*. Max used his hands to part my middle as he continued to devour me. I wanted to feel him, to touch him, but my hands were wrapped up in the fabric, and I couldn't reach him.

It was driving me crazy.

I felt the orgasm building in my belly, but I wasn't there yet. I needed pressure.

"Please," I said the word without realizing it. Max looked up at me from between my thighs. His face glistened with my arousal. His eyes were dark from lust.

"If I put my fingers in you, I expect you to come for me. Are you going to do that?" Max asked.

"Yes, yes, I will," I responded.

"Good girl," he said.

My back arched, and a loud, low moan escaped my throat as Max slid a finger deep inside me. God, I was so wet. His finger slipped in easily, but I needed more. He must have understood my silent request because I stiffened slightly as Max added another finger.

With his tongue back on my clit and two fingers pumping in and out of me, I wouldn't last long. I felt myself dripping down my thighs, no doubt making a mess. All I wanted to do was touch him. To hold on to him. But I was given an order, and I would follow it.

I ground myself into his hand and face as the feeling in my belly built up. I was close. Sweat clung to my forehead and slid down my back. My chest was flushed and hot. Max turned his hand, adding a third finger, and cupped my wet pussy as he fingered me. This was it.

"Oh, god, Max." I couldn't even think straight.

My toes were tingling, and my thighs were tightening up. I flexed around his fingers, and I let out a loud moan as I exploded. I chased the waves of my orgasm as Max lazily slid his fingers in and out, his mouth on my clit. Everything was so sensitive. So warm.

I squirmed as he removed his fingers but then slid his tongue down my middle, lapping me up. He hummed his approval in my core, and the vibrations rattled the shockwaves of my orgasm.

"You taste so good, Isabella, exactly how I've been dreaming." Max sighed into me as he placed light kisses on my inner thighs. He stood and walked around me to gently release my arms and thighs from the straps, then slid his arm around my waist to help me stand. I was wobbly on my feet, but Max leaned me against his shoulder.

He had picked my panties up off the floor and held me upright as he slid them back on me. Max picked up my dress next and brought it up my thighs, around my hips, and up over my shoulders. The sound of the zipper being pulled up was all I could hear.

"I guess I get to keep these?" I said as the fabric of my panties settled back on my waist.

Max smirked at me in a way that said he might just change his mind about that. He brought his hand to the side of my face, swiping gently at my cheek. "How do you feel?"

I smiled up at him, still in a daze from my orgasm. "Like it's going to be hard to concentrate on work when I know how fun this stage can be," I said, deciding to answer him honestly.

He smiled. "Yeah, fair warning, I plan to make every room in this club hard for you to concentrate in."

My eyes widened at his promise. "Oh?"

"We still have a couple of hours before the crowd starts coming into the Prism Society. I'm going to take you home so you can rest before our shift, okay?" Max guided me down the steps and helped me slip my shoes on.

"I think a nap and some snacks will do you good," he said as we made our way through the bookshelf entrance and into the tavern. I nodded in agreement, the bliss of my orgasm threatening to take me under as I walked.

There were a few construction guys mingling around, wrapping up a few details. It was crazy to me how stepping through that bookcase was like walking into an entirely different world.

It felt like Vegas back there. Without any windows, you lost your sense of time, and I was surprised to see the sun was still out, almost ready to set, once we walked through the door of the tavern.

Max ushered me to his car and started the drive back to my parents' house. He rested his hand on my thigh as he wove through traffic, and it felt like, just maybe, it was always supposed to be there. Things with Max had never felt awkward or uncomfortable. I wasn't sure how much longer I could keep what was going on between us hidden from everyone else. Heck, I wasn't even sure *what* was going on between us.

All I knew was that when Max took control, I felt at ease. When he gave me directions, I wanted to listen. I would have never guessed this would be my thing, but with Max, it felt safe. It felt good. When Max spoke his desires to me, they somehow helped my overthinking brain shut off. Every insecurity and over-analyzation seemed to evaporate out of my mind when I allowed myself to trust him.

"Can you walk up the stairs, or do you need help?" Max asked as we pulled up to the house.

I had the front steps and two flights of stairs to tackle. As much as I wanted his help up the stairs, I would have some explaining to do if my parents saw him. Plus, I wasn't sure I'd be able to send Max away once he was in the room with me.

I'm not going to lie, I *love* when his focus is solely on me. His touch, his gaze . . . all trained on me. But when he also lets himself unravel and shut out everything else? It's intoxicating.

"No, I've got it," I said. Max looked doubtful. "I promise," I added. "I'll see you in a couple of hours. Um," I hesitated, "thank you. For this afternoon."

Max's eyes had a twinkle to them when he smiled. "You're welcome. I like taking care of you."

I smiled, opened the car door, and began the trek upstairs.

TWENTY

MAX

The past few weeks had been a blur of relentless activity and mounting pressure for me. Between my intense study sessions for the upcoming Advanced Sommelier Exam and the myriad responsibilities at the Mirage Guild, every moment embodied a race against time. My exam, now three days away, had consumed me, my mind constantly replaying wine regions, grape varieties, and tasting notes.

To say I was stressed would be an understatement. The exam was a massive hurdle, but even clearing it meant only a brief respite. Just one week later, the grand opening of the Mirage Guild loomed on the horizon.

The lounge of the club still resembled a work in progress. Furniture lay unboxed, strewn around haphazardly, while some wires dangled ominously from the walls, awaiting the elegant sconces Emma had carefully chosen. The club's transformation was underway, but there was still so much to be done.

And so I'd been dividing my time between the two clubs. Helping bring one to life and passing over the baton to the new staff at the other. Every day I could feel the flutter of pressure beating in my chest, but I knew only time would ease it.

Isabella, meanwhile, had been engrossed in finalizing the RSVPs for the grand opening. The guest list was a who's who of the city's elite, and every detail had to be perfect. I wanted to ensure they would be walking into a club that lived up to its hype and promise.

This afternoon, Izzy and I were at the Mirage Guild. I was engrossed in studying my flashcards and occasionally muttering wine-related terms under my breath. Isabella, on the other hand, was tracing lines on architectural blueprints, mumbling about the arrangement of tables for the grand opening. I felt guilty for all the time my studying was taking out of my schedule. As much as I wished I could fully focus on the excitement of the grand opening, my brain was currently swimming in pop quiz questions.

"That layout looks incredible, Izzy," I said, leaning in to get a closer look at the blueprints. "Our clients are going to be thrilled with your designs."

She glanced up, a flicker of uncertainty in her eyes. "You really think so? I was thinking that maybe I could move some of these arrangements around—"

"Iz," I cut in, hoping to ground her swirling thoughts.

"You're doing great. The way you've envisioned the space, it's going to bring this place to life. Trust in that."

A sudden vibration from my phone interrupted my focus. The glow from the screen lit up with a message from my sister: "Hey, Fancy Boy, remember family dinner tonight. You better not be late!"

I let out an exasperated groan, rubbing my temples. "Damn it," I whispered, having completely forgotten about my familial commitment amidst the chaos of work. I glanced at Isabella, debating internally.

"You okay?" she asked, looking up from where she stood.

I hesitated. "I completely forgot about my family dinner tonight. And I'm nowhere near prepared for it mentally."

Isabella chuckled. "I take it this is something you can't skip out on?"

I nodded. "Not a chance. My phone would probably overheat with all the calls and texts my sisters would send my way if I didn't show."

Noticing the growl in my stomach and the way her eyes had started to glaze over, I smirked. "You know, it's a well-known fact that plotting grand openings works better on a full stomach. How do you feel about gate-crashing a slightly intimidating, always unpredictable, family dinner?"

Isabella caught the playful glint in my eyes. "Is Max Kingsley actually inviting me to meet the fam? I mean, I don't usually do dinners until the fifth . . . work meeting."

I chuckled. "It's . . . uncharted territory for me too. But, given how the day is going, I thought, why not? Besides, it could be fun, watching my three sisters trying to decipher the enigma that is Isabella."

"Flattery will get you everywhere." She flirted back. "All right, I'm in. But two conditions: one, there has to be copious amounts of wine, and two, you have to show me at least one picture of baby Max."

I grinned, the tension melting away. "Deal. And thank you. Truly. Having you there might just make the evening bearable."

"I hope that's not all I bring to the table," she replied with a wink, her voice a mix of jest and sincerity.

"You know it's not, sweetheart," I said, eyebrows raised.

"We have an hour or so before we need to leave. So, before we brave the familial battleground," I began with a smirk, shifting my gaze back to Isabella, "how about a quick taste test? I've been working on a signature cocktail for the grand opening."

"Oh, now you have my attention. Show me whatcha got," she said as she stood and headed over to the bar, sliding into one of the new chairs that had recently arrived.

I selected a few ingredients, a shaker, and two champagne glasses. "Okay, I'm thinking this could be called Midnight Carousel. It's a blend of elderflower, crème de violette, lemon, and Champagne. We could always sub out the Champagne for sparkling soda."

"Okay, that sounds *amazing*," she said.

I felt her eyes on me as I added the ingredients to the shaker, popped the lid on it, and shook it vicariously.

"Oh, Max, it's beautiful," Isabella said as I poured the

concoction into our glasses, the purple liquid swirling with a smidge of activated charcoal I added to give it a deeper purple color. I rubbed a few flakes of edible gold over the top and slid a glass over to her.

She gripped the stem. "Cheers," she said, raising her glass.

"Cheers, Isabella," I responded.

I watched her reaction as she parted her lips and tasted the drink. Her eyes widened. I was hoping for a good reaction, and the way her eyes widened told me I'd hit the mark.

"Oh my god, Max, this is so good," she said, taking another sip.

"You think it'll work for the signature drink?" I asked. "I have this one planned and some other mocktails, too."

"Absolutely," she said, "This is amazing."

Isabella's eyes landed on the stack of flashcards. "I'm sorry if my drink requests distracted you from studying. I know your test is coming up."

I shook my head. "It's no problem, really. It gave me something other than tannins and wine notes to think about."

"Okay, I feel like I've taken up a lot of your time lately. With the event and . . ." Her cheeks flushed, no doubt remembering about what we'd done on the stage last time we were here. "I shouldn't be distracting you when you need to focus."

I set down my glass and rested my palms on the bar top. "You are not a distraction, Isabella. Not in the least."

She sucked in her bottom lip. "Okay. I just don't want

anything to compromise your focus for your exam. This is a big deal."

"Trust me, you help my brain calm itself. In the same way that I think it helps you," I said.

She tilted her head. "You mean, you stress out about being a thirty-five-year-old single woman with no clear path for the future, too?"

"I know there's a lot of overthinking that goes on in here." I came around from the back of the bar and walked over to where she sat. "And, right now, it sounds like you're in your head. And as beautiful of a place that would be to hang out, I don't want you overthinking about our time together."

"It also seems to me," I continued, "that you've achieved quite a bit since you got back not *that* long ago. Do you give yourself credit for your achievements or do you just focus on the things you haven't perfected?"

"Fair point," she said.

"Is this your way of asking me to help you refocus?" I asked as I slid my palm over her thigh.

"You do have a knack for that," she said, holding my eyes as my hand pushed up under the fabric of her dress.

"You could just ask me though," I said teasingly. "You could just say, 'Hey, Max, will you get me off real quick so I can stop overthinking?'"

"Oh, is that what I can do?" she asked as she widened her legs.

"I wouldn't mind hearing it," I admitted.

"Max, will you slip your fingers inside me so I can come before meeting your family?" Isabella asked.

"I know you think you're being cute, but, Isabella, that is music to my ears," I said as I pushed the fabric of her panties to the side. I tugged her hips toward the edge of the leather seat and pushed her knees out wide.

"Mmm, already wet for me, huh?" I asked.

I trailed a finger down her middle, and I grinned as she gasped when I slipped past her folds. I added a second finger and began pumping them in and out as my thumb pressed down on her clit. Aware of what she liked now, I knew what would get her over the edge.

She gripped the bar top with one hand and my shoulder with the other. I hooked my fingers to hit the spot to bring her there.

"Are you close? Are you going to come for me, baby?"

"Yes, oh, I'm almost—"

Her voice cut off as I slid my fingers out of her and out from under her dress. Her eyes darted in confusion as I wiped my fingers on a cocktail napkin.

"I want you to start practicing asking for what you want," I said as I leaned down close to whisper in her ear, "and trust that I will give it to you." Her mouth fell open as I took a step back.

"But we're going to dinner at your mom's house. I'm all worked up now," she said with a whine.

I shrugged. "I don't think it'll take long for you to get up the nerve to start verbalizing what you need then, huh?"

I chuckled as she let out an aggravated sigh. Family dinner was about to get entertaining for me.

On our way out through the secret bookcase, I brought out my phone, thumbing quickly over the screen. "Just need to give them a heads up. You know, so they don't, uh, ambush you or anything."

Izzy peeked over my shoulder and saw the text I was composing for the family chat:

> Max: Hey, bringing a friend over for dinner. Please, do NOT make a big deal out of it. And no teasing. Seriously.

Almost instantly, there was a reply.

> Lara: Ooh, a "friend"! Must be serious if you're warning us in advance.

> Ellie: Oh, I promise to be on my best behavior. winking emoji

> Naomi: No promises here.

I sighed, rubbing my forehead. "Well, I tried."

Isabella chuckled. "Should I be worried?"

"You? No." I smiled as I held open the tavern door for Isabella. "Me? Abso-freakin-lutely. My sisters are ruthless."

"Oh, I love ruthless women," she said as she followed me down the sidewalk. "How far away did you have to park today?"

I stopped abruptly. "Uh, I don't typically drive out to my

mom's. I was just heading to Penn Station on autopilot, but we can call a taxi or a car if you—"

She rested her hand on my forearm. "Max, it's fine. I've taken the subway plenty of times. We don't need to call a car."

"I'm sorry, I should've thought about it," I said.

"Thought about what? That I might think I'm too good for the subway?"

I chuckled. "Well, I mean, look at you. You're all dressed up and fancy. Not that the subway isn't full of all kinds of people, but—"

She smirked, nudging me lightly with her elbow. "Oh, so now I'm too glamorous for the subway? Better be careful, Mr. Sommelier. Next thing you know, I'll start demanding my wine be poured from a golden decanter."

I laughed, visibly relaxing. "Just remember, once we get to my mom's, you're drinking that fancy wine from plastic cups. So, soak up all this fanciness while you can."

"I'll make sure to savor every single moment then," she quipped, giving me a playful wink.

The subway ride was a blend of casual chatter and comfortable silence. As we swayed with the rhythm of the train, I found myself enjoying the mundane normalcy of it all, the simple way in which Isabella and I existed together. We stepped off at the designated station, the city's pulse humming around us as we ascended to street level.

Emerging into the fresh air, we were greeted by the charming residential character of Jackson Heights. The transition from the hustle of urban streets to the serene ambiance of a residential neighborhood was almost instantaneous. Tree-lined avenues unfurled before us, each brick home nestled against its neighbor like chapters in a storybook.

I guided Isabella, my hand wrapped around hers with an ease that spoke of years walking these streets, each step taking us closer to my childhood home. The familiar sights eased some of the tension from my shoulders, my steps becoming more assured as we approached.

I led us up a short set of stairs to a modest, welcoming home. Its warm, golden lights glowed from the inside, illuminating the porch. Before I could even knock, the door flew open to reveal a bubbly young woman with a shock of curly hair similar to mine.

"Maxie!" Lara squealed, wrapping me in a tight hug.

Isabella chuckled from behind us, stepping back. As Lara's eyes landed on the woman beside me, Isabella lifted her hand and waved. "Hi, I'm Izzy."

My sister's eyes widened, and with an impish grin, she said, "I'm Lara. And it's Izzy? As in *Isabella*, Izzy?"

"Yep, that's me," Isabella replied, slightly taken aback but smiling nonetheless.

Lara's eyes danced with mischief. "Oh! Isabella! Are you the one who Max couldn't—"

I body-blocked my sister as I pushed her back inside, mumbling against her head. "Lara, I told you all to be nice."

Isabella's gaze flickered between us, clearly intrigued.

I was flustered and tried to steer the topic elsewhere. "Where's Mom? And the rest of the chaos brigade?"

Lara rolled her eyes, escaping my grasp. "Inside, getting

the roast out. But, oh boy, are they gonna be excited to meet *Isabella*." With a final wink, she turned and sauntered back inside.

From the heart of the kitchen echoed a lively voice, "Max, is that you? Don't just stand there trying to impress. Come and set the table!"

My eyes rolled dramatically. "I'm on it, Mom!" Yet, the warm, playful smile I exchanged with Isabella was a testament to the deep-rooted affection I held for the playful ribbing.

The scent of a roast, mingled with the heady aroma of various spices, filled the air, prompting a subtle rumble from my stomach. As Isabella ventured further into the cozy space, a broad smile stretched across her face. Walls adorned with memories showcased a younger me and my sisters, captured haphazardly in a collection of mismatched frames. I heard a chuckle as she smiled at the little kid with glasses staring back at her.

My parents' home, even though it was just my mother's since my dad passed away all those years ago, had always exuded a vintage charm. Nearly every surface was decked with trinkets, quaint curios stood in corners, and lace runners elegantly laid over a polished wooden buffet. Here, my sisters, already engaged in a lively chat, looked up and beamed as Isabella entered. The round of warm introductions culminated with her being ushered to a seat directly across from them.

I pulled out her chair and gave her a soft smile that hopefully conveyed my apologies for the barrage of questions my sisters were, no doubt, about to pepper her with. I pushed through the swinging kitchen door to help my mom. Our tiny galley kitchen was muggy from the steam of pots on the stove and warmth of the oven toasting my mom's handmade rolls.

I grabbed trivets and dishes to take out to the dining table after kissing my mom on her head as she added salt to the pot of stew.

"I brought Isabella for dinner, Mom, don't make a big deal out of it," I said as I grabbed a stack of linen napkins.

"Isabella? *The* Isabella?" she asked teasingly. "It's about time, Maxwell."

Throughout dinner, it was probably evident to Isabella that I played the role of the beloved but often teased youngest brother even if it was against my will most times. My sisters soaked it up and had me summoned for the most trivial tasks: from sending the basket of rolls around to being the one to fetch the forgotten butter. Her eyes twinkled with laughter to see me bending to every whim and fancy of my family without a hint of reluctance.

As I went to open another bottle of wine, this one a Caymus Cabernet Sauvignon from Napa I'd brought from the bar, my mother shooed me away. "Max, you don't need to waste that stuff here. I've got plenty of red back in the kitchen."

"It's not a waste mom. It pairs well with the roast," I said as I twisted the cork out. "Besides, your red comes *from a box.*"

"Well, we wouldn't be able to tell the difference if we

tried. No sense in wasting such an expensive bottle on us," she said. "We don't need any of that fancy wine here."

I schooled my mouth into a grin and poured my mother a glass anyway. My mom liked to distance herself from the world I worked in and the friends I kept. A lot of it stemmed from insecurities about our house, our lifestyle, but now that it was part of my world, her separation hurt.

"Speak for yourself, Mom," Lara said. "I personally enjoy the wine that Fancy Boy here brings."

From across the table, I caught Isabella's eye, raising an eyebrow to ask if she was surviving the family onslaught. She nodded once, smiling behind her raised glass. It was odd having her with me in this element. I don't know why I didn't think she'd fit in, but it was a pleasant surprise to see her interact with my loud family with such ease.

As the clock chimed, signaling the late hour, I began gathering empty plates, and Isabella, eager to help, joined in. We could still hear my sisters' laughter from the dining room as we moved into the kitchen.

With plates washed and the counter wiped down, I turned to her, my eyes filled with gratitude. "Thanks for coming tonight," I murmured. "It means a lot."

She smiled gently, placing a reassuring hand on my arm. "Thank you for inviting me. It was . . . enlightening." With a playful wink, she added, "I've got enough stories to tease you for a lifetime now."

TWENTY-ONE

MAX

The moment my feet crossed the threshold into the Mirage Guild, the familiar weight of anticipation and nerves that had been my constant companions over the past months dissolved, leaving a buoyant sense of accomplishment in its wake. The door, cleverly disguised as a bookshelf, closed behind me with a soft click, a symbolic gesture that seemed to seal away the external pressures and doubts that had dogged me throughout my sommelier certification journey.

The Guild, bathed in the golden warmth of carefully placed lighting, was more than simply a space. It became a witness to the transformation quietly taking place within me. Each step I took toward Isabella, who was engrossed in the meticulous task of arranging name plates, felt like a step into a new chapter of my life.

Her back was to me, but it was as if she could sense my presence, turning with a smile that effortlessly bridged the gap between us. In that smile, I found not just a friend, but a pillar of support, a confidante who had seen beyond the façade of confidence I often projected. It was to her, this beacon of unwavering belief and encouragement, that I wanted to first reveal the news of my passing.

"I did it, Isabella," the words spilled out, tinged with a mixture of disbelief and pride. For a moment, I allowed myself to fully absorb the gravity of what this achievement meant.

Passing the sommelier exam wasn't just about earning a title. It was a validation of my passion, a testament to the endless hours of study, the sacrifices, and the singular focus that had defined my life recently. It was a credential that placed me firmly within the world I had long admired from the fringes, a mark of expertise I could now bring to both the Prism Society and the Mirage Guild.

Her reaction was immediate: her eyes lit up, and a cheer escaped her lips. "Max, that's incredible! I knew you could do it!" She jumped up from her seat and came over to throw her arms around my neck in excitement. Her enthusiasm was infectious, and for a moment, I basked in the glow of her praise, a stark contrast to the doubts and critiques I'd become accustomed to.

This achievement opened more than just professional doors. It was an opportunity to redefine my role within our circle, to bring a new depth of knowledge and passion to our endeavors. With my certification, I could now elevate our wine programs, curating experiences that were not only luxurious but also deeply informed and personalized. It was a chance to blend the art and science of wine in ways that would enchant our patrons, creating moments of connection and discovery that transcended the ordinary.

In that moment, surrounded by the soft hum of preparation and the tangible sense of anticipation for what the Mirage Guild would become, I felt an alignment between my personal aspirations and the collective vision we were building. It was a confirmation that my journey hadn't been just about obtaining a title, but about finding my place in a world where my passion for wine could flourish and contribute to something truly extraordinary.

And as we broke away from the embrace, the future felt bright with possibility, not just for me, but for all of us who were pouring our hearts into the creation of something magical. The Mirage Guild, with its promise of sensuality and discovery, was not just a project; it was a canvas for us to express our deepest passions and to invite others to explore alongside us.

Relief sagged my shoulders at finally being past this hurdle.

We stood there for a moment, her arms still loosely circling my neck, my hands resting comfortably at her hips. Her eyes held that impossible mix of green and gray, like ocean water churning beneath a stormy sky.

God, she was beautiful. And kind, and whip-smart, and . . . everything I never knew I wanted. The realization hit me like a blow, nearly knocking the wind from my lungs. I was falling for her. Hard.

The revelation struck with the intensity of a physical

force, leaving me momentarily breathless. As I stood there, watching Isabella navigate the preparations with a mix of grace and determination, the truth of my feelings for her crystallized. She was not just a flicker of adolescent longing reignited. She had become the epicenter of my world, embodying qualities I hadn't even known to long for.

It wasn't just her beauty, which was undeniable, or her intelligence and kindness, which were evident to anyone who spent more than a few moments in her company. It was the depth of her compassion, her unwavering support that had quietly woven itself into the fabric of my daily existence, making her indispensable to me.

Over the past few months, as we collaborated and faced challenges together, Isabella had shown up for me in ways that went beyond mere professional courtesy or friendship. She had become my confidante, my cheerleader, someone who saw beyond the façade I often presented to the world. Her presence had become a balm to the chaotic nature of my life, grounding me with her steadfastness and understanding.

The realization that my feelings had evolved, deepening into something more profound and enduring than a mere crush, was both exhilarating and daunting. Isabella had become everything I never knew I needed, her strength and vulnerability intertwining in a way that drew me closer, compelling me to reconsider the nature of my affections for her.

It was in the small moments, the exchanges that others might overlook, that the breadth of my feelings became apparent. The way she listened, truly listened, when I spoke about my aspirations and fears. The way her laughter could light up the darkest of days, and how her mere presence seemed to make any challenge surmountable.

I kept my eyes locked on Isabella as I slowly brought my face down to hers, lightly brushing my lips over her own. Her mouth opened for me, and I greedily leaned in for more. Her mouth was warm and tasted like cinnamon and orange from the tea she had sitting next to her. I slid my tongue over her teeth and felt her melt into me.

A groan escaped my mouth as she tilted her hips forward to grind against the bulge forming in my jeans. "If you don't stop that, I'm going to have to take you in one of those rooms, Isabella," I said into her mouth.

Her hands left my neck and trailed down my chest, one snaking down to rub me through my jeans. "Is that a promise?" she asked.

She let out a laugh and huff of air as I quickly scooped her up and threw her over my shoulder, stalking around the stage. There were small rooms that lined either side of the stage, each with a distinct theme and accessories to match. I turned the knob of the room with the golden lion head on it.

Inside, I pressed a brass button to turn the lights on. The lights were all programmed to be set to dim so we could keep the mood intimate. The entire room glowed with the light bouncing off the mirrored walls and ceiling.

It felt like a sexy funhouse with the black silk sheet-lined bed in the middle of the room that had a low upholstered bench at the foot. She let the palm of my hand trail up her ass, her spine, and eventually cup the back of her head as I slowly sat Isabella down. Her lips were red and puffy from where my mouth had claimed hers a moment ago.

"Take off your clothes," I said. "I want to see you from every angle." Our last time had been hurried and I hadn't gotten to take my time with her. I wanted to watch every inch of her tremble beneath me. I wanted to see how good she looked when she took all of me. I wanted to watch myself slide in and out of her. God, I wanted to make her mine.

Isabella obeyed and began lifting the oversized sweatshirt she wore over her leggings. She pressed her hands into the waistband of her pants and tugged them down and soon she was left in just a thin sports bra and panties.

"Take everything off," I said.

I circled her as she finally stood in front of me fully bare for me. Her olive skin glowed in the dim light of the room and her curls fell heavy over her shoulders. I traced the indent her yoga pants had left at her hips, and I smiled when she sucked in a breath at my touch.

"You are so beautiful, Isabella," I whispered. "I want you to be able to see just how incredible you look as I'm fucking you."

I watched as her eyes fluttered around the room, noting glimpses of herself on every wall. I could tell her eyes wouldn't linger over one place on her body for too long and that bothered me.

I'd heard her not-so-subtle comments that she'd make about herself, her age, her place in life. I had thought it was just awkward filler conversation at first but now seeing the way she didn't soak in how incredible she really was told me it was real.

"When you're excited, there's a tiny triangle shape of redness that shows up right here," I said as I traced the base of her throat. "I can't keep my eyes off it when you talk."

I trailed my fingertip down between her breasts before scooping one up and running my thumb off my nipple. I smiled as goosebumps popped up on her skin and she sucked in a breath.

"*Max*," she whispered.

"There's this green dress you wear that holds your tits in the perfect way. It's when I first saw this mole you have," I said as my finger tapped the darkened spot on her skin above her nipple.

I moved to stand behind her and wrapped an arm around her soft belly. I ran my other hand softly down her ribs, slowing when I reached the curve of her hips.

"These right here," I said as I gripped the flesh tightly, tugging her back against me, "have me in a goddamn choke-hold." I placed a gentle kiss at the top of her shoulder as Isabella let out a slow breath.

"And if all of these don't make you stare in wonder at yourself like I want to," I continued, "then I guess I'm just going to have to spend some more time worshiping it." I gripped and pulled at the softness of her inner thighs, my eyes dark as I watched her body move in the mirror in front of us.

My eyes narrowed in on the shine of the sticky wetness I could see coating her inner thighs. I slid two fingers over the wetness and traced them along her flesh and over the crease of her leg.

"*Max, please,*" Isabella said.

I grinned as I spread her lips with my two fingers and gently traced along her outer edges. "Look at how fucking wet you are watching me talk about you. I don't think you *want* to be insecure Isabella. I think you feel like you're *supposed* to be."

"*Max,*" Isabella said as she began shivering beneath me.

"What is it sweetheart? What do you need?" I asked.

"Touch me, *please,*" she said as she locked eyes with me in the mirror.

"I *am* touching you." I chuckled as she groaned and shifted her hips to grind against my hardness pressing against my zipper. "We're not ready for that yet, sweetheart, you're going to watch yourself come first."

I dropped to my knees behind Isabella, placing kisses down her spine and over her ass on the way down. She was nearly up on her tiptoes when I traced two fingers down her wet middle. With one hand wrapped around the front and the other coming between her legs from behind I set my sights on hearing all of her moans.

Two fingers pressed down firmly and made small circles around her clit. I used two more to slide into her warm pussy from behind. Isabella bent over me, barely able to hold herself up.

"Watch yourself," I said, "I don't want your eyes leaving the mirror. I want you to watch as I pound my fingers into you, making you come all over my hand."

Her moans and whines were delicious, but she listened. She lifted her gaze and her eyes locked in on my hands. I slid two fingers in slowly at first, pushing them in and turning them slightly. Then I added a third.

The way she stretched for me was making my cock strain painfully. The sounds of her sweet, wet pussy filled the air as I picked up my speed. My other hand never left her clit. I rubbed and pinched it gently, bringing her closer and closer to the edge.

"Oh god, Max, *please*," she begged from above me. It was a sound I'd never get tired of.

I pressed those three fingers in deep and slowly flicked them as I went to work on her clit. I pressed two fingers into the sensitive bundle of nerves and rubbed back and forth as Isabella wiggled and moaned above me.

Both of our eyes were locked onto my hands working their magic on her pussy. I looked up and spotted that triangle of redness on her neck and knew she was close. Isabella let out a low, long moan as her pussy clenched around my fingers and held onto me tightly.

I felt the goosebumps on her thighs as she rocked herself on my hands, bringing herself down to get deeper. Liquid flooded my hand as I continued to rub even as her moans got wilder.

"Okay, okay, okay," Isabella repeated. "I need you inside me."

I pulled my fingers away and slid each in my mouth, sucking them clean, before tugging off my shirt over my head. Isabella swayed, unsteady on her feet. I slid my pants down next, relieving some of the pressure against my cock.

"Get on your knees," I said. "I've dreamt of what you would look like taking my cock in this room and I can't leave without seeing it."

I pulled my cock out of my black briefs, feeling the heat of myself in my hand as I gave myself a few strokes. I tightened more at the sight of Isabella, wordlessly getting down on her knees next to the mirror.

"I desperately want to be inside that pussy, but I've got to see those lips wrapped around my cock again," I said as I walked closer to her, bringing the tip of me to her lips.

Isabella reached out with her tongue to lap up the precum beading at the tip as shivers ran down my spine. She ran her tongue up and down the sides, coating my cock in her saliva. Then she lined up her mouth, opened wide, gripped my hips, and sank my cock deep in her mouth.

I almost came right then and there. My eyes danced between Isabella beneath me and the sight of her taking me in the mirror. *God, she was something.* I could watch her swallow my cock every day. But I didn't want it to end here. I gently released her grip on me and slid myself out.

"Get on the bench, on your knees," I said, lifting her up off the floor. Isabella positioned herself exactly how I wanted her. Her knees were pressed down into the fabric, her ass was in the air, and her elbows rested on the edge of the bed. She turned back to me and grinned as she wiggled her hips.

I was on her in an instant, laying a warm smack of my palm against the smooth skin of her ass. I kept my eyes on her face as she closed her eyes and grinned softly. *Exactly how I'd hope she'd react.*

"Turn around and watch, Isabella," I said. "Your pussy is about to be wrapped around my cock."

She rewarded me with a small arch of her back, pressing her ass against the tip of my swollen cock as she turned her cheek to watch our reflections. I reached down and spread her cheeks out with my hands. I lined my cock up to her entrance and sank myself into her. I relished in the soft moan that came from beneath me.

I gripped Isabella's hips tightly as I pulled myself away only to slam back in. My hips smacked against her ass making her skin jiggle. *She was mesmerizing.* My eyes moved between watching myself slide into her and watching *her*. Isabella's eyes were heavy and glassy as she stared over her shoulder at the mirror beside us.

God, she felt so good beneath me. She was so soft and warm. So willing to play the games I liked playing. I knew, right now, she wasn't stressed about everything going on outside these mirrored walls. That, for once, she wasn't over-thinking about where she was in life, where she lived, or what her ex was up to.

"God, I could be inside you *all night*, Isabella," I said. "But right now, I want to see my cum dripping out of you."

I knew Isabella liked my dirty talk because I could feel her pussy clench around me as I spoke.

I picked up my pace and gripped her hips. I felt my orgasm quickly building so I slammed into her one more time before exploding. I let myself catch my breath before slowly sliding out, my eyes locked onto her dripping pussy. I didn't miss how Isabella's eyes tracked my movement or how they widened when I spread her wide so I could see me dripping out of her.

I could never get enough of Isabella.

I helped her lay down on the bench and brought a warm rag to clean up the mess we had made.

"Well, that was one way of celebrating you passing your exam," Isabella said as she tugged back on her pants.

"Wanna go test out another room?" I joked, half-serious. Her laughter, light and airy, filled the space between us, but my suggestion seemed to tap into a deeper, unresolved tension.

"I think we've pushed our luck enough for one day," she replied. The humor in her voice didn't mask the underlying concern about getting caught. It struck a chord. Was our secrecy necessary, or was it a barrier I hadn't acknowledged until now?

Reflecting on our hidden moments, a sense of déjà vu washed over me. I'd been here before—kept in the shadows, deemed not quite right to be brought into the light. Isabella's earlier words, designed to keep a distance between us, now resonated like a repeating pattern. Was I falling into old habits, hoping for more from someone who might not be ready to offer it in full view?

As we cleaned up, my mind wrestled with these doubts. This wasn't about being discreet. It was about feeling valued, seen, and unashamed. I had promised myself not to fall for someone who wouldn't openly stand by me, rich girl or not.

Yet here I was, caught in the gravity of someone who made me reconsider all my rules.

This conversation needed a proper time and place, not in the aftermath of our closeness but in the clear light of day. It wasn't just about wanting to be seen with Isabella. I wanted to be chosen by her, publicly and privately.

Navigating these feelings felt like walking a tightrope—exhilarating but perilous. And as we merged back into the real world, I had some thinking to do. Was I content in the shadows, or did I deserve more? The thought lingered, a challenge to my own worth and what I truly wanted from Isabella and myself.

The Mirage Guild was a hive of activity, a symphony of last-minute preparations echoing through its ornate halls before the grand opening tomorrow. Moments like this, the calm before the storm, they were what I cherished. It was the culmination of all the overanalyzing and stress, the tangible manifestation of our collective dreams and hard work.

And it was breathtakingly beautiful.

I paused, taking in the sight of our unlikely group of friends.

Emma and Liam sat nestled together on a plush couch, a picture of a contented partnership. Liam's fingers gently played with a strand of Emma's hair, a tender gesture that spoke volumes, while he engaged in light conversation with Jessie. She sat across from them, her knees pulled up close, her eyes twinkling.

Then there was Dom, who strolled over to the edge of

the tufted couch, exuding a quiet strength. His hand reached out to Jessie, his touch gentle yet firm on her shoulder. I tried to decipher the layers of meaning behind Dom's effortless, nonchalant demeanor. He was an enigma, always keeping his emotions carefully guarded, locked away beneath a calm exterior. My gaze then landed on Natalia and Max. They were engaged in a spirited yet friendly debate. Their voices rose and fell in a dance of words, each trying to outwit the other, yet there was an underlying current of mutual respect and fondness.

These moments, surrounded by friends who had become family, grounded me. Amid the chaos of planning and preparation, there was a sense of belonging, a shared purpose connecting us all.

The Mirage Guild stood as a testament to our unity, a club where our individual talents and quirks intertwined to craft something extraordinary. Standing there among this dynamic and vibrant group, I felt prepared for whatever the future might hold, knowing we would face it together.

"Okay, I think we've perfected everything to death. It's time to just trust that tomorrow night is going to go well," I said.

"What if we pre-celebrate with some drinks?" Max asked from the bar.

"Yes!" Jessie said, turning in her spot on the couch. "Definitely drinks. Also, I already analyzed our horoscopes and tomorrow is looking bright for all of us." Jessie, with a dramatic flourish, held her glass aloft and declared, "According to the stars, tomorrow aligns with a rare cosmic convergence that promises success, deep connections, and unexpected revelations for us all."

"Well, I'll take whatever good luck we can get," Emma said.

I plopped down in one of the swivel chairs and turned to where everyone else sat around low mercury glass-topped tables. Max navigated back from the bar, each step exuding a calm confidence, balancing a tray of artfully prepared drinks. In each glass, a mesmerizing mix of purple, deep black, and gold flakes swirled.

"As the resident sommelier and mixologist," Max announced, his tone imbued with a playful showmanship, "I present the Midnight Carousel, a concoction designed to capture the essence of the Mirage Guild—enchanting, vibrant, and a touch mysterious." His eyes shone with a mixture of pride and excitement as he distributed the drinks, his passion for his craft visible in every gesture.

I watched him, a smile playing on my lips, impressed by his transformation from a studious sommelier into a charismatic host. As he handed me a glass, our fingers brushed, a fleeting but charged touch that sent a subtle current running through my fingertips. My heart fluttered, a sensation I tried to quell but couldn't completely hide.

From the corner of my eye, I caught Natalia's knowing wink. A silent acknowledgment of the unspoken electricity between me and Max. My cheeks warmed slightly, but I masked it with a sip of the exquisite cocktail, letting the rich flavors distract me from the butterflies in my stomach.

Two cocktails and one Champagne toast later, we'd all

kicked off our shoes and were animatedly talking about how tomorrow might go. There were guesses and bets on who might show up and what rooms certain people might try out. There were predictions for how the entertainment might go and hopes that all their members would enjoy it.

Dom had decided to oversee the Prism Society and had since entrusted Natalia and Liam to do the same for the Mirage Guild. It was reassuring knowing there could be an element of this world that I could be a part of without my younger brother and his friend's presence. Well, except for Max.

Max had long since passed the blurred lines of fitting in the boundary of just "my brother's friend." And I had no idea what to do with that change. I wasn't ready to fully admit to Dom something was going on between us, especially since it was most likely a fling. Something that, especially if we kept working together, would need to come to a stop.

I was asking for heartbreak and trouble the longer I kept up our charade. I was at a place in my life where I needed to be looking for a partner who was ready to settle down and move into the next phase of life. There were a lot of things on the to-do list of my life that still needed to be checked off.

I *did* want to get married, become a parent, move out of my freaking parents' house.

A few months ago, I still had all the time in the world to do those things, but for every day that goes by, that pressure gets heavier and heavier.

"Earth to Izzy." Natalia's voice cut through my over-thinking, and my eyes refocused on her face in front of me.

"Oh, sorry," I said, "lost in thought for a minute. What's up?"

"We're going around and answering the question, 'What's one thing you've always wanted to do but haven't yet?'" she said.

"Oh, uh," I said, vying for time, "well, there's a lot of things, actually. But not enough time to do them in." I laughed and shrugged, hoping that was a sufficient enough answer.

Natalia's raised eyebrows told me otherwise.

"Come on, you're in a safe space, like what?" Emma asked.

I took another sip of my cocktail, hoping for a bit of clarity. "Well, there's this little brownstone in Washington Square that I've had my eye on to redesign, but that would involve actually moving out of my parents' guest room."

"I didn't know you were looking at buying," Dom said.

I laughed. "I'm not. I'm not in a place where it makes sense to do so, it probably won't happen."

"Why not?" Jessie asked.

My eyes darted around the group. What was this, grill Izzy hour?

"It doesn't really make sense for a single woman to buy a place meant for a family," I said, knocking back the rest of my drink.

"Well, it would make a great spot for a family one day," Natalia said.

"Come on, Nat, you and I both know the odds of *that* ever happening, I don't really make the best choices when it comes to the men in my life, now, do I?" I said.

Natalia's eyes widened at my admission.

Shit, Max was right here. He must know I don't mean him. Even though I kind of do. We both knew we were just keeping each other company until we both found someone better suited for us.

I dared a glance his way and immediately regretted it.

Not just for the look of confusion on his face but because Dom was looking his way too. In a way, that told me he was apologizing for my behavior. That meant Dom *did* know something was going on between us. Realizing that Dom might know about us felt like being doused with cold water.

My initial embarrassment about the situation with Max morphed into a deeper discomfort, knowing my brother might be privy to my personal life in ways I hadn't intended. The thought of Dom judging me for engaging with someone younger, especially someone as close to him as Max, knotted my stomach. It wasn't just the age difference that made me uneasy. It was the fear of being seen as irresponsible or flippant in my brother's eyes, someone whose opinion I valued deeply. The potential for his disappointment added a layer of anxiety to an already complex mix of emotions.

"Well, I personally think that women can make whatever investment they choose to make with or without the excuse or desire of a family," Emma said, saving me from the awkward silence that filled the air.

"Yeah, maybe," I said.

The rest of the group went around answering the question for themselves. Even as my ears buzzed with embarrassment. My brain picked up on tiny details as they spoke. Jessie had always dreamed of going to the Himalayan salt caves for a retreat, and Liam mentioned something about rescuing a specific kind of dog.

Sitting there, my mind whirled with conflicting emotions, the words I'd uttered hanging heavy in the air. Max's posture had stiffened slightly. Was he hurt by my words? Disappointed? Or was I reading too much into it? I shifted my focus back to the group, trying to engage in the conversation and laugh at the right moments. But my laughter felt hollow, my smile forced. I couldn't shake off the sense that I'd inadvertently created a rift, however slight, between Max and me.

Finally, I stood and gathered up a couple of empty glasses to take to the bar. I dumped the ice down the sink and pushed the glasses on the water spigot to rinse them before turning to load them in the dishwasher. Dom's body blocked me from opening the stainless steel door.

"I'm going to cut some of the awkwardness that I'm sure you're feeling," he said.

"Gee, thanks, bro," I said.

"I know that you and Max have been hooking up," he said, not making eye contact with me. "And that's whatever, but I wanted you to know that I knew so you would stop being all weird about it. And maybe you could actually give it a real chance since I don't have a problem with it."

My face was warm. I didn't know, and didn't need to

know, how Dominic had found out about Max and me. But did his knowing help make my feelings about Max any clearer?

"It's not just that, Dom, he's . . ." I glanced over at the group, who were all huddled over Jessie's phone as she showed them the inside of the caves she wanted to visit. "He's *younger.*"

Dom's eyebrows scrunched in a scowl. "Oh, I was waiting for you to say more."

I rolled my eyes and scoffed. "That's plenty of a reason, you know. If *he* were dating someone seven years younger than him, it would be no problem, but for me?"

"Listen, I'm not going to pretend to understand the ins and outs of how age gaps are different for men and women," he said. "I'm going to trust that you're the expert on that, but if that's the *one* thing holding this up, I think that's a pretty weak argument."

"There's a lot to it, Dom," I said.

"Have you actually shared about these concerns with Max?" Dom asked. "You know, *talked* about them?"

I fixed my eyes on Dom.

"Thought so," he said, shaking his head. "You always do this, Iz, you make assumptions about what everyone else is thinking and feeling so you can make the choice for them. That's not fair. *Talk to him.*"

"When did *you* become so introspective?" I grumbled.

Dom grinned back at me, shrugged, and headed back out to the lounge. If Dom was bringing this up, that meant he *actually* didn't have a problem with us dating or whatever we were doing.

Wasn't that the hangup I'd been dreading? And now, if that's not a problem . . .

I shook my head to clear my thoughts. Dom was right. All of this *should* be a conversation with Max. But having an intentional conversation about whatever was going on was admitting that there was more to the hookup.

That maybe I did want more.

And that was a hell of a lot scarier than I wanted to admit.

TWENTY-THREE
ISABELLA

"Looking good, guys," I said, carefully placing the brushed brass tabletop nameplates Dom had specially engraved.

I ran my fingers over the embossed letters, pausing for a second to take it all in. It was the grand opening of the Mirage Guild, and the air was thick with anticipation. Dominic and Liam heaved cases of wine, their muscles flexing under the strain, laughter escaping them in short bursts. Emma, ever the perfectionist, adjusted the pillows and scrutinized every angle of my interior design masterpiece. Jessie, with my keen eye, polished each glass to sparkle, ensuring every reflection shone as bright as the future of this place.

Max stood behind the bar, his hands moving deftly as he stocked it with the new bottles we'd tasted together. His face was a picture of concentration.

I felt bad that we hadn't chatted yet, but I hadn't trusted

myself last night after one too many cocktails. And, like the coward I was, I had avoided him, slipping away as everyone else had said good night.

I did one final sweep of the lounge, ensuring everything was perfectly in place. The rich jewel tones of the furnishings looked striking against the dark wood accents. Overhead, the antique lighting cast a sultry glow across each booth and table. I stood for a moment on the small stage, picturing it coming to life later: the buzz of conversation, the tinkle of glasses, the energy of people out to enjoy themselves.

"It's really coming together," Max said, coming up behind me.

Normally, he'd place his hand on the small of my back. A subtle gesture I didn't realize I missed until now that he hadn't done it.

I forced a smile. "It is. I can hardly believe this is real."

We both gazed out at the room. This vintage circus, secret speakeasy vibe had been quickly coming together for the last few months. Seeing his excitement now made my heart swell.

"Gather round, everyone!" Dom called out, waving us over. "I'll be heading over to the Prism Society tonight to make sure things run smoothly there. I trust that you all will handle the opening tonight perfectly."

We clustered around the bar, giddy with anticipation. I was happy my brother wouldn't be here tonight. He'd let Liam take the lead on this space as he spent more time at Prism. Dom popped open a bottle of Champagne with a theatrical flourish and began filling flutes.

"To the Mirage Guild!" He held his glass aloft. "To new beginnings and to Max, for not only passing his sommelier exam but truly embodying what it means to excel in his craft. Here's to raising the bar higher."

"To new adventures," Jessie chimed in, clinking her glass against Emma's.

Max lingered near me, yet there was an unspoken distance between us, a tension that felt heavier than the air around us. It was clear what I'd said last night had landed poorly, his usual warmth replaced by a careful, measured silence. The moment passed, and the conversation flowed around me, but I couldn't shake off the disquieting feeling of Max's withdrawal. It hurt more than I expected, the absence of his casual touches, his smiles directed elsewhere, avoiding any interaction that might bridge the gap between us.

The instinctive need to maintain a façade of indifference in front of our friends had driven my actions, but at what cost? Max and I hadn't defined what was happening between us, true, but the connection, the unspoken understanding we'd shared, seemed fractured now.

And it was my doing.

Max's hurt, his deliberate isolation, was a reflection of my own fears, my own uncertainties about what we were to each other. I brushed the anxieties away. Now wasn't the time to spiral about this—not minutes before the grand opening. I had worked too hard and invested too much of myself into this project to have it derailed. The conversation with Max would have to wait.

Max cleared his throat, pulling me from my inner

turmoil. "To new beginnings!" he announced, his voice steady, but I sensed the underlying strain.

"To new beginnings," I repeated mechanically, my voice barely above a whisper, my glass clinking against his a little too sharply. As I watched Max mingle with the others, laughter, and lightness in his demeanor, a part of me ached to pull him aside, to explain, to bridge the gap I had widened. But fear held me back, fear of what acknowledging my feelings for Max meant, fear of stepping out of the safety of "casual."

Why does this feel so complicated? I thought, taking a deep breath and trying to focus on the night ahead. But no matter how hard I tried, my gaze kept drifting back to Max, and with each glance, the knot in my gut tightened, a silent reminder of the internal conflict I couldn't escape.

Not yet, I pleaded silently, glancing at Max's handsome face. Give me tonight.

Within the hour, the energy in the club had shifted dramatically. From behind the hidden bookshelf door, a stream of elegantly dressed guests flowed into the intimate space, their faces alight with anticipation and curiosity. Couples clasped hands, friends whispered excitedly, their eyes sparkling under the dim, golden lighting that bathed the room in a warm, inviting glow.

Soft music drifted from the sound system and the clinking of glasses could be heard around the room as people sipped on Max's signature cocktail. He was held up behind the bar, pouring glass after glass of the purple and gold drink.

Liam navigated the crowd of VIP guests with ease, shaking hands and explaining the concept of the new space. Unlike the Prism Society, the Mirage Guild gave the opportunity for more public displays of lust and passion.

Everyone's eyes kept drifting to the center stage where the entertainment for the evening was set up. I'd planned circus-themed vignettes to grace the stage to entertain our guests. It was a play on the circus acts that traveling shows put on, but instead of traditional juggling or trapeze artists, we had topless jugglers walking around the lounge, on-stage masturbation, and aerial sex.

Right now, the stage showcased a woman lying back on a red velvet chaise. Her brown hair was pinned back with gold clips and a deep red stain marked her lips. Her body was draped in a black, sheer mesh fabric that bunched at her hips in waves as she moved. She cupped her breasts with slender hands and trailed red-painted fingernails down to her inner thighs.

She had no toys, no accessories, just herself. Guests watched from comfortable seats or from across the room as the woman hummed while she explored herself. She was just what we needed to set the tone for the rest of the evening.

I kept pace with our guests, refilling glasses and fetching snacks as needed. Every time I made my way up to the bar I tried to communicate as much as I could with a glance at Max. He grinned at me, and part of my brain told me that I'd made up for the hurt I saw in his eyes last night, but deep down I knew I'd seen it.

The soft ringing we'd set up to announce a shift in the stage set rang out from the speakers, alerting the entertainment and staff. I watched as the curtain dropped around the stage and the anticipation in the room built.

Within minutes, the curtains were pulled back again. On the stage now rested a bed with clean creamy silk sheets, a small wooden table within arm's reach of the bed, and a couple. On top of the table rested various toys and accessories that would be used on stage, for everyone to see.

The Mirage Guild was more than exploring fantasies, it was about putting them out in the open for everyone to enjoy and experience. It was about removing the judgment and stigma about enjoying watching others in pleasure. And by the grins on the faces of our VIP guests, I think we got it right.

I leaned against the bar for a few minutes and watched the couple. Everyone in the room seemed to be holding their breath waiting for them to get started. The woman sat up on her knees, wearing only a tiny lace thong. Her creamy skin glowed in the dim light of the room and was a contrast to the tan hand of the man who palmed her belly.

The man knelt behind her, placing soft kisses up and down her neck as she smiled. His other hand reached around to grab her full breasts and she moaned when he tweaked her nipples. More guests came to take their seats to watch the show.

The man slid a palm down her toned belly and cupped

her between her legs, grinding his palm into her. She rolled her head back against his shoulder, her breath coming out heavy. He reached over to the table and selected a palm-sized vibrator and turned it on.

He rolled the buzzing device all over her body, making her tremble. He ran it down her neck, in between her breasts, over her stomach, and pressed it between her legs. He ran it over her panties, and we all watched as she lifted her hips to press herself into it.

The man was only wearing small, tight shorts, revealing a bulge pressed into the woman's back. Everyone watched with rapt attention as the man tugged down her panties and pulled them off her. She sat up, bare for all of us and we greedily soaked her in.

He reached again for the table, this time selecting a thick, veiny dildo from the options of toys. He trailed it up her thighs, up between her breasts, and brought it up to her mouth. She immediately parted her lips and I let out a small gasp as he slid the dildo in her mouth.

I swallowed, hoping it would clear my head, and turned from the stage. I reached for a glass of water and caught Max's eyes. They were dark and his brows were furrowed as he took me in. My chest grew warm, both from the display on the stage, and his stare.

"I'm sorry about earlier," I said. What better time to apologize than when everyone else was distracted by what's happening on the stage? "I don't know why, I just . . ." I let my voice trail off, not really sure *what* I mean.

"It's fine," Max said. "Truly, I get it." He smiled at me, so I smiled back.

"I just don't know . . ." I said, not really saying anything.

"You don't need to overthink this, Isabella, I'm fine, I promise," he said. "Now turn around and watch the show. It's getting to the good part."

I swallowed at his firm direction. Maybe things would be okay between us. Just because I wasn't ready to do a deep dive into our situation didn't mean we couldn't keep whatever it was that we were doing, right?

My eyes scanned the room making sure no one needed anything, but all eyes were on the stage, so I followed their lead. My eyes widened as I watched the man slowly slide the dildo in and out of the woman as he held her up with his other arm, wrapped under her breasts. Her chest was red, and her breath came out in moans as it pressed past her entrance.

The man kept the dildo inside her, lowering her hips down on it. He reached for the small vibrator he was using earlier and placed it on her clit. Immediately she started rocking her hips and moaning louder.

The entire room watched as the woman crested over the edge. Her body pulsed on the dildo shoved between her legs as the man held her up. Their set was about to wrap up, so I took a deep breath and started to make my way around the room.

As the lights dimmed and the sultry ambiance of the Mirage Guild embraced us, I found myself caught in the mesmerizing spectacle unfolding on stage. The performers moved with a grace and intimacy that echoed the thrum of desire pulsing through the club. Out of the corner of my eye, I caught glimpses of Max, his attention fixed on the stage, yet a palpable distance hung between us—a chasm widened by my words earlier.

The vibrant energy of the performance, meant to draw people together, highlighted the space growing between us. In that moment, amid the seductive allure of the Guild, all I wanted was to bridge that gap, to lean into the warmth between us. Yet, as the performers intertwined in a dance of shadows and light, I remained rooted in place, the weight of unspoken emotions anchoring me firmly to the spot.

TWENTY-FOUR
MAX

Caught in the whirl of sultry performances at the Mirage Guild, I found myself relenting to the pull of desire, the need to be close to Isabella overpowering the awkward tension that lingered between us since last night. The charged atmosphere, the captivating acts on stage, all of it attempted to melt away the walls I'd wanted to maintain.

Even as every rational thought urged me to put distance between us, to protect myself from the inevitable downfall we'd experience, the moment our eyes locked—a mix of relief and evident desire swirling within hers as the echo of a climax reverberated through the club—I felt an irresistible pull toward her. In that charged silence, filled with the raw intensity of everything unfolding around us, words became redundant.

Seeing her get all worked up as the performers were on the stage had made me unbearably hard. Luckily, I could hide behind the coverage of the bar all evening. Watching the next performance would bring back memories of the last time I had Isabella on that stage.

The charm sounded through the club, and the curtains closed, shutting off the trance everyone was in. Chatter and giggles filled the room as the stage was reset behind the curtain. This was the gap where people would order new drinks and snacks, so I shook my head and focused on the crowd walking up to the bar.

Seven signature cocktails, two mock-aritas, and four bowls of snack mix later, the room was ready for the next and final set. After this one was over, the rooms would book up quickly with couples who required a more private experience. But the rules of the Mirage Guild stated that open displays of passion, lust, and even sex were all allowed.

As I watched Isabella make her way around the lounge, dropping off drinks and picking up empty glasses, the curtains on the stage parted again. This was perhaps our most elaborate scene of the evening.

Two anchors came down from the ceiling holding black silk bands that floated down to the floor. Two women, fully nude, stepped up to the bands and began winding them around their limbs. One man and another woman joined them on stage, helping the aerialists get secure. As they helped wrap the bands, their hands roamed over their bodies and placed kisses on their mouths.

This scene was going to overwhelm all of my senses. I didn't know exactly what to expect, but based on the bodies on the stage and a heavy-breathing Isabella next to me at the bar, I was in for a show. I decided to focus on one pairing at a time, taking in what they were doing before moving to the next.

The first aerialist, a black-haired, pale-skinned woman, wound herself in the shimmery black silk bands. Her body was strong and toned as she wrapped herself up, the flesh of her thighs squeezing out through the edges of the fabric.

Her partner walked up to her, grazing his hands across her skin as she spun slightly from the anchor. I moved my eyes to the next woman, already secured in the silk bands, her red hair trailing down her back. Another woman with short cropped blonde hair circled her, running a black-painted fingernail down the middle of her chest.

Soft music played from the speakers as the scene unfolded. My eyes flicked over to Isabella, who leaned against the end of the bar. She swallowed hard as she took everything in. The crowd was quiet in respectful anticipation. Soon, the aerialists began to twirl slightly in the silk bands.

Their partners trailed hands over their flesh as they helped guide their movements. I wasn't totally sure of the protocol, but I figured my tasks shouldn't include standing here staring like a gaping fool. Especially as the man's cock slipped out of his tight shorts, and the black-haired woman took it in her mouth as she stretched back.

To break the spell the scene had on me I focused on some tasks behind the bar. I would need to be quiet, but with everyone's full focus on the stage, I had a little bit of leeway. As I glanced down the bar at Isabella, no longer looking at the stage but staring over at me instead, my plans shifted.

This, right here, is what I was good at. Giving one last show for the road.

I tilted my head back and silently directed her to come closer. She walked to me like she was in a trance. My hands were on her hips instantly, guiding her to stand at the counter, facing the stage. I pressed my body against hers without hesitation. I grinned at the intake of breath as she felt me press into her back. Even if I knew where she stood on things, I was confident I could give her this.

"Watch," I said as she turned her head back to me to say something. "Just watch."

Izzy might want to walk away like our time together meant nothing. Like I meant nothing.

But I wouldn't make it easy for her.

My hands slid up her thighs.

God, I loved the feel of her warm, soft skin. I would never forget it. But when I felt her trembling against me, I smirked.

She wouldn't forget how I felt either.

Good.

"Keep your eyes forward, and don't make a sound," I said. I trailed a finger over her panties. "Can you do that?"

Isabella nervously nodded.

I pushed the material to the side and ran a finger up and down her middle. Her arousal coated my fingertips, and I grinned like a maniac in her hair. This woman was just as filthy as me.

"Do you enjoy watching them up there?" I asked. "Do you like it when he pushes his cock down her throat?"

Isabella trembled beneath me. "Do you like watching when she rubs her partner's clit?"

Isabella shuddered as I pressed a single finger past her entrance and into her warmth. On the stage, the man pulled himself out of the black-haired woman's mouth and helped her sit more upright in the silk bands. She repositioned the bands around her wrists and thighs so she could use the bands as leverage.

Then, the man walked closer to her, and she sank herself down onto his waiting cock. As she began fucking him, I timed the push of my finger to their movements. Isabella's hands pressed against the edge of the bar top as she watched it all unfold.

My eyes flicked over to the other aerialist as she lay back comfortably in the bands as her partner knelt in front of her. Her face was buried in her pussy, and her fingers pumped in and out of her. Moans and wet sounds came from the stage as the tension intensified.

I took advantage of the distraction and added a second finger inside Isabella. Only the slightest gasp left her mouth as she adjusted to the new sensation. I rubbed my knuckles against her clit right before I buried my fingers deep inside, and based on the soft shakes of her legs, Isabella was close.

"You're going to come all over my fingers, but you can't make a sound, got it?" I whispered in her ear.

She nodded furiously, her knuckles white in their grip on the counter. Based on the slapping of skin coming from the stage, our performers were also close. I needed to get Isabella there with enough time for me to rinse my hands and slow my breathing before the crowd's attention was again pulled to the bar.

I curved my fingers in the way she liked and pressed tightly into her clit. The walls of her pussy clenched around my fingers, and her body arched forward in a wave as the orgasm hit her. I held her up with one arm wrapped around her middle, but she kept her word and stayed quiet.

I waited until the goosebumps faded from her skin to pull my fingers out. I was washing my hands as our performers on stage were reaching their own climaxes. Isabella's eyes were full of fire as she glanced up at me, and I wanted nothing more than to push myself into one of the side rooms and sink myself inside her.

I had to tear my gaze away from her before I did exactly that.

The charm sounded from the speakers, and the heavy curtain dropped from the ceiling, signaling the end of the on-stage acts. Now, the club would transition to private rooms and public displays from members who weren't shy.

As I glanced at Isabella, taking a deep, steadying breath, I noted the subtle signs of our recent closeness—a faint blush on her neck, the nervous bite of her lip. The lounge buzzed back to life, murmurs of excitement and desire filling the space as the performance concluded. The grand opening was a success. The club's new daring direction was resonating with our guests.

Couples nestled into secluded spots, the room alive with whispers and laughter, a testament to our club's unique appeal to both exhibitionists and voyeurs. Our communication about the openness of the Mirage had clearly emboldened them. Already, the club buzzed with energy, guests exploring their desires openly.

Izzy quickly put herself back together, grabbing her tray to head back into the fray of the lobby. Watching her from my spot behind the bar, a pang of sadness hit me. It was time to be up-front with her, to let her know that, for me, this couldn't continue. We needed boundaries. Izzy had made it clear enough times that I wasn't in her long-term picture, so it was better for both of us to start moving on now.

As she headed back to the bar, the familiar tension that had wrapped around us since our last encounter tightened. It wasn't just the events of the evening that were weighing heavily on me. It was her words, the boundaries she had set without saying them directly. I understood her hesitations, her need to protect herself from whatever complications our relationship could bring, especially given the age difference. But understanding didn't ease the sting of rejection, the sense of being placed in a box marked "temporary."

Her gaze, always so piercing and revealing, met mine as she navigated her way back through the lobby. I often wondered if she realized how transparent she was to me, how her eyes were the windows to the tumultuous thoughts swirling in her head. It seemed we had both reached a silent agreement on where we stood, but I felt the weight of voicing it fall heavily on my shoulders.

Drawing a steady breath, I prepared myself for what had to be said. "I think it's time we set some new boundaries," I began, my voice steady, even if my heart wasn't. She stopped in her tracks, a testament to the seriousness of our conversation. "I understand where you're coming from," I continued, gesturing vaguely in the space between us, the physical representation of our undefined relationship. "And so, I think it's best I give you the space you seem to need."

Her response was immediate, a quick inhalation of breath, and then her lips pressed together in thought. "Yeah, I think you're right," she said, her voice tinged with a resignation that didn't sit well with me.

It was a strange dance of giving and taking, of opening up only to pull back. Isabella was cautious, wary of rushing into something neither of us was ready for, especially with the looming reality of our age difference and what she perceived as my lack of readiness for the kind of commitment she envisioned. On my end, it was a protective measure, a way to shield myself from the potential hurt of being another temporary thrill in her life. My decision to step back wasn't just about respecting her boundaries. It was about safeguarding my heart from the ache of being seen as not enough for someone I was, against all logic, falling deeply for.

As she nodded in agreement, I couldn't help but wonder if she truly understood the depth of what I was offering—space, yes, but also a silent plea for her to see me as more than a momentary diversion.

The crisp morning air mingled with the aroma of fresh coffee as we found our spot in the bustling brunch café, a well-earned treat after the whirlwind of the Mirage Guild's grand opening. As we settled into the cozy corner, the chatter and clink of dishes surrounded us, a comforting backdrop to our gathering. The girls were already animatedly discussing the night before, their excitement palpable. Yet, amidst the laughter and lively conversation, I found my thoughts wandering, detached from the celebration unfolding around me.

The girls buzzed with energy, rehashing each detail of the Mirage Guild's grand opening, their voices blending into the background noise of the brunch spot. Natalia was gesturing broadly, recounting a particularly daring performance, while Jessie nodded, her laughter filling our corner of the café. I should have been right there with them, basking in the afterglow of our triumph, yet I found myself disengaged, my focus drifting.

I half-heartedly pushed around the hollandaise sauce on my plate, the rich, creamy texture suddenly unappealing. Last night should have been purely a cause for celebration, the culmination of our hard work and daring vision. And it was, to everyone else. But for me, it also marked something much more personal—a final chapter with Max.

"That event was a game-changer," Emma enthused, sipping her iced latte. "I've never seen anything quite like it. The energy, the décor . . . it was all so spot-on. "Iz, I'm serious, you *need* to consider event planning as your career. You thought of *everything*."

Jessie, eyes sparkling with a mixture of pride and inspiration, nodded in agreement. "Truly, when Emma started creating custom events for the Prism Society, our members loved it."

"Yeah, and I definitely don't have time to do both with my design work. Honestly, I'd love to offload the events to someone else," Emma said, her eyes twinkling.

The mention of passing the baton jolted me from my reverie. I blinked, focusing back on the conversation as Emma's gaze settled on me expectantly.

"Really?" I asked. "You think there's enough there to create something from?"

"My work on the Prism Society had me creating my own design firm that's got a six-month-long waitlist for just a CAD sketch," Emma said.

I had been craving direction the last few months, hell the last few years. Was this the direction I was meant to go in?

"Stop overthinking it, Iz," Natalia's voice cut in. She knew my reactions better than anyone.

"You're right," I said with a laugh, "Okay, yeah, I actually think that would be really fun. I know you guys are wanting to expand even more so I could help with those grand openings, club events, VIP member events . . ." My voice trailed off as my brain went into overdrive.

I was sick of floundering and waiting for overly obvious signs of what to do. It might not be the perfect decision, the best decision, the forever decision, but I'd be good at it. I wanted to be the person who allowed myself to make a decision without the full ten-year plan mapped out right along with it.

"Now that the club's success is out of the way, when are we celebrating you and Max officially becoming a thing?" Emma teased, a sly grin spreading across her face.

"Wait, you all knew about Max and me?" I blurted out, the revelation catching me completely off guard. A flush of embarrassment warmed my cheeks as I realized our attempts at secrecy might not have been as successful as I thought. "Here I was thinking we were being sneaky."

Laughter bubbled around the table, their knowing looks suddenly making sense. "Izzy, it was the worst-kept secret," Jessie said with a chuckle. "Seriously, anyone paying even a little bit of attention could see what was happening between you two."

My embarrassment morphed into a mix of amusement and resignation. So much for discretion. I let out a small sigh, the weight of last night pressing down on me. "Well, I hate to be the bearer of bad news . . . Max and I . . . we decided to end things," I admitted, the words tasting bitter as they left my mouth.

Silence enveloped our little corner of the café, their playful smiles fading into looks of surprise and concern.

"End things? I thought you guys were cute together," Natalia said, her brows knitting together in confusion.

I managed a small, resigned smile. "Yeah, well, it was his call. I guess . . . it's for the best. We're at different places in our lives, you know? There's an age difference and . . ."

Jessie reached across the table, her touch reassuring. "Izzy, don't let something like age dictate your happiness. What matters is how you feel about each other."

Natalia leaned in, her gaze earnest. "Iz, I know you. And if I can be honest, sometimes it feels like you're the one holding yourself back, convincing yourself someone's not right for you even when they're standing right there."

Emma nodded, her voice gentle. "It's tough, isn't it? We grow up with all these voices telling us how our lives should unfold. Sometimes, without even realizing it, we start believing those voices more than our own desires. I mean, look at me: I left what I thought was my dream job for something completely different. Scary, yes, but so worth it."

Their words, a blend of challenge and support, forced me to confront my own barriers. Was I the one pushing Max away, veiled under the guise of protecting myself from potential judgment? Their insights, wrapped in layers of friendship and understanding, left me pondering the choices I had made—and the ones still before me.

TWENTY-SIX
ISABELLA

Twenty-three days. That's how long it had been since Max had set his boundaries about us.

Not that I was keeping track.

With the encouragement of the girls and my growing desire to release the expectations others had placed on me, it was time to create something of my own. This desire for a new beginning led me to the concept of WanderLand, my own event-planning venture. It was a name and idea that surfaced after nights of introspection and scribbled notes in my journal during moments of hope and ambition. WanderLand was more than a business—it was my declaration of independence, a promise to pursue what brought joy and creativity into my life and the lives of others.

Embarking on this entrepreneurial journey felt like diving into uncharted waters. I dedicated days to researching, plotting out services, and connecting with potential clients, driven by a blend of nerves and excitement. Securing my first event, a private wine and cheese party my mom would host, felt like a victory, a tangible sign that WanderLand wasn't just a dream but a reality taking shape.

As I sat in the bustling coffee shop, the hum of conversation and the clatter of cups forming a backdrop to my focused intent, I couldn't help but feel a twinge of something like liberation. With each sip of my latte, I felt more grounded in my decision, more certain this venture was not just a distraction but a meaningful step forward, a way to blend creativity with connection, weaving the magical with the tangible.

The coffee shop, with its rustic charm and the aroma of freshly ground beans, was the perfect spot for creativity to flourish. I chose a corner table, a strategic spot allowing me to observe the ebb and flow of city life through the large, paneled windows, while still offering a semblance of privacy.

Across from me sat Cara, the artsy vibe evident in her vibrant scarf and the array of colorful tattoos peeking out from her rolled-up sleeves. Her hair was a cascade of loose curls, and her eyes sparkled with creativity as they focused intently on the digital tablet before her. Her fingers moved with a dancer's grace, tapping and swiping as she brought our ideas to life.

"Okay, Izzy, think whimsical journeys, enchanted escapes, but with a touch of urban sophistication," Cara said, her voice a melodious blend of excitement and concentration.

I leaned in, my eyes scanning the array of logo concepts she had compiled. Each design was unique, yet they all captured the essence of what I envisioned for WanderLand. "Yes, exactly that," I replied, my voice tinged with awe and a hint of relief. "It's like you've plucked the ideas right out of my head."

Cara chuckled, her fingers pausing momentarily. "Well, that's the goal, isn't it? To make WanderLand not just a name but a story in itself. Something that instantly transports people."

I nodded, my mind momentarily drifting to those evenings spent under foreign skies, the thrill of discovering the unknown. This sense of adventure, mingled with the elegance of curated experiences, was what I wanted to encapsulate.

Cara tapped on her tablet, bringing up a design that immediately caught my eye. The logo seemed to swirl and dance, its lines flowing like trails on a map yet forming a cohesive, elegant image. "How about this one?" she asked, her voice laced with a hint of pride.

"That's it," I breathed out, a smile spreading across my face. "It's perfect."

After finalizing the logo and discussing branding colors, I hugged Cara and settled back into my corner seat. I'd ordered another latte. Whoever said four espresso shots in one day was a bad idea? There, amidst the grind of coffee beans, I filled out the online paperwork to officially file WanderLand as an LLC. My fingers hesitated for a moment before hitting the "submit" button. This was more than just a formality. It was a commitment to a new chapter, a leap into the unknown.

Once I was sufficiently jittery from way too much caffeine, I stepped out of the coffee shop, the new logo for WanderLand in my hands acting as a beacon for my growing business. With every step, my stride grew more confident. WanderLand, once just a concept, was now becoming a reality, a tangible expression of my passions and dreams.

As I walked, my phone buzzed with a reminder of the photoshoot scheduled for tomorrow. It was with Luca, an old school friend-turned-professional photographer. The thought of capturing the essence of WanderLand through his lens was exhilarating.

Lingering in that thought, I found myself tempted to reach out to Max. My fingers hovered over my phone, itching to send him a screenshot of the newly finalized logo or ask his opinion on the final locations for tomorrow's photoshoot. I imagined his reaction—that easy smile spreading across his face, the gentle teasing laced with genuine interest. Max always had a way of making even the smallest achievements feel monumental.

But then I hesitated, my thumb hovering over the send button. This was the line I had drawn, wasn't it? To keep things casual, to not entangle our lives more than they already were. And deep down, there was a part of me that suspected Max's feelings ran deeper than I thought. It wasn't just fun and games for him. There was something in the way he looked at me, a certain earnestness that I couldn't quite return.

Sending him updates, and sharing these snippets of my life, it wouldn't be fair. Not when each exchange might give him hope and might lead him to believe there was more to us than there really was. It was a selfish comfort to want his support and his enthusiasm when I wasn't ready to offer him the same in return.

I locked my phone and slipped it back into my purse, a small pang of regret echoing in my chest. I wanted to share these moments with him, to include him in this journey I was so passionate about. But that wasn't the choice I had made. I had to respect the boundaries I had set, even if it meant walking through these milestones alone.

As I continued down the street, my mind filled with plans and possibilities, there was a small, nagging voice in the back of my head. It murmured of what could be, of shared dreams and mutual support. But those were whispers in the wind, fleeting and intangible. I was building something of my own, and that had to be enough. For now.

The next day dawned bright and beautiful, the perfect setting for a photoshoot. I dressed with careful consideration, aiming for a look both professional and inviting, reflecting the essence of my new venture. I settled on a crisp black pantsuit, its blazer boasting a deep V-cut that added an edge to the ensemble. To complete the look, I chose a simple gold necklace, allowing it to glimmer subtly against the dark fabric. My hair, rebellious in its curls, framed my face in a way I was hoping came across as effortless.

Stepping outside, I was enveloped by the vibrant energy

of New York City. The streets were alive with the rhythm of daily life—people bustling by, the distant honk of taxis, and the faint rustle of trees lining the block. I made my way down the stoop of my parents' home in Gramercy Park, an ideal location for the shoot.

Luca was already there, setting up his camera against the urban backdrop. The historic brownstones and leafy streets of Gramercy Park offered a quintessentially New York scene —a blend of timeless charm and modern dynamism.

"Hey, Izzy!" Luca greeted, his camera slung around his neck. "You look sharp. Ready to capture some headshots that'll wow your clients?"

I nodded, feeling a surge of excitement mixed with a touch of nerves. "Definitely. Let's do this."

Luca was a natural behind the lens, guiding me with ease. "Let's start with some shots right here on the stoop," he suggested. "The brownstone makes for a classic New York backdrop."

I perched on the edge of the stoop, trying to appear relaxed yet poised. Luca clicked away, occasionally asking me to change my pose or look in a different direction. "Think about your business, your goals," he advised. "Let that ambition shine in your eyes."

As we moved through the shoot, Luca's easy banter helped me loosen up. We captured a variety of shots—some with me looking directly at the camera, others more candid, as I gazed down the street or laughed at a joke he made.

"Perfect, Izzy," Luca said, reviewing a few shots on his camera. "These are going to be great for your website. You're embodying that confident, savvy entrepreneur vibe perfectly."

Standing there on that stoop, amidst the heartbeat of the city, I felt a deep sense of belonging and purpose. This was where I was meant to be, building something of my own in the city that had always been my home. For the first time in forever, I was starting to feel hopeful about the future, believing that everything was unfolding exactly how it should be.

What do I do when the person criticizing my place in life is myself? How do I come to terms with the fact that it's been my own self holding me to the ridiculous standards of others? How do I untangle my own expectations for myself and what I think other people expect of me?

The click of the camera shutter zapped away each realization. I *wanted* to free myself of the stress of playing catch-up. When I looked back at how I'd spent the last decade of my life, I didn't *actually* have any regrets. I wouldn't change anything.

I only wish I could've paused time so that, when I was ready, I could pick back up where everyone else had left off. But plenty of people, *women*, had been in my position before. This wasn't new. Thirty-five wasn't a freaking death sentence for everything else I wanted to check off my list. I just needed to start believing that.

As we adjusted for the last few shots, I couldn't help but feel a mix of excitement and nerves about everything coming together. "Thanks, Luca. I'm really looking forward to seeing the final shots," I said, hoping my appreciation shone through despite the whirlwind of emotions about the upcoming event.

"You've got this, Izzy. And hey, isn't your first big event under the WanderLand banner happening soon? You feeling ready for it?" Luca asked, packing away his camera gear.

I paused, taking a moment to gather my thoughts. This week marked the official launch of WanderLand with an event that felt more personal than I had anticipated. Not only was it my debut as an independent event planner, but it was also a gathering for a group my mom was deeply involved with—let's call it the Women's Leadership Circle. It was an influential network of women who led various boards across the city, and they were the exact clientele I dreamed of impressing.

It didn't exactly soothe my nerves knowing my mom had specifically requested Max to helm the wine and cheese segment of the evening. Max, with his effortless charm and deep knowledge of wine, was perfect for the event's wine and cheese theme. But our recent history, the carefully maintained distance since he'd set those boundaries, made the idea of working closely with him again both daunting and strangely exhilarating.

"Yeah, it's coming up in just a couple of days," I responded, forcing a smile as Luca looked on. "Just finalizing some last-minute details tonight. Should be . . . interesting." My voice trailed off, hinting at the unspoken emotions tied to the event but not delving too deep. Luca nodded, understandingly, offering a supportive smile as we wrapped up the session.

Back inside the house, the quiet hum of the city outside my window became the soundtrack to my afternoon. I had a mountain of logistics to work out today, and I knew that a good bottle of wine would do the trick. A smile tugged at the corners of my mouth as I remembered the last time I was down in the wine cellar with Max.

Descending the stairs, the cool, earthy scent of the cellar enveloped me. Rows of meticulously arranged bottles lined the walls, each a testament to my family's love for fine wine. My fingers trailed over the labels, and I selected a bottle of Pinot Noir, one of my favorites. As I held the bottle, a blush crept up my cheeks, recalling the stolen moments with Max in this very room. It all seemed so daring, so unlike me, yet so undeniably thrilling.

Returning upstairs, I uncorked the bottle and poured myself a glass. The rich aroma of the wine filled the air, bringing a sense of comfort. I took a sip, letting the flavors dance on my tongue as I contemplated my next steps.

I settled at the dining room table, laptop open, and took a deep breath. It was time to make things official. I logged into the website for the Department of State and began the process of opening my first business bank account for WanderLand. The clicking of the keys felt almost ceremonial, each stroke a step closer to a dream realized.

I clicked over to my inbox and a tab I still had open made me pause. The invitation I'd created for Max's wine event stared back at me and it made the flutters in my stomach start all over again. Working on that with him had been so easy. So effortless. Even when I'd royally fucked up with the wine selections, Max had taken it in stride and walked me through his passion again. He'd welcomed me into his world with ease.

Excitement tinged with a bit of apprehension bubbled within me at the thought of collaborating with Max later this week. Our schedules at the Mirage Guild had grown increasingly hectic, transforming our interactions into fleeting moments of acknowledgment as we passed each other by. The success of the events we had orchestrated together leading up to the grand opening had not only bolstered the club's profile but had also ignited a surge in membership, culminating in an ever-growing waitlist. This newfound popularity meant our paths rarely crossed in more than a professional capacity, yet the prospect of working closely with him again stirred something within me that I couldn't quite ignore.

Was it really that ridiculous to want someone like Max? And even more absurd to think he might want me too? The idea of us, together, seemed like a leap into the unknown, yet it was a leap my heart yearned to take. But there were so many uncertainties, so many "what ifs." The age difference, our different backgrounds, the fear of what others might think . . .

There was a connection between us I couldn't deny, a pull that went beyond the physical. It was scary, but it was real. Maybe, just maybe, it was worth exploring.

The thought of him brought a mix of emotions. There was an undeniable pull toward him, a connection that went beyond the physical. But then, there was the fear—the fear of what it meant to truly open up to someone, to let them see the real me, with all my uncertainties and insecurities.

I shook my head, trying to dispel the doubts. This was my life, and I had to start living it on my terms, without the constraints of societal expectations or self-imposed limitations.

Returning to my laptop, I messaged the web designer, approving a couple of layouts from the wireframes they'd sent. Each decision felt empowering, a step toward carving out my own path. I was creating something uniquely mine, a reflection of all the experiences, the journeys, and the dreams that had shaped me.

With a deep breath, I sent off the final approvals and closed my laptop. The evening stretched before me, a blank canvas for my thoughts and reflections. I sipped my wine, the rich flavor a comforting companion as I mulled over my feelings.

I picked up my phone, my finger hovering over Max's contact. I wanted to tell him about the business, about the steps I was taking toward my dreams. But more than that, I wanted to tell him about everything swirling in my brain about us, about the longing I felt every time I thought of him.

But I hesitated, the fear of vulnerability holding me back. I set the phone down, deciding tonight was not the night for such confessions. Tonight, I would focus on WanderLand, on the future I was building. But sooner or later, I would have to face the feelings I had for Max. And when that time came, I hoped I'd be ready.

As I flitted around our family's elegant Gramercy Park townhouse, the flurry of preparations for tonight's wine-tasting event enveloped me. It was the first official event under the banner of WanderLand, and my stomach was a knot of excited nerves.

In the six weeks since the Mirage Guild had opened, I'd poured myself into getting WanderLand off the ground. Amidst all the business, my mom asked me to orchestrate a wine-tasting event at our family's Gramercy Park home, a gathering aimed at bringing together the influential and dynamic women who, like her, held positions on various boards across the city. The event promised an evening brimming with the kind of energy and empowerment that only a room full of powerhouse women could generate.

The prospect of Max's involvement in the event had stirred a complex whirl of emotions within me. On one hand, his expertise in wine was unmatched, making him the obvious choice for ensuring the event's success. On the other, the thought of seeing him again, especially here, in the home that held memories of our past interactions, filled me with a blend of nervous anticipation and excitement.

Over the last six weeks, we had maintained the careful distance we'd agreed upon, a boundary that had not once been breached. Yet, his impending presence tonight threatened to blur those lines and reawaken feelings and tensions we had both worked hard to navigate.

Now, the house bustled with beautiful chaos. Caterers, florists, and lighting technicians streamed in and out, each contributing to the transformation of our stately home into a luxurious venue for the evening.

"Isabella, everything looks fantastic!" My mom's voice floated down the grand staircase, her tone infused with pride and a hint of awe. I glanced up, offering my grateful smile. The house, already beautiful in its own right, was now adorned with delicate floral arrangements, soft glowing lights, and elegantly arranged tables, each element melding into a harmonious vision of sophistication and warmth.

"Thanks, Mom! I just hope everything goes smoothly," I replied, smoothing down my blouse, a stylish silk number that struck the perfect balance between professional and chic.

As I adjusted a vase on the main table, the doorbell rang. I rushed to answer it, my heart skipping a beat. It was Max, arriving with his sommelier tools and a selection of wines cradled in his arms. Our eyes met, and for a moment, the world around us seemed to pause. The air between us was charged with an unspoken connection, a current that neither of us had yet dared to fully acknowledge.

"Hey, Max. Come on in," I said, stepping aside to let him pass.

"Isabella. Good to see you," he said with a smile.

"Max!" my mom called out. "So good to have you here tonight."

Max responded with one of his gorgeous smiles. "I'm honored to be a part of tonight, Ms. Esposito."

"The wine cellar is all ready for you," I said, my voice betraying a hint of the fluttering in my chest. He nodded, a small, knowing smile playing on his lips as he stepped inside.

"Great," he said with a smile. "Is there perhaps a table down there, large enough to hold the wine I brought?"

Heat flooded my cheeks and I cast my eyes down to avoid the smirk I knew he was delivering.

"Oh yes," my mom replied totally oblivious to Max's silent teasing. "It's strong enough to hold whatever you sit on it."

My throat hitched and I tried to mask it with a cough. I walked to the kitchen for a glass of water and Max whistled as he walked to the stairs that led down to the cellar. Tonight should be *interesting*.

As the evening unfolded, the house transformed under the skilled hands of various vendors, each adding a layer of elegance and ambiance to the event. The florist arrived with armfuls of fresh blooms, their sweet fragrance filling the air. Delicate roses in shades of blush and cream, intertwined with sprigs of eucalyptus and soft lavender, were artfully arranged in vases of varying heights, adding a touch of natural beauty to each table. The floral arrangements were strategically placed around the room, some on the mantelpiece, and others on side tables, creating a cohesive, garden-like feel throughout the space.

The lighting technicians worked their magic, enhancing the mood with strategically placed lighting. Lanterns filled with flickering candles were scattered around the room, casting a warm, inviting glow. In the garden, twinkle lights were strung amongst the trees and along the pathways, transforming the outdoor space into an enchanting, fairy-tale setting. The soft light from the lanterns and twinkle lights created a magical atmosphere, perfect for an evening of wine tasting and intimate conversations.

As I oversaw these final touches, a sense of satisfaction washed over me. Everything was coming together as I had envisioned. The blend of elegant florals and warm, ambient lighting created an atmosphere that was both luxurious and inviting—a perfect backdrop for Max's wine-tasting expertise.

My attention was momentarily caught by the garden. The way the lights twinkled in the dimming light of the evening gave the space a dreamlike quality. I could already picture the guests stepping out into the garden, wineglasses in hand, enchanted by the beauty of the night.

Returning my focus to the interior, I made my way through the house, double-checking every detail. The warm glow of candle-lit lanterns added a sense of intimacy to the space. Each flicker of their flames seemed to invite guests to relax, to indulge in the sensory experiences that awaited them.

As more guests arrived, the energy in the room shifted. The blend of lively conversations, the clinking of glasses, and the soft background music created a symphony of sounds that was music to my ears. Everything was just as I had hoped—perfect, yet effortless. It was the ideal setting for an evening of exploration and enjoyment, a testament to the hard work and passion I had poured into WanderLand.

And through it all, my thoughts kept drifting back to Max. His presence added an undeniable spark to the event, his expertise and charm enhancing the entire experience. I found myself eagerly anticipating our next interaction, curious and slightly apprehensive about the chemistry growing between us, a chemistry that was both exciting and unnerving.

At one point, as I navigated through the crowd to check on the catering, our paths crossed in the narrow corridor leading to the wine cellar. We both paused, the close proximity sending a jolt of electricity through me. For a second, we were the only two people in the world, caught in a moment of intense connection.

"Everything's going great, Izzy," Max whispered, his voice low and husky. His gaze lingered on mine, filled with an unspoken question, an invitation to something more.

I swallowed hard, my breath catching in my throat. The air around us felt thick, charged with a tension that was both exhilarating and terrifying. I wanted to lean into him, to close

the gap between us, but I hesitated, the weight of our unacknowledged feelings heavy in the air.

"Thanks, Max. You're doing amazing," I managed to say,
stepping back to put some distance between us. The moment
passed, but the lingering heat of it stayed with me as I
returned to the hustle of the event.

As the night progressed, the energy in the house was
palpable. The décor I had chosen created an intimate and
luxurious atmosphere, the lighting casting a soft glow that
made everyone look their best. The music, a carefully curated
playlist of jazz and soft contemporary tunes, added to the
ambiance, creating a backdrop of relaxed sophistication.

Amidst the laughter and the clinking of wineglasses, the
atmosphere in the room shifted ever so slightly as a new guest
arrived. She moved through the crowd with an effortless
grace and confidence, her presence commanding attention. I
found myself observing her, struck by a sense of familiarity in
her poise and style. She approached Max, and I felt a sudden
twist in my stomach as he stiffened, his usually relaxed
demeanor replaced by a visible tension.

The woman, radiant and engaging, extended her hand to
Max, her smile warm. There was a moment of hesitation
before he responded, a fleeting look of discomfort crossing
his face before he masked it with a polite smile. It was unlike
Max to be so guarded, and it piqued my curiosity.

I drifted closer, under the guise of checking on the floral
arrangements, watching them from a distance. My heart
raced as I observed their interaction. Max's body language
was rigid, his usually easygoing nature nowhere in sight. The

woman seemed oblivious to his discomfort, her laughter light and carefree as she touched his arm in a familiar manner.

Just then, Mrs. Harrington, a longtime friend of my mother's from my charity work, beckoned the young woman away from Max. She caught sight of me and waved me over. I moved closer, blending into the crowd, my role as the event organizer providing the perfect cover.

"Isabella, darling, come meet my niece," Mrs. Harrington said, her voice filled with pride. "This is Ana. She's just finished her studies in international business."

Ana. The name clicked in my mind, a piece of a puzzle falling into place. I had heard that name before, in passing conversations. Max's ex. I stole a glance at Max, noticing the way his jaw was clenched, his gaze fixed on a distant point as he tried to appear engaged in another conversation.

Before I could process this revelation further or approach Max, another guest pulled me into a conversation. I excused myself, my mind swirling with questions and uncertainties. Why did Max seem so affected by Ana's presence? And why did it bother me so much?

As I moved through the room, attending to guests and ensuring everything was running smoothly, I couldn't shake the uneasy ache that had settled in my chest. I realized, perhaps for the first time, my feelings for Max might run deeper than I had admitted to myself. The sight of him with Ana, and the tension it caused within him, affected me more than I wanted to acknowledge.

Jealousy, insecurity, and a sense of loss tangled within me. I had told myself what Max and I had was casual, just some fun. But watching him with Ana, I couldn't deny the sharp pang of longing that pierced through me. Had I made a mistake in pushing him away? Was there more between us than just a fleeting connection?

The evening progressed with a seamless blend of elegance and warmth, each guest seemingly enchanted by the atmosphere I had meticulously created. Compliments flowed as freely as the wine, and several of my parents' friends even inquired about reserving my services for their upcoming events. It was more than I could have hoped for, yet my mind was distracted, caught in the undercurrents of emotion stirred up by Ana's presence.

As I circulated among the guests, silently checking in on everyone, I spotted Ana pulling Max into a secluded corner. They stood close, their conversation hushed and intimate. My heart ached at the sight, a cocktail of emotions swirling inside me. Why did it matter so much? I had no claim over Max, yet the sight of them together sent a pang of longing through me.

Mrs. Harrington's touch on my shoulder snapped me back to reality. Her knowing eyes met mine, and she leaned in, her voice a whisper. "Ana misses Max, you know. They used to date. They were quite the pair. Ana ended it a few months ago, but I think she's having second thoughts."

My gaze drifted back to them, watching as Max's posture relaxed slightly, a small smile tugging at his lips in response to something Ana said. It was as if I was watching a scene from a life I was no longer a part of, yet desperately wanted to be.

"Looks like my niece is trying her best to win him back,"

Mrs. Harrington continued, her voice laced with a hint of mischief.

I forced a smile, my heart sinking further as Ana stepped closer to Max, her hand gently grazing his arm. Then, as if in a slow-motion scene from a movie, she rose on her toes and planted a soft kiss on his cheek. Max didn't pull away. Instead, he listened attentively, his eyes locked on hers.

The sinking feeling in my gut intensified. Watching them, a realization dawned on me: Max's softened demeanor, his gentle smile, it all seemed to suggest that perhaps Ana's attempts were not unwelcome. Maybe there was still something there between them.

For a moment, I was an outsider looking in, aching, and witnessing a moment that was both intimate and foreign. The air around me felt heavier, each breath a struggle as I grappled with the whirlwind of emotions inside me.

I turned away, needing a moment to compose myself. I busied myself with the last-minute details of the event, but my mind was elsewhere. The evening that had started with such promise was now clouded with a sense of loss and confusion.

I couldn't shake the image of Max and Ana together, couldn't silence the nagging voice in my head that whispered of missed opportunities and unspoken thoughts. I had pushed Max away, convinced myself that what we had was casual, but now, seeing him with Ana, I couldn't deny the depth of my feelings.

As the guests departed, leaving behind a trail of laughter and fond farewells, I realized that tonight had been more than just a successful event. It had been a revelation, a painful yet necessary insight into my own heart. The realization that what I felt for Max was real, and perhaps, it was time to confront those feelings head-on. But as I watched Ana linger by Max's side, I couldn't help but wonder if it was already too late.

TWENTY-EIGHT
ISABELLA

The next morning, I walked the bustling streets of Manhattan, heading from Greenwich Village down to the East Village. The familiar sounds and sights of the city wrapped around me like a comforting embrace.

I hadn't slept well and had snuck in an extra cup of coffee before leaving my parents' house, but with the morning came a sense of calm. And an answer to the question that had kept me tossing and turning last night.

Max.

The way his eyes had locked onto mine in the wine cellar, the unspoken words hanging between us, the soft warmth of his smile that seemed to reach deep into my heart.

We had a connection I couldn't deny, yet I didn't know how to navigate it.

Being around Max, and witnessing his interaction with Ana, had stirred something in me—a tangled mess of feelings

I wasn't prepared to untangle just yet. My involvement in the Mirage Guild had blurred lines I hadn't even realized were there, and now, it was time to redraw them.

As the cityscape blurred past my window on the way to a business meeting, my mind couldn't help but drift back to the wine-tasting event and the brief moments shared with Max. Those fleeting interactions had reignited a yearning I thought I'd managed to quell, a yearning for something more with him, something beyond the constraints we had placed on ourselves. The idea of distancing myself from the Mirage Guild surfaced, carrying with it a bittersweet blend of freedom and loss.

Leaving the club would carve out a significant chunk of time, time that could be devoted to expanding WanderLand into the empire I envisioned. Yet, the thought of stepping away also meant potentially sacrificing the sultry, adrenaline-fueled world that had become a part of me, a world where Max and I had danced around each other in a complicated ballet of desire and restraint.

It would make things easier for Max, wouldn't it? To not have me there every night, a constant reminder of what we had decided to leave behind. Sure, our paths would cross occasionally, given our shared circle and the small universe we operated in, but it wouldn't be with the same frequency, the same intensity.

And maybe, that distance would allow us both the space to truly consider what we wanted, individually and possibly together. The Mirage Guild had been a crucible for us, a place where we both had shone brightly, yet it also held the shadows of our hesitations and fears. Walking away could mean giving us both a chance to find our own footing.

This meeting wasn't just another business engagement. It was a step toward defining my path, a path I was determined to tread on my terms, even if it meant navigating the complexities of my feelings for Max from a new vantage point.

I couldn't escape Max entirely. Natalia wouldn't let me off the hook for organizing club events, and our paths were bound to cross. But stepping back from the day-to-day operations was a boundary I desperately needed. It was a chance to regain some semblance of control over the chaos of emotions swirling inside me.

And as I made my way to my meeting, a sense of determination settled within me. Whatever the future held, I was ready to face it—on my own terms.

This was my world, where I belonged.

I was scheduled to meet with Mrs. Langley, my old art teacher from St. Catherine's Private School. The woman had a knack for fostering creativity and pushing boundaries, and I owed much of my passion for design to her encouragement during my school years.

We met at the Reading Room, a quaint little café nestled in the heart of the East Village, known for its cozy ambiance and shelves lined with classic literature. The place was a favorite spot for book lovers and provided the perfect backdrop for our discussion.

Mrs. Langley was already there when I arrived, her silver hair elegantly tied up, her eyes as sharp and observant as I remembered. She greeted me with a warm hug, her eyes twinkling behind her glasses.

"Izzy, my dear, look at you! All grown up and making waves in the world," she exclaimed, her voice tinged with pride.

We settled into a corner booth, surrounded by the soft hum of hushed conversations and the occasional clink of coffee cups. Mrs. Langley wasted no time diving into the reason for our meeting.

"Izzy, I came across WanderLand on your social media, and it's just spectacular. The school is hosting a fundraiser for our arts department, and I immediately thought of you," she began, her eyes gleaming with excitement. "We're planning an event at the school's library. It's a beautiful space, as you remember, but it needs your touch to bring it to life."

The school's library was a place I held dear to my heart. It was where I had spent countless hours lost in books, dreaming up worlds far beyond the confines of the classroom. The idea of transforming that space for a cause so close to my heart sparked an instant connection.

"That sounds incredible, Mrs. Langley. I'd be honored to help. Tell me more about the event. What are you envisioning?" I asked, my mind already racing with ideas.

Mrs. Langley outlined her vision for the fundraiser. It was to be an evening event, combining elegance with an artistic flair, aiming to attract donors and alumni to support the arts program.

"We want to create an atmosphere that's both sophisticated and inspiring. Something that reflects the creativity we're trying to nurture in our students," she explained.

I nodded, jotting down notes as ideas took shape in my mind. I imagined transforming the library into an enchanting haven, where art and literature blended seamlessly, creating an immersive experience for the guests.

"I'm thinking of a theme that intertwines classic literature with modern art. Perhaps we can have installations that represent different books, but with a contemporary twist," I suggested, my excitement growing with each word.

Mrs. Langley's eyes lit up. "That's exactly why I wanted you for this, Izzy. Your creativity knows no bounds."

We spent the next hour discussing logistics, budget, and potential challenges. By the time we finished our coffees, a detailed plan was beginning to take shape, and I felt a surge of enthusiasm for the project.

Walking home from the Reading Room, wrapped in the city's relentless energy, I was brimming with new plans and possibilities for WanderLand. Each step seemed to echo with potential, the idea of contributing something meaningful to the fabric of New York igniting a fire within me. It wasn't just another project, but a culmination of everything I'd been working toward, a true reflection of my passion and ambition.

As I navigated the bustling streets, a thought that had been lurking in the back of my mind surfaced, growing clearer with each block I passed. Perhaps it was time for me to step away from the Mirage Guild. The realization wasn't accompanied by fanfare or dramatics. Instead, it settled quietly but firmly, like the final piece of a puzzle clicking into place. Acknowledging this possibility was the last step in fully committing to my new venture, a necessary shift to align my daily actions with my larger goals and values.

But as I turned the corner onto the familiar street of my childhood home, the sight of Natalia waiting for me on the stoop brought a sudden shift in my thoughts. There she was, as though no time had passed since our high school days of dreaming and scheming on these very steps. Her presence, both comforting and somehow confrontational, forced the swirling emotions to the forefront.

Dropping beside Natalia on the stoop, I bumped shoulders with her, offering a lopsided smile. "Just had a 'business meeting,'" I said, air quoting with a dramatic flourish, "with Mrs. Langley."

"From school?" Nat asked, her eyebrows arching in mock seriousness.

"Yeah." I nodded, excitement bubbling up as I briefly outlined the event Mrs. Langley wanted me to run. It felt surreal, discussing such grown-up ventures where we used to gossip about school crushes and homework assignments.

We settled into a comfortable silence, the familiar rhythm of our friendship wrapping around me like a warm blanket. Then, with a deep breath, I found the courage to voice the thought that had been shadowing me. "I think . . . I might need to leave Mirage Guild," I murmured, the words both heavy and liberating as they hung in the air between us. Like opening a valve, the confession released a pressure I hadn't fully acknowledged.

Natalia turned to me, her expression a blend of surprise and understanding. "Really? That's a big move. What's got you leaning that way?"

I shrugged, the reasons both clear as crystal and murky as the Hudson. "WanderLand . . . it's starting to feel like something real, something I could really pour myself into. And then there's . . ." I hesitated, the unspoken name hanging between us.

Natalia nodded, her gaze gentle but unwavering. "Max."

I let out a long breath. "Yeah. Max. I think it might be easier for both of us if I . . . if we had some space to focus on what we really want, you know?"

Natalia nodded slowly. "What do you mean, 'what we really want'? It seems to me that you're really missing him."

I sighed, feeling a tangle of emotions at the mention of his name. "I don't know, Nat. It's complicated. I saw him with his ex last night, Ana. The way he reacted when she first showed up, it was like he still had feelings for her."

"And by the end of the night?" Natalia prodded gently.

"He seemed . . . okay with her, comfortable. They were laughing, and she kissed him on the cheek. It's clear they're not over each other." I felt a lump forming in my throat, the words sounding more like a confession than an observation.

Natalia reached out, her hand finding mine. "Izzy, are you sure you're not just assuming things? Have you talked to Max about how you feel?"

I shook my head, feeling a familiar fear creeping in. "No, I haven't. It's just . . . I'm scared, Nat. What if I'm not what he wants? What if I'm just a fling to him?"

Natalia's grip on my hand tightened. "Izzy, I think *he* feels like a fling to *you*! Don't you think it's only fair to lay it out there? To actually talk to him?"

I looked down, feeling vulnerable and exposed under her gaze. "I'm just so scared that I've missed the boat, Nat. That it's too late to get all the things I thought I had so much more time for. The house, the partner, the kids . . ." I sighed deeply as it all came to the surface. "It's not fair for me to put that timeline on someone like Max. Someone who has so much more time to figure it all out."

Natalia pulled me into a hug, and I allowed myself to lean into her embrace. "You won't know until you have that conversation, Iz. And you owe it to yourself, and to Max, to be honest about what you're feeling."

Natalia's words lingered in the air as we sat there on the stoop, the city sounds providing a soft backdrop to our conversation. Her advice echoed in my mind, stirring a mix of apprehension and resolve within me.

"I know you're right, Nat. I just . . . I don't want to open up old wounds or create new ones," I admitted, my voice quivering slightly. "But you're right. I need to talk to Max. I need to know where we stand."

Natalia nodded, understanding etched in her features. "It's the only way you'll find peace, Iz. And who knows? Maybe it'll lead to something beautiful."

I let out a half-hearted chuckle, the idea seeming both terrifying and exhilarating. "I just wish I could be as confident about this as you are."

Natalia gave my hand a reassuring squeeze. "Confidence

comes with taking that first step, even when it's scary. You've always been braver than you give yourself credit for, Iz."

We sat in silence for a moment, the weight of the decision ahead pressing down on me. I knew what I had to do, yet the idea of laying my feelings bare to Max was daunting. The possibility of rejection, of misunderstanding, loomed large in my mind.

But then, I thought about the alternative: living with the "what-ifs," never knowing if there could have been something more between us. That possibility was even more unbearable.

As I sat there, in the comfort of Natalia's understanding, my fear of being alone battled my fear of being in a relationship that wasn't right. I had made so many assumptions about Max and his feelings, about Ana and their history. I had let my insecurities dictate my actions without truly comprehending his perspective.

"I just . . . I don't want to make a mistake, Nat. I don't want to invest my heart in something that isn't going to last," I confessed, my voice barely above a whisper.

Natalia pulled back, looking me in the eyes. "Izzy, love is always a risk. But it's a risk worth taking. Talk to Max. Be honest with him, and with yourself. You might be surprised at what you find out."

As Natalia stood up, ready to leave, she gave me a knowing look. "You've got this, Izzy. Just be honest and open. The rest will follow."

I watched her walk away, her words echoing in my mind. It was time to face my fears, to take that leap of faith. I needed to talk to Max, to lay all my cards on the table. It was the only way I'd ever find out if there was a chance for something real between us.

Her words resonated within me, a mix of fear and hope swirling in my chest. Maybe it was time to confront these feelings head-on, to stop hiding behind assumptions and fears. Maybe it was time to have that conversation with Max, to truly understand where we stood. And maybe it was time to be brave.

I woke up with a determination that felt foreign yet necessary. Today was the day I needed to reach out to Max, to clear the air and confront whatever was brewing between us. The uncertainty of it all had been gnawing at me, and I couldn't shake the feeling that I needed to make things right.

Lying in bed, I stared at the ceiling, my heart pounding with a mix of anxiety and resolve. I grabbed my phone from the nightstand, its screen lighting up the dim room. Drafting the text took longer than I expected, each word weighed down by the gravity of what I was about to do. I settled on something simple yet direct:

> Isabella: Hey, Max, can we grab lunch today? There are some things I feel like I need to clear the air on.

I hit send before I could second-guess myself. The

message was delivered, leaving me in a state of suspense. I tossed the phone aside and got out of bed, trying to shake off the jitters.

The morning passed in a blur. I busied myself with WanderLand tasks, but my mind kept drifting back to Max and the impending conversation. When the response finally came, my anxiety eased enough to trick myself into thinking the conversation would be easy.

> Max: Would love to meet up. Cafe Lune
> at 1?

Café Lune was a quaint, cozy spot tucked away on a quiet street, its charm accentuated by the warm lighting and rustic décor. The aroma of freshly brewed coffee mingled with the sweet scent of pastries, creating an inviting atmosphere. I had been here once before, lured in by their reputation for the city's best almond croissants. The flaky, buttery layers had left a lasting impression, and it was a perfect spot for a quiet, uninterrupted conversation.

As I walked into Café Lune, the familiar scent of espresso and pastries offered a small comfort. Max was already there, sitting at a corner table, looking casually handsome as always. His presence commanded the room, and my heart skipped a beat as our eyes met.

"Hey," I greeted, my voice steady despite the butterflies in my stomach.

"Hi, Isabella," Max replied, his eyes searching mine. There was a warmth there, but also a hint of caution.

I took a seat across from him, my hands fidgeting in my

lap. The initial small talk felt awkward but necessary. We spoke about inconsequential things until the weight of the unspoken filled the space between us.

Taking a deep breath, I broke the silence. "Max, I've been doing some thinking about the Mirage Guild and my involvement there. I haven't made any decisions yet, but I'm considering stepping back."

He looked at me, his face a blend of understanding and mild surprise. "Oh? I wasn't expecting that."

"I've just been so wrapped up with WanderLust lately—I landed three new events at my parents' place alone. It's getting to the point where I might not be able to give Mirage the attention it deserves. I should've brought this up with you sooner," I admitted.

"I never expected you to stick around forever," Max said, his voice soft but carrying a weight of acceptance.

My breath hitched. That was the crux of all of this, wasn't it? Classic Izzy of being flighty and never sticking around in one place for too long, afraid to put down some roots. And Max had seen it from a mile away and I'd proved him right.

"Isabella." Max's stern tone forced me to glance up from the swirling caramel-colored liquid in my mug. "Stop swimming around in your head. Talk to me."

The words tumbled out of me then, a mix of honesty and vulnerability I hadn't planned on revealing. I told him about my confusion after seeing him with Ana, and how it made me question everything about what we had—or didn't have. I spoke of my fears, my insecurities about being alone and refusing to settle, and how all of it had clouded my judgment.

I talked about all the big dreams I *do* have and how I'm afraid I might scare away anyone who wants to be with me because I long to achieve them all right *now*. I shared my goals for WanderLust and how I *really* wanted to buy that brownstone in Washington Square and fix it up. How I yearned to get married and throw an amazing party and have babies and have *fun*.

Max listened quietly, his gaze never leaving mine.

"And so when it came to you, to *us*," I said, "I—you're so much younger than me, Max. You're at a totally different place in life and you want different things. It's not fair for me to rush you into being a grown-up just because of where I'm at."

Max took a deep breath. "I know we didn't have a traditional *courting* phase, or whatever it's called, but if we had, we would've talked about these things. I would've shared with you that Ana made me feel like I was never good enough, that nothing I did was ever serious enough for her, and how that made me feel like shit.

"I would've told you," he continued, "that I've had my grandmother's ring in a small box in the back of my sock drawer for three years ready to pull it out for the right person. You would've discovered that I had to learn how to drywall when I was fifteen because our laundry room flooded into our kitchen and we couldn't afford to rent it out, so I'm really handy in renos."

He reached across the table, his hand tentatively covering

mine. "We just didn't get to have those conversations because, well, we were busy doing other things," he said with a smirk.

I grinned back at him. "You're right, I didn't know those things," I said.

"I know that beautiful brain is going a million miles an hour with all the what-if scenarios that *could* happen but what do you *want*?" he asked.

"You've been the only person who has been able to shut off the buzzing in my brain, the flutter in my chest when I get overwhelmed . . . seriously, just looking at you eases something here," I said, tapping my chest.

"I want," I continued, "to see what doing this life with you would look like."

Max grinned from across the table, his hands still covering mine. "I'd love to see what doing this life would look like, too," he replied.

"All I ask moving forward," Max continued, "is that you *talk* to me about your concerns, Isabella. I know you can achieve every single thing on your to-do list in life by yourself, but you'll have way more fun if you share that with someone. Specifically, with me." He shrugged his shoulders in mock modesty. "I know you're used to taking care of yourself, but watching you come undone when that beautiful brain finally shuts off has been the highlight of my year."

Heat flooded my face as I remembered how well Max played that role.

His words, sincere and heartfelt, washed over me like a soothing balm. Maybe we didn't have all the answers, but the possibility of exploring this—whatever this was—with Max suddenly felt like a risk worth taking.

I intertwined my fingers with his as we stretched across the linen tablecloth. His thumb rubbed small circles over the back of my hand as the nerves in my belly settled. A piece of me, deep down inside, was telling me that this man was *made* for me. His calmness helped reflect my anxiety away long enough so I could get a chance to think straight.

In his ease, I was able to see clearly and breathe calmly. He anchored me when my brain wanted to sail me away in a wind of overthinking. He'd been nothing but supportive of every idea I'd shared or dream I revealed. I was committed to not letting my brain trick me out of this one again.

"Okay, so for the sake of just getting it all out there," I said. "My goal is to buy that brownstone this year and get married next year. Ideally, I'd like to start trying for babies, well pretty much immediately, given my age, but we can get on the same page about that. I'll be knocking on forty's door sooner than I realize but there's not much I can do about that."

I swallowed the excuses for why that probably didn't work for him I wanted to hurl his way. Excuses he could pick up and read off like a cue card as the reason this was all too much for him.

"When do you want to go look at the house?" he asked. "That way we can see how much work it's really going to need."

I laughed and shook my head. "We might get to look at it now. I know it's empty and the agent is a family friend," I said, pulling out my cell phone to text my mom for Sandra's number. Mom replied quickly with her contact information.

I sent the text to Sandra, feeling a buzz of excitement mixed with nerves. She responded immediately, giving us the go-ahead to visit the brownstone.

"Looks like we can go now," I said, standing up. "Sandra just sent me the code to let ourselves in. She warned that the place is a mess, so we'll have to look past that."

Max grinned, his eyes lighting up. "I love messes," he said as he stood.

We left the café, hand in hand, and I felt an unexpected sense of comfort settle over me. The streets of New York were bustling with activity, but in Max's presence, everything seemed a bit more serene, a bit more manageable.

The walk to the brownstone was filled with light conversation and comfortable silence. The late afternoon sun cast a warm, golden hue over the city, adding a picturesque quality to the day. Leaves rustled gently in the breeze, and the sounds of the city played a soft, rhythmic backdrop to our stroll. For the first time since leaving my globe-trotting days, I felt content.

Approaching the brownstone, I was struck by its potential. The building had a classic charm, with its aged brick façade and the promise of hidden stories within its walls. It stood proudly among its neighbors, a testament to the enduring beauty of old New York architecture.

"This is it," I said, gesturing toward the building. "It needs a lot of love, but I can see it being transformed into something really special."

Max peered up at the brownstone, his expression thoughtful. "It's got character, that's for sure. I can already see your touch on it. Let's take a look inside."

We made our way up the steps, and I punched in the code Sandra had provided, 0104, with Max peering over my shoulder.

"0104?" he asked. "Hmm, that's my birthday." He side-eyed me with a grin as we stepped forward.

The door creaked open, revealing the dusty, untouched interior of the brownstone. We stepped inside, and I was immediately struck by the potential of the space, despite the layer of neglect.

As we walked through the double-door foyer and into the front entrance hall, my eyes sparkled with the potential. Stairs led up to the second floor and underneath layers of dust and old paint was, undoubtedly, a charming wooden railing. To our right was a small sitting room with a pocket door that hung haphazardly from its track and to our left was a dining room that had peeling red paint hanging in strips.

"Perhaps some water damage here, but we can fix that," Max said as he poked and tapped at the walls.

As we explored each room on the lower level, we discussed possibilities and ideas, and the vision of what could be took shape in my mind. The high ceilings, the spacious rooms, and even the worn-out floorboards seemed to whisper promises of a future filled with love and laughter.

We tentatively took the worn-out steps up to the second level and glimpsed into bedrooms where trash was piled in the corners. Intricately carved trim lay hidden beneath layers of dirt and the wooden floors creaked beneath our feet. Max kept assessing walls with a tap of his knuckles as I pushed open the door to the room at the end of the hall.

"Oh, my gosh, look at this, Max," I said as my breath hitched in my throat. A gorgeous fireplace flanked one wall of what must be the primary bedroom.

"Wow, that's incredible. I bet if I scraped this paint off, we'd find marble," Max replied. "It has to match the one downstairs in that small room at the back. You should use that one for your office, it will get really good morning sun since it faces east."

I smiled at the implication of his words. I glanced at him, seeing the sincerity in his eyes. The realization that he was envisioning a future with me here, in this space, filled me with a sense of warmth and possibility.

As we stood there, in what could one day be our bedroom, the significance of the moment wasn't lost on me. Max's vision for the house wasn't just about renovations and décor—it was about us, about a life we could build together. It was both exhilarating and grounding, a feeling of coming home not just to a place, but to a person.

"We have a lot of work ahead of us," I said, my voice tinged with a mixture of awe and excitement.

Max wrapped his arms around me, pulling me close. "We do, but think of all the memories we'll create turning this house into a home," he whispered, his breath warm against my ear.

I leaned back into his embrace, allowing myself to fully absorb the weight and beauty of his words. Here, in this dilapidated brownstone that held so much potential, I saw a future I hadn't dared to imagine before—one filled with love, laughter, and the shared joy of creating something beautiful together.

As we left the brownstone, locking the door behind us, I felt a profound sense of rightness. The path ahead was uncertain and would undoubtedly be filled with challenges, but for the first time, I wasn't facing it alone. With Max by my side, I felt capable of facing whatever came our way.

There are moments in life when leveraging one's family name feels not just advantageous, but almost necessary. This was one of those moments. Navigating the complex terrain of New York City's real estate, I found myself drawing upon the Esposito legacy to secure what was soon to become much more than a mere property—it was the manifestation of a dream, a cornerstone of my future. It took a flurry of phone calls, a whirlwind of paperwork, and a few strategically placed conversations, but forty-two days after Max and I first explored the dusty, forgotten corridors of the old brownstone, the keys dangled heavily in my hand, a symbol of new beginnings.

In those early days, I didn't wait for the fanfare or assistance. With the ink barely dry on the paperwork, I ordered a dumpster, slipped into a pair of rugged overalls, and dove into the chaos of renovation. The house, once a relic hidden under layers of neglect, now stood bare and echoing, ready for transformation.

I stood amidst the empty rooms, the sledgehammer feeling almost surreal in my grip. The walls, stripped of their old, peeling wallpaper, loomed around me like blank canvases. Sunlight streamed through the grimy windows, casting a hopeful glow on the faded wooden floors. I could almost hear the echoes of laughter and conversation that would soon fill these spaces, transforming them from hollow echoes to warm, vibrant scenes of life.

The deep-cleaning crew had done wonders, erasing years of dust and grime, and leaving behind a sense of purity and potential. Now, as I roamed from room to room, each step resonated with possibility. The high ceilings and spacious rooms whispered secrets of elegant dinner parties, cozy winter nights by the fireplace, and sunny afternoons with sunlight streaming through the windows.

My phone vibrated against the fabric of my overalls, snapping me out of my daydream. It was Max, his message a simple yet exciting prompt: "On my way. Ready to bust some walls?"

A grin spread across my face as I typed a quick response. His enthusiasm was infectious, and I could already feel the adrenaline kicking in, a heady mix of excitement and anticipation.

We had decided to go all-in on each other over the last month or so. We were kind of going backward and actually *dating* and getting to know each other. I hadn't missed a Sunday dinner at his mom's house since.

I'd learned Max loved the big family he came from and had always talked about wanting a mess of kids running around. One of his sisters had shared with me how hard it was when their dad had died when all the kids were so young and how Max had stepped up to help out. He had played Dad at such a young age but had been really good at it. Like he was meant for that role.

I also learned less serious things, like how he hated green peppers and loved popcorn as a midnight snack. One time, when I was snuggled up on his couch, he had randomly decided to make cinnamon rolls from scratch so we could have them for breakfast. All of these little things filtered through to let me know who Max was at his core. And all of those things were making me fall for him.

As I waited for Max, my gaze drifted over the expanse of the main room. The grand fireplace stood as a stoic centerpiece, its mantel dusty but dignified, a silent witness to the home's storied past and its promising future. I imagined where we might place the furniture, how the light would look streaming in during the golden hour, and where we might hang the art that would bring our personalities into the space.

Max's arrival brought a new energy to the house. His presence seemed to fill the rooms, his laughter and optimism infectious. Together, we stood, side by side, on the threshold of our shared project. This wasn't just about renovating a house. It was about building a life, a future that was as exciting as it was unknown.

With a deep breath and a shared look of determination,

we raised our sledgehammers. The walls that had confined the brownstone's potential would soon fall away, opening up a world of possibilities. This was more than just a physical undertaking. It was a leap into a new chapter of our lives, one filled with hope, hard work, and the promise of something beautiful to be built together.

But first, we needed to tear them down. The walls that were too damaged had been marked with an X from an inspector. They would all need to come down, but Max had promised he'd be the one to put them back up.

We made our way through the living room, swinging our sledgehammers and forcing sections of wall to crumble down. After tackling the downstairs, we both turned to face each other, covered in dust, chunks of wall, and sweat. My stomach growled loudly.

Luckily, we had working plumbing, so we were able to wash up in the kitchen even though the sink had chunks of porcelain taken out. I'd brought a stack of rags and soaked one to wipe down my face, chest, and arms. I swear I could taste plaster in the back of my throat.

"Wine and snack break?" Max asked, pulling out a small cooler and bottle of wine he'd brought in.

"Absolutely," I replied.

Life hack: date a sommelier and you'll always have a glass of wine ready every time you turn around.

Max poured a buttery Chardonnay into plastic cups. He held his cup up as he said, "To you, to the house, to your hard work."

I smiled like a maniac at him. Everything was truly

coming together exactly how I'd wanted it to even though I was too afraid to admit it just a few months ago. I tapped my cup against his before drinking. I couldn't fight the giddiness I felt in my gut.

Tipping the wine back, I swallowed my pour in one gulp and set my cup down on the counter. I pressed myself into Max's chest, standing on my tiptoes so I could wrap my arms around his neck. I pressed a kiss against his lips, both our mouths cold from the wine. My tongue parted his lips and slipped in his mouth, and I smiled against him as he groaned.

"I think it's time we christened the house, don't you think?" I asked as my hand trailed down his chest to the waist of his pants.

"We can count it as christening the kitchen because I plan on taking you in *every single* room of this house," Max replied.

I hurriedly unfastened my overalls and pushed them down to the floor. There was a fever in me that only Max could ease. Max tugged his shirt off and I couldn't help the way my eyes tracked his every movement. God, this man was sexy. He had a small sprinkling of dark hair below his belly button that made my stomach do flips.

I looped my fingers in his waistband and tugged him toward me. My kisses were frenzied, and my hands moved everywhere. Max reached between us to unbutton his pants and stepped away slightly to kick them off. The sight of him, even underneath the fabric of his black briefs, had me swallowing deeply.

Max scooped me up, and I wrapped my legs around his

waist. His mouth was on mine, matching my energy, as he pushed us against the counter.

"Please," I said, "I need you inside me."

He reached in between us to pull himself out and pressed himself against my entrance. I shifted my hips so I could slide down on him. My hips stilled as I adjusted to the feel of him between my legs, my breath finally releasing.

Max held my hips as he pulled me back only to bring me back down. This wasn't slow or sweet. This was frenzied and full of emotions. All the anxiety I'd held onto about Max, about *us*, was unraveling with every thrust. I pressed my mouth against his and tangled my fingers in his hair. I wanted to be closer, *closer*.

Max leaned me against the counter so he could release one hand from my hip. He brought his fingers in between us and pressed firmly against my clit, rubbing in small circles with two fingers. With one roll of his hips, he hit the spot he knew would bring me over the edge. I shivered as my orgasm flowed through me, Max never releasing his hold.

As I came down, Max increased his pace. His fingers dug into the flesh of my hips as he pushed himself inside me over and over. Sweat dripped down my lower back and Max moved furiously between us. I clenched around him and felt a low hum leave his chest as he found his own release.

He stayed inside me and leaned his forehead against mine as his breathing evened out. I placed light kisses against his jawline and ran my palm over his cheek.

"I think that I might love you, Max Kingsley," I whispered.

I felt the grin before I actually saw it. Max leaned his head back and looked into my eyes.

"You say that now, with me buried inside you?" he asked teasingly.

"Oh my god, it's not just because of that!" I said, pushing myself away from him. But Max held on tighter, pulling me close. He kissed along my neck, up my chin, and finally found my lips.

"I *know* that I love you, Isabella Esposito," he said. I felt him stirring inside me, his cock twitching.

I grinned and narrowed my eyes as I shifted my hips, grinding myself against him.

"Fuck, baby, you really are going to be the death of me," Max said. But he only put his arms back around me and walked us into the living room. I was thankful the cleaning crew hadn't wiped down the windows; we could use all the grimy privacy we could get.

Max sat me down on my feet and slipped out of me. Within seconds he fanned out a clean drop cloth on the living floor, scooped me back up, laid me down, and settled himself in between my legs.

"I never want to leave this spot," he said as he pushed himself back in.

His hands found my breasts and palmed them through the thin layer of my bralette. My nipples hardened at the touch, and I arched into him. This time was slower, and more intentional. Max's eyes scanned my face and my body as he gently pushed himself inside me.

His fingers were slow as they danced over my clit, his

tongue lazy as it explored my mouth and my neck. Max tugged the material of my bralette down and sighed as my breasts spilled out over the edge. His warm mouth was on them in an instant.

My second orgasm started slowly with a tingling in my toes and a tightness in my legs. Max didn't let up on the pressure on my clit or the tugging on my nipples as I moaned into him. I squeezed around him in waves as the pleasure rolled through me.

"God, you feel so good as you come around me, baby," Max said. "Let me feel you squeeze me."

Max fucked me through the aftershocks, my soft screams filling the air of my empty living room. My chest was hot and my breath ragged as he found his release again, spilling inside me. He gave himself a minute before pulling out and lying back on the drop cloth next to me, his large hand thrown over his heaving chest.

"It's going to take us three times as long to get through the demo if we keep taking breaks like this," Max said.

I laughed and covered my face with my hands. "I couldn't help it. You don't know what you look like in those pants with a sledgehammer," I replied.

"Oh, a working man, what does it mean for Miss Isabella?" he asked. "Noted," he said, tapping his temple.

Max got up to grab tissues from the bathroom and handed me a water bottle. I gratefully accepted and chugged most of it. Dust and drywall clung to my hair, and I desperately wanted a hot shower. I also wanted Max to come back with me to my parents' and join me in the shower. I don't know what had gotten into me.

Perhaps admitting my anxieties to someone who wouldn't judge me freed something in me. Maybe hearing that Max was here for everything on my to-do list and actually believed we'd make it happen allowed me to finally let my guard down.

Whatever it was, I was crossing my fingers that this feeling wouldn't go away.

I wasn't exactly sure what I was expecting to find when I walked through the brownstone's doors on a random Monday morning, but it certainly wasn't Isabella slouched down in the hallway upstairs with tears running down her face.

"Hey, baby, what's wrong?" I asked, "What happened?" I slouched down beside her.

She sniffled and grinned up at me, relief flooding her face. I loved watching the calmness spread over her when she laid eyes on me. She treated me like her own security blanket, but she was my life force.

"We passed the first round of inspections," she said, more tears spilling from her eyes. We'd been hard at work the last three months tearing down walls so new electricity and plumbing could come in. Those teams along with the floor refinishers had wrapped up last week and we'd been waiting on pins and needles for the go-ahead from the city to move on to the next phase.

"Okay, that's great! Right?" I asked, confusion lacing my tone.

"Yeah, it's great," she said through more tears, "it means we can actually work on remodeling the bathrooms and the kitchen."

"Okay, so why all the tears, baby?" I asked, wrapping my arms around her shoulders and pulling her toward me.

"It just makes me," she said through sobs, "really happy."

"Oh, baby," I said, chuckling as I rubbed her back. "Everything is coming together, isn't it?"

"It's scary for me to ask for what I want because then what if it doesn't happen?" she asked through her sniffles. "But it's happening and that's exciting and really scary."

"I know," I said. "But it's okay for things to go right, to go perfectly, to go exactly how you want them. That doesn't mean anything is going to mess that up."

"Don't jinx us, Max," she said, her breath finally even.

"I wouldn't dare," I said, crossing my heart with a grin.

Isabella leaned her head back against my chest. "Ugh, I don't know what has gotten into me," she said. "Maybe home ownership makes me emotional."

"Hey, how about," I said, "we don't work on the house today. Let's get out, let's go explore the city, find a new place to eat or something."

She tilted her face toward mine and smiled. "Okay, yeah, let's do that."

We'd been able to use one of the bedroom closets for storage for the last couple of weeks so we could keep our work clothes here and have a change of fresh clothes when we left. We both swapped out our work clothes for something less dusty and tattered and spruced up with what we had in the small bathroom off the room.

"I think it's so cute that this bathroom connects to these rooms," Isabella said as she fluffed her hair and dabbed at her eyes with a makeup brush.

"The Jack and Jill bathroom?" I asked, "Yeah, it'll be perfect for when kids are up here; they can have their own bathroom and we won't have to see it."

I caught her eyes in the bathroom mirror. It would definitely need to be replaced. It had a large crack that ran across it diagonally and little rusted corners. But Isabella's eyes were shining through the grimy mirror anyway.

"When do you want to get married?" I asked. The question came out of nowhere but considering it was on Isabella's to-do list, I knew that *she* had a preference for the ideal timeline. I'd marry her today, tomorrow, next Thursday, it didn't matter to me.

She chuckled and said, "Uh, I don't know."

I raised my eyebrows to let her know I did not believe that for a second.

"Okay," she said, "I was thinking after the house is ready. I really don't want to do anything big. Maybe our housewarming party can be a small wedding. Knock both out at the same time."

"So *that's* why you were crying," I said teasingly. "The closer we get to finishing the house the closer you are to marrying me."

"Oh, please, Max," she said, "if I could have done it perfectly, I would've bought this house, gone down to the courthouse to get married, and gotten knocked up. All on the same day."

"I do forget that I have a sugar mama," I said, wrapping my arms around her waist and tugging her toward me.

She threw her head back and laughed. It was something I could finally tease about without getting in my head thinking our age gap bothered her. The only thing that bothered me was thinking all those years ago when I'd first laid eyes on her at her mother's birthday party, I could've snagged her then. We could've both grown up together and I would've gotten to enjoy her in my life for that much longer.

But, I knew, deep down, the time Isabella had taken to travel and meet new people was what made her . . . *her*. Those experiences are what led her to fall in love with event planning and design and it's certainly what makes her such a kick-ass business owner now. And for all of that, I wouldn't go back to change a thing.

We found each other at exactly the right time. And everything else was going to line up exactly how Isabella wanted it to. I just knew it.

"All right, sugar mama, let me take you to lunch," I said, tugging on her hand and putting myself behind her so she could walk through the bathroom. As Isabella stepped out of the bedroom to head downstairs, I tugged out the small velvet box I'd kept hidden in the back of my duffle bag on the floor of the closet.

Isabella scrolled her phone as we walked down the city streets, her thumb pausing on a note she'd kept tucked away in her phone—a list of all the hidden gems in NYC she'd been meaning to try. She settled on the Nook, a tiny hole-in-the-wall spot known for its unassuming façade but incredible fusion tacos. It was nestled in an alley off the beaten path, promising a culinary adventure. We agreed without a word, making our way to the nearest subway station.

When we got to the Nook, it was exactly as Izzy had described: a narrow entrance wedged between two larger buildings, with a faded sign swinging gently above the door. Inside, the smell of spices and sizzling meat hit us, a warm welcome that made my mouth water instantly. The clatter of dishes and the low murmur of conversations created a cozy cacophony, a soundtrack to the vibrant energy of the place.

The Nook was dimly lit, with mismatched chairs and tables crammed into every available space. Strings of fairy lights crisscrossed the ceiling, casting a soft, inviting glow over the patrons. We found a small table near the back, the intimate space encouraging closeness. As we took our seats, I watched Izzy's face light up with anticipation, her excitement infectious. It was this, her ability to find joy in the new and unfamiliar, that drew me to her again and again.

As we sat, our knees brushing under the table, I couldn't help but marvel at how easy it was to be with Izzy. There was no pretense, no need to fill every silence with words. We simply existed together, comfortably inhabiting the same space.

Ordering was a shared task; our selections were a mix of recommendations from the staff and adventurous choices from Izzy's list. As the food was delivered to our table, the rich aroma of spices and sizzling meat filled the air. I watched as Izzy's face twisted slightly, her nose wrinkling as if the smell was somehow off to her.

She shook her head , as though to clear away the sensation, and reached for a taco, one of the Nook's signature dishes, filled with an inventive blend of flavors. She hesitated for a moment as if the mere act of shaking her head could dispel the unsettling sensation that had crept upon her. Then, with a resolve that seemed to push past her discomfort, Izzy again reached out for a taco.

This wasn't just any taco. The concoction was the Nook's claim to culinary fame and promised an explosion of flavors in every bite. The tortilla, perfectly charred at the edges, cradled a vibrant mix of ingredients both familiar and daringly innovative. Bright, fresh cilantro contrasted with the deep, smoky undertones of chipotle, while the tanginess of pickled red onions cut through the richness of the succulent, slow-cooked pork.

Her expression morphed into one of confusion as she chewed, eyebrows knitting together in a clear sign of distress. "I think I'm getting sick," she said, pushing the plate away slightly. "I'm sorry, this all sounded so good a minute ago, but smelling it and seeing it now? I can't eat it."

I couldn't help but feel a pang of concern. "Hey, no big deal," I assured her, quickly flagging down the waiter to grab to-go boxes and settle the bill. By the time I'd turned back to grab Izzy, she was already outside on the sidewalk, taking deep breaths of the fresh air.

"Let's get you back to your parents' house," I suggested gently, slipping an arm around her shoulders for support. Izzy nodded, still taking deep, steadying breaths.

The walk back was quiet, the bustling energy of the city somehow muted. Izzy leaned into me, her steps slow and deliberate. I couldn't shake the worry nagging at me, her sudden shift from excitement to discomfort too abrupt to ignore.

Reaching her parents' townhouse, I helped her inside, the familiarity of the space offering a small comfort. Izzy managed a weak smile, her usual vibrancy dimmed. "Thanks, Max," she whispered, her voice soft. "I just need to rest, I think."

Watching her slowly ascend the stairs, my mind raced with concerns and questions. Whatever was affecting Izzy seemed sudden, but I knew better than to press for answers she might not have. Instead, I resolved to be there, to offer whatever support she needed.

I felt the weight of the box in my jacket pocket. I gently patted it, a gesture that was becoming a habit. Today was supposed to be the day I turned an ordinary lunch date into a moment we'd remember forever. I had pictured it clearly: amidst our animated discussions of who had picked the better dish, I'd slide the box across the table, making the mundane magnificent.

Finding magic didn't come from grand gestures or the right timing but rather from the simple, everyday moments we shared together. All I had to do was wait for another one of those ordinary moments to come along.

I had two problems: One, the only semblance of a meal I could keep down consisted of oyster crackers and chicken broth. And two, I was undeniably, unquestionably, going to be late for my annual doctor's appointment that had somehow snuck up on me in the chaos of everything going down at the brownstone.

Yesterday, Max had dropped me off at my parents' house and I'd slept long and hard for the rest of the day. I padded downstairs around nine in the evening to raid the kitchen cabinets in hopes of finding something that didn't make my stomach turn. Was the flu going around?

My plan was to lay in bed all day today. I'd already sent out a canned email response to all my clients informing them I'd be out of touch for a minute while I recovered from a light illness. Well, I was hoping it was light, I still didn't really know what was going on. I'd been snuggled deep in my covers, *You've Got Mail* playing on a low volume in the background, when my phone buzzed.

It wasn't the sound of a text, but rather a calendar reminder. Picking up the phone, my eyes squinted in the dimly lit room and flew open when I realized I had exactly twenty-three minutes to get over to my doctor's office.

I wouldn't normally care about needing to reschedule at the last minute, but with an upset stomach, I'd decided to pull it together. I threw on an oversized hoodie and yoga pants before stuffing my feet into some old sneakers.

I barely glanced in the mirror, knowing time was of the essence. There was no way I could wait for my parents' car service—there simply wasn't time. So, I dashed out the door, my steps quick and determined as I hailed a taxi on the busy streets outside. It was just my luck the first one to stop reeked of stale cigarettes; the driver attempted to mask the smell with an overpowering, cheap car freshener. The combination made my stomach churn even more, and I cracked the window open, trying to breathe in some fresh air amidst the traffic.

The drive was a slow crawl, the city's traffic unforgiving. I had to focus on my breathing to keep the nausea at bay with each lurching stop and start of the cab. The minutes ticked by, my anxiety rising with each passing second. By some miracle, I made it to the doctor's office with a minute to spare. I handed the driver a wad of cash, not bothering to wait for change, and stumbled out onto the sidewalk.

The cool air was a relief after the stifling atmosphere of the cab, but I had no time to enjoy it. I rushed inside, checking in at the front desk with hurried, clipped words. The receptionist took one look at my pale face and directed me to the waiting room for sick patients, a quieter area with plush chairs that felt like a haven in my current state.

I sank into one of the chairs, grateful for the relative calm and the gentle hum of the air-conditioning. The waiting room was dimly lit, a deliberate choice to soothe the senses, and I found myself closing my eyes, trying to steady my breathing. The plush fabric of the chair felt soft against my skin, a small comfort as I waited to be called back.

My mind raced with possibilities, the uncertainty of what was wrong with me nagging at the back of my thoughts. Yet, at that moment, surrounded by the soft sounds of the waiting room, I allowed myself a moment of rest, hoping for answers soon.

I barely had time to settle into the sterile, brightly lit examination room before the nurse came in. She took my vitals with a practiced ease, the blood pressure cuff tightening around my arm with a familiar squeeze. I barely listened to the numbers she rattled off. My mind was elsewhere, fixated on the queasiness that had taken up residence in my stomach.

After an eternity, or more likely a few minutes, my doctor breezed into the room with a cheerful, "Good afternoon, Izzy! Ready to get that IUD swapped out, or are we thinking of other family plans?"

I blinked, certain I'd misheard her. "I'm sorry, what?"

She chuckled, flipping through my medical file on my tablet. "Yup, it's been in there for . . . ninety-six, oh actually, ninety-eight months now. It's time to replace it for maximum efficacy."

My mind reeled, trying to grasp the timeline she was outlining. Has it really been eight years since I had the IUD inserted? My doctor's words from back then echoed in my memory: "Izzy, make sure you use backup birth control in the last few months before you get it replaced. We haven't really narrowed it down to exactly when efficacy begins to dip."

Oh no.

A wave of panic washed over me, cold and relentless. "I think I might need a pregnancy test first," I blurted out, my voice barely above a whisper. My heart hammered in my chest, and I felt my face drain of color.

The doctor's demeanor shifted instantly from cheerful to calm, professional concern etched on her face. "Okay, let's take a step back. Tell me what's been going on," she said, her tone soothing, as she pulled up a chair next to the examination table.

I recounted the past few days, the sudden aversion to food, the overwhelming nausea, and the incident at the Nook. The realization that I might have overlooked the critical timing of my IUD replacement loomed over me like a dark cloud.

The doctor listened intently, nodding as I spoke. When I finished, she placed a reassuring hand on my shoulder. "Let's not get ahead of ourselves. The first step is to take a pregnancy test. Whatever the result, we'll figure out the next steps together," she said, her voice imbued with a calm certainty that helped steady my fraying nerves.

I nodded, a lump forming in my throat. The possibility of being pregnant hadn't even crossed my mind until now, and the reality of the situation was beginning to sink in. The doctor left the room to give me some privacy, and I sat there in the paper gown, feeling more vulnerable than I ever had before.

Here I was, having meticulously laid out a plan for my life, ticking off each milestone with precision. Buy the house, fix it up with Max, a small wedding once it feels like home, then start trying for a family. Everything was supposed to happen in a certain order, a sequence I had convinced myself was the right path.

And yet, as I sat there, I couldn't help but feel the weight of the surprise. Pregnancy was the furthest thing from my mind, a distant "next step" that suddenly felt like it might be thrust upon me without warning. The concept of motherhood wasn't something I was opposed to. It was the timing and the sheer surprise of it all that threw me.

I had envisioned a certain timeline for these milestones, a way to ensure everything was perfect and Max and I were ready. But life had its own plans, and the realization left me adrift in a sea of uncertainty. It was a reminder of life's unpredictability, a lesson in the futility of trying to control every aspect of our existence. How would Max react? Were we ready for this? Could we handle the accelerated timeline fate seemed to be pushing us toward?

As the doctor returned, her expression unreadable, I took a deep breath, ready to face whatever news she had for me.

When I walked through the door of my parents' house, my mother was there, her presence both a comfort and a reminder of the conversation I dreaded having. Her keen eyes missed nothing, and she immediately sensed the storm of emotions brewing within me.

"Isabella, what's on your mind?" she asked, her voice gentle yet probing as she guided me to sit beside her on the plush sofa that faced the panoramic windows overlooking Gramercy Park.

The words tumbled out with a chuckle before I could stop them. "Mom, I'm pregnant." My voice was a mix of fear and anticipation, bracing for her disappointment or judgment, especially since Max and I weren't even engaged.

Her reaction was nothing like I expected. She chuckled softly, shaking her head with a mixture of amusement and pride. "Isabella, you're not sixteen. Did you think I was going to scold you?" she asked.

I raised my eyebrows at her. "I mean, *kind of*. We're not even engaged, Mom," I said, leaning back into the sofa.

"Isabella, do you want to be a mother? Do you want that right now?" she asked.

"I actually told Max the other day that if I could've planned it perfectly, I would've bought the brownstone, fixed it up, gotten married, and pregnant all in the same day," I admitted.

She laughed. "Okay, sweetheart, this seems right in line with what you wanted, is it not? Who cares if you and Max aren't engaged? This is your life, your journey, your happiness. Don't let outdated societal norms dictate how you feel about this wonderful news."

Her words washed over me, a soothing salve to the turmoil I felt. My mother, a world-renowned sex therapist, had spent her career challenging societal norms and advocating for personal freedom in matters of sex and relationships. Her support at this moment was unwavering, and my belief in the right to choose one's own path was clear.

"If you strip away everyone else's expectations, Iz, would you be happy about this?" she asked, her gaze locking onto mine, searching for the truth beneath the layers of societal conditioning.

Her question pierced through the fog of my uncertainties, forcing me to confront what I truly felt, absent the weight of expectation. Would I be happy? The answer came from a place deep within, a resounding *yes* that filled me with a sense of clarity and purpose. Yes, the timing was unexpected, but the more I allowed myself to feel without the shadow of "shoulds" and "supposed tos," the more I realized how much I wanted this—how much I wanted a family with Max.

My mother's smile widened, my eyes sparkling with unshed tears as she reached for my hand, squeezing it gently. "Then that's all that matters, Izzy. This baby is a blessing, a new chapter in your incredible story. And you have my full support, every step of the way."

Her acceptance and encouragement felt like a balm to my soul, the fears and doubts that had clouded my mind beginning to dissipate. In their place, excitement and anticipation bloomed, the possibilities of what lay ahead filling me with a newfound sense of joy.

"We'll navigate this together," she continued, her voice firm yet tender. "You're not alone, sweetheart. You have a family, a partner who loves you, and now, a little one on the way. There's nothing more beautiful than that."

As we sat together, the sun dipping below the horizon, the sense of peace that enveloped me was profound. My mother's words had given me the strength to embrace my future with open arms, free from the constraints of societal expectations. This wasn't about following a prescribed order of milestones. It was about carving out my own path, one filled with love, laughter, and now, a new life. And in that moment, I knew everything was going to be just fine.

THIRTY-THREE
MAX

The morning air was crisp as I made my way to the brownstone, a sense of anticipation thrumming through me. Isabella's text had been a simple one, asking if I planned to come over to work on the house today. Of course, I did.

The messy stage of drywall awaited; sections of walls needed to be completely redone and others required a bit of patching. It was tedious work, but necessary, and I was eager to get started. More than that, I was excited to see Izzy again. She'd been lying low the past few days, presumably shaking off the tail end of what I had suspected was the flu. I hoped she was feeling better.

As I approached the house, the tangible progress we'd made filled me with a deep sense of pride and excitement for our future. The new electricity and plumbing were in, a significant milestone that brought the old building back to life and made our dreams for it seem all the more attainable.

Some walls were still missing, a stark reminder of how much work lay ahead, but the floors had been beautifully refinished, now protected under layers of paper to shield them from the chaos of renovation.

Stepping through the double foyer, the potential of the space tugged at something in my gut. The downstairs area, which would eventually become a blend of living and entertainment spaces, was a canvas waiting for our touch. Light streamed through the dust-covered windows, illuminating the raw beauty of the exposed brick and the smooth expanse of the hardwood floors. Despite the disarray, the essence of what the house could become was palpable—a place filled with warmth, laughter, and shared memories we had yet to make.

I set down my tools and took a moment to envision the future. The living room, with its high ceilings and large windows, would be the heart of the home, a cozy space where we could unwind after long days. The adjoining dining area, currently nothing more than outlined by chalk lines on the floor, would one day host dinners with friends and family, the air rich with the aroma of home-cooked meals and the sound of animated conversations.

I smiled at the sound of Isabella's voice filtering down from upstairs. She was humming to herself in one of the rooms on the second level. Moments like this gave me little glimpses into what our future was going to look like. Isabella could overthink and overanalyze, but I had known since one of our very first conversations.

Sometimes Isabella gives herself a hard time for taking a

decade "off" to travel and explore but I know, at the time, she was just waiting for me. I patted the small velvet box in my jacket pocket as I ascended the stairs. I had wanted to make my proposal a cute moment for us at one of our many hole-in-the-wall lunch dates but after the last few days, I couldn't wait any longer.

My steps rustled the paper covering the wooden steps as I rounded the stairs and stepped out into the hall. I heard Isabella still humming from one of the bedrooms, so I made my way to her. There might actually not be a better place to get down on one knee with my grandmother's ring than in the home we're creating together.

"Hey, love," I said as I leaned against the doorframe. My forehead scrunched as I realized what was in her hand. "Already picking out paint colors?" I asked. "Baby, I've got walls to still put up." I chuckled as I walked over to her. Her jasmine and vanilla perfume instantly put me at ease as I wrapped my arms around her hips and tugged at her.

"I know it's early," she said, "but this room needs the least amount of work, and I thought it would be cool to start thinking of what this room could be."

"Well," I said, making a show of looking around the room, "it could be a guest room, a workout room, a room to sit and ponder all of life's mysteries." I kissed the top of her forehead.

Isabella leaned back a little so she could look at my face. "What if it's a baby's room?"

"I definitely see it as a baby's room," I said with a smile. "Do you want to start now?" I walk us over to the wall, pressing my back against it. "Are you asking me to put a baby in you Isabella Esposito because I will gladly lie you down right here and—"

"Max," she stopped where my mind was going, "Max, I didn't have the flu." She smiled up at me with a mix of excitement and fear in her eyes.

My eyebrows scrunched as my brain slowly took in what she was saying, but I was slow to put it together. I looked at her, needing her to keep talking. To say it.

"Max, I'm pregnant," she said.

For a moment, everything else faded into the background, the noise, the chaos of the city around us. It was just Izzy, standing there with vulnerability and hope mingling in her eyes, and me, suddenly feeling like the ground had shifted beneath my feet. "Are you serious?" The question came out as a breath, a whisper really, carried on a wave of sudden, unexpected joy that surged up from somewhere deep inside. My heart raced, not with panic, but with a growing sense of wonder and elation, at the magnitude of what she was telling me.

Izzy simply nodded.

I crashed my lips to hers to quiet the many versions of the what-ifs that must be going through her mind right now. She was warm and soft in my hands and her mouth opened to let me in, only the small tremor in her bottom lip gave her anxiety away.

"Isabella, oh my god, how are you feeling?" I asked, pulling away from her mouth. "I want to check in with you before I bombard you with everything that's going through my mind."

She chuckled and sighed, not pulling away from my arms. "I freaked out at first, obviously. I was supposed to get my IUD replaced this year. I guess its efficacy dipped down in its last year and I was behind on the timing. I'm sorry, I just—"

"Why are *you* apologizing?" I asked. "I took sex ed. I know what it takes to make a baby. You don't carry all the responsibility of prevention, Isabella."

"I know." She continued, "But the timing of everything, I mean, we still have walls to put up, for goodness' sake. And I wanted to give us more time. We were going to get engaged and . . ." Her voice trailed off with a sigh.

I reached up to push back some of her curls and rested my palm on my cheek. "Fuck the timeline. Who gives a shit about it? Will it be chaotic and wild for a bit? Hell, yeah. But we've got this. I'm here for you no matter what you decide."

Izzy nodded and pressed her forehead to my chest.

"Not to steal your thunder," I continued, "but reach into my jacket pocket."

She looked at me confused but raised her hand to slip it into my jacket. She felt around until her hands found the small box and she froze.

"Take it out," I said.

Her fingers slid into a small holding spot and pulled out the velvet box.

"You can put it back if you want something bigger than this," I said with a gesture around the empty room. "I was planning on asking when we went for lunch the other day, but I guess you wanted to one-up me," I said.

She flipped open the box as I stepped back and got down on one knee. "Isabella Esposito, I couldn't have predicted how our lives would intertwine when I saw you, rain-soaked and determined, when you walked into the Prism Society. Since then, every moment with you has been an adventure. You've shown me the beauty of spontaneity, teaching me to find joy in the unexpected, like when we decided to buy this brownstone on a whim," I said with a chuckle. "Dreaming of the life we could build within these walls. Your passion for life, your dedication to following your heart, even when it leads you down uncharted paths, inspires me every day."

I couldn't hide the grin that spread across my face even as tears streamed down her cheeks. "Your laughter is my favorite sound, even if it's echoing through all these rooms with walls I still need to patch." Isabella chuckled from above and I took a deep breath. "I love that you can find happiness in the smallest things, like the perfect almond croissant or the way the light filters through our windows in the morning. Isabella, you challenge me, support me, and love me in ways I didn't even know I needed. And it's in the mundane, the everyday moments of our life together, that I find the most magic. I want to build with you, dream with you, and face every up and down by your side."

"So," I said, clearing my throat, "I want to ask you: Will you marry me? Will you continue this incredible journey with me, as my wife, my partner, and my best friend? Let's make this house our home, fill it with laughter, love, and maybe a little chaos, but most of all, let's fill it with us."

I pretended I didn't notice the way her head had been nodding during my entire speech and waited until I heard her excited "yes" before I slipped the ring on her finger. I'd already snuck one of her rings out to get this one sized months ago, so it slid on perfectly. She sucked in a breath as I pushed it back over her knuckle.

I leaned forward, resting my head on her belly. Despite it being too early to feel anything yet, I was so happy to share this moment with what would one day be our baby. Isabella's fingers threaded in my hair as she let me rest there. I placed kisses over her shirt and spread my hands over her hips.

I used my nose to nudge up the fabric of her shirt and kissed the warm sliver of skin under her belly button. "I can never get enough of you, Isabella, you smell so good," I said. I kept going because of the small hum that left her throat, the one that told me she was relaxing, shutting off her brain, and ready to be taken care of.

My fingers slipped into the waistband of her soft pants and tugged them down. Isabella lifted each foot, one by one, as I pulled the fabric away. My hands roamed up the back of her calves, her knees, her upper thighs, and finally her backside. I pulled her toward me gently.

I let my nose press into her core, over the fabric of her underwear, and smiled at the gentle tug of my hair. "I can't *wait* to taste my fiancèe's pussy, slip my fingers in its warmth," I said. "Do you think it'll taste different when my fiancée comes all over my face?"

Isabella shivered above me. "You are ridiculous," she said.

I tugged down her underwear and brought my mouth up to her middle. My tongue slipped out and I ran it from her entrance to her clit, feeling Isabella buckle slightly. I used my hands to help hold her up by her hips as I set my mouth on her warm pussy and devoured her.

I thrust my tongue inside her, tasting her arousal, and used broad strokes to run up and down her middle. She hummed and bucked against my face as she tugged my hair and brought me closer. I could never get enough of this.

I wrapped one hand around her waist, holding her steady so I could use my other hand to finger her gently. I started with one finger before quickly adding another and gently brought them in and out as my tongue flicked over her clit.

"Max," she said my name like she was begging, "please, you don't have to go so easy on me."

I pushed two fingers deep inside her and looked up. "Are you asking for it to be harder, Isabella?"

She nodded. "Yes, *please*, I want it harder."

I sucked her clit in between my lips sharply as my fingers picked up their pace. She was dripping wet, and my hand glistened with her arousal. I knew she was close as she started moaning above me. I kept fucking her with my fingers as my tongue flicked over her sensitive nub to bring her over the edge.

Her legs began trembling and her pussy started clenching my fingers, locking me inside. I felt the waves of her orgasm roll through her body as she soaked my hand and mouth. I lapped up every bit of it because she had never tasted sweeter.

I slipped my fingers out of her and in between my lips to clean them off.

"Well, I'm glad you didn't propose at the Nook now," she said. "It would've been really awkward if you'd tried *that* afterward."

I chuckled as I helped her slip back into her underwear and pants, bringing the waistband up with a kiss on her belly before standing.

"How are you feeling?" I asked.

"Right now? Really blissed out. And tired. Really tired," Isabella replied.

I kissed her forehead and grabbed her hand, leading me out of the room. "Let's get you out of here and into a warm bed. I'll keep working on the drywall so the dust can settle before you're back here."

"Can you take me back to your apartment?" she asked. "I kind of just want to live in our own bubble for a couple of days before the chaos sets in."

"I would take you to go nap on the moon if that's what you wanted," I replied. "Isabella, I'm not sure you totally realize everything that I would do for you."

As we walked out of the room, her hand in mine, I couldn't help but marvel at the turn our lives had taken. There, in the midst of renovation dust and the echoes of our future, everything felt right. The prospect of becoming a father, of stepping into this new chapter with Isabella, filled me with a sense of purpose and joy I hadn't known was missing.

It wasn't just the excitement of the baby or the thrill of

our engagement; it was the profound realization that this—us, our growing family, and the life we were building—was everything I'd ever wanted. The world outside, with its expectations and chaos, faded into insignificance. At that moment, as we stepped into the future together, as long as we had each other, we could face anything. This wasn't just a new chapter. It was our greatest adventure yet, and I was ready for every moment of it.

THIRTY-FOUR
ISABELLA

The weeks that followed, marking quite possibly the biggest change in both Max's and my life, were a whirlwind of morning sickness, picking out paint colors, napping, and juggling all the events I had committed to before my entire life changed.

The weeks turned into months, and as my belly grew, so did the support system around us. Max and I were overwhelmed by the love and assistance we received, not just in readying the brownstone but also in preparing for our new arrival. It seemed everyone wanted to play a part in this next chapter of our lives.

As soon as Max and I shared our news, it was as if a switch had been flipped. Our family and friends, including Natalia, Emma, Jessie, Liam, and my brother Dominic, rallied around us in a way that left me both overwhelmed and incredibly grateful. The brownstone, which had been a labor of love and, at times, a source of stress, became a hive of activity. Everyone pitched in to help get it ready for our little one's arrival. I was touched by the generosity and the sense of community that enveloped us.

During the sanding and painting process, I was unceremoniously evicted from the premises, with everyone citing concerns about what I should and shouldn't be breathing in. Despite my protests, I knew they were right. The health and safety of our baby were paramount, and I was willing to take all necessary precautions—even if it meant stepping back and letting others take the lead.

Natalia, always the organizer, had taken charge of scheduling the work that needed to be done on the house. She had a knack for rallying the troops, ensuring there was always someone present to oversee the contractors or to paint a room. Her ability to manage and delegate made the renovation process smoother than I could have ever imagined.

My mom, the epic problem-solver, tapped into my extensive network and found me an assistant. This was a first for me, and honestly, it was a game-changer. My ability to focus had taken a nosedive, a casualty of the pregnancy brain that seemed to have taken over my cognitive functions. My new assistant was a godsend, adeptly handling client communication for WanderLand and ensuring no detail, no matter how small, was overlooked. It was a relief to know my business was in capable hands, allowing me to focus on my health and the monumental changes on the horizon.

Emma, with her impeccable taste and design expertise, had offered to help decorate the nursery. Together, we pored over color swatches and furniture catalogs, choosing each piece with care. She had this incredible way of turning my vague ideas into a coherent vision, creating a space that was both beautiful and comforting.

Jessie, our group's creative spirit, had surprised us by handcrafting some of the most adorable decorations for the nursery. From painted canvases to a mobile she had assembled herself, her contributions added a personal touch that made the room feel even more special.

Max, ever my rock, took the lead on the renovation front, coordinating with our friends and overseeing the endless list of tasks that needed to be completed before we could move in. It was heartening to see him so involved, his excitement about becoming a dad evident in everything he did. He was already talking about babyproofing the house and researching the best strollers and cribs, his enthusiasm boundless.

In the midst of all this, there were moments of pure joy —choosing the color for the nursery, feeling the first fluttering kicks, and envisioning our future as a family. There were also moments of sheer panic—wondering if we were truly ready, if we could handle the responsibilities that lay ahead.

The more the swell of my belly grew, so did the strength of my confidence in how our life was unfolding. I had this sudden focus on something so much bigger than myself, even though, at this point, it was the size of a mango. Each kick and flutter was a reminder of the new life Max and I were about to welcome into the world, and with it, a clarity that what we were building together was meant to be.

Today was the day I was allowed back into the brownstone. Max stood at the front door, his face a mixture of excitement and nerves, as if he was presenting me with a gift he desperately hoped I'd love. God, this man was something else. My hormones kicked into overdrive, and I was ready to jump his bones with even the slightest look from him.

He reached for my hand, his palm warm and reassuring against mine. "Ready for the grand tour?" he asked, his voice laced with hope.

As we stepped through the vestibule—a term Max had proudly learned and insisted on using—I was immediately struck by the transformation. The entranceway opened into a bright, airy space where the living room flowed seamlessly into a hallway leading to the kitchen at the back. The walls, once bare and peeling, were now adorned with vibrant colors and covered with patterned wallpaper.

Memories from around the world found their new home here. A tapestry from Morocco draped elegantly over a vintage couch, colorful lanterns from Turkey hung from the ceiling casting soft patterns on the walls, and a collection of framed photos from my travels adorned the walls, each telling a story of adventure and discovery. Natalia had outdone herself, digging through my parents' storage to bring these treasures to our new home, infusing the space with warmth and personality.

Max watched me closely as I took it all in, his anticipation palpable. "Do you like it?" he asked, his eyes searching mine for approval.

I turned to him, my heart full. "I love it," I whispered,

the words barely capturing the depth of my emotion. "It feels like home."

He exhaled, relief washing over his face, and pulled me into a hug. "Good, because this is just the beginning. There's so much more I want to show you."

I gasped when Max led me to the kitchen. The green cabinets and bright mosaic floor were exactly what I'd envisioned for this space. Emma and I had spent hours combing through inspiration photos as I laid in bed with crackers and Emma sketched. Large terracotta pots and clay vases lined the upper cabinet area, each one reminding me of who I was when I came across it.

That's the joy about traveling and picking up pieces along the journey. One day, they'll get to be on display, serving as a reminder of who you once were. I chuckled at the memory of a salsa-dancing addict version of myself as I took in a display of colorful tiles hanging on the wall that we picked up in Havana. I smiled at the worn rug under my feet by the breakfast nook that Natalia and I came across on a severely hungover stroll through a market in Turkey.

"Max, this is absolutely perfect," I said as my eyes continued to take in all the tiny details.

"Wait until you see upstairs," he said.

He grabbed my hand and led me back down the hall and up the freshly polished stairs. The wall leading upstairs was covered in mismatched frames, small tapestries, and woven art. It all led to a bright hallway with navy-painted doors.

"Do you want to see our room or the baby's room first?" Max asked.

"Show me the nursery because I don't think I'll be able to stop myself from ravaging you if we see our room first," I said.

Max threw his head back and laughed. "Well, by all means, then," he said, directing me toward the middle door.

I pushed it open, and tears sprung to my eyes. We'd decided to be surprised about the anatomy of our baby and I hadn't wanted anything too kitschy anyways. Inside, a deep emerald board and batten flanked each wall, and a gorgeous rug of reds, pinks, and greens covered the floor. An organic rattan shape hung from the ceiling to light the room and a low dresser, already stocked with a few baby necessities, stood to the side.

"Oh my god, I can't wait to bring our baby home here," I said through quiet tears.

Max walked in behind me, closing me in with a hug. "Natalia went and picked up your things from your parents. The house is officially ours to stay in," he said.

"Show me our room," I said, turning to face him.

I followed him out of the nursery and down the hall. Our room looked over the backyard and spanned the width of the second floor. I pushed open the door and sighed at how beautiful everything was. Warm white walls fell back so the beautiful citron velvet upholstered head and footboard could shine. Lacquered navy nightstands stood on the side of the bed and a massive intricate wooden mirror leaned against the wall.

A tasseled chandelier hung from the ceiling and lit the room with golden dim light. I spun on my heel taking in the room. It would take me days to uncover all the tiny details that Emma put into each of our spaces. My heart was bursting with the love and care that went into putting this space together.

"If there's anything you want to change, I'm sure—"

"I don't want to change a thing," I said, "I couldn't have created a better space if I'd done it myself. This is our *home*, Max. We *live* here."

He grinned at me as he leaned against the doorframe. "Yeah, I still don't think my brain has caught up to it all yet," he said.

I sat down on the edge of the bed, facing Max. I just looked at him for a minute, my brain trying to piece together the people we were barely over a year ago with who we've become. I never would have imagined, in a million years, that the to-do list of my life, that once felt so out of reach, would all fall into my lap so quickly. Staring back at me was a partner, an amazing person to share this wild life with, and the man who would soon be the father of our children.

His dark hair fell into his eyes with a tilt of his head as he pushed himself off the doorframe and filled the space between us. Max's hand was warm as it cupped my chin and brought my face up to look at him as he stood before me. This man knew exactly how to light a fire in my belly. I could tell with the smallest shift in his bottom eyelid that he was trying to rein in his control.

I kicked my shoes off, brought my bare feet to the ledge that ran the length of the bed, and spread my knees out wide. I let the desire shine through my own eyes as I smirked up at

Max. He grinned back at me, a willing participant in our games. Quickly, he dropped to his knees and buried his mouth in my hair, against my neck. I threw my head back as he made his way down the front of my loose dress, his breath warming my collarbone, in between my breasts, and the top of my belly.

He placed a trail of kisses over every inch of me as his large hands snaked up my thighs, pushing the fabric of my dress up around my waist. Max reached behind me and tugged me toward the edge so that I perched on the edge of the mattress. His head dipped below my line of sight, my belly now protruding out enough to block any view of him.

I leaned back on my elbows so I could see as Max pressed his face in between my legs. His warm breath immediately sent goosebumps over my skin, but heat pooled to my core as he tugged off my underwear and tossed them to the side.

"God, you're so fucking sexy," Max said, the last part of his sentence muffled as he dove back in between my legs. His tongue ran up and down my pussy as he hummed his approval into me, the vibrations causing me to shiver.

"You taste so damn sweet," he said in between kisses and licks.

My hips twisted and pushed forward into his face, craving more friction, more touch, just *more*. I gripped the hair on the back of his head in between my fingers as I tugged him forward.

"Max," I said breathily, "I need you inside me."

With a final lick, he sat back on his heels. I stood, pulling my dress over my head, leaving me in only a too small black bra. I hadn't decided when it made the most sense for me to buy a larger size, unsure of how long the next one would even fit. My swollen breasts spilled over the edges of the fabric.

Max stood, unfastened his pants, pushed them off his feet, and took my place on the edge of the bed. I tugged at the hem of his shirt and brought it up over his head. My hands found their home over his chest, running down his muscles and over the small patch of hair below his belly button.

"These need to go," I said, pulling at the edge of his black briefs. Max lifted and slid them off with ease.

"This needs to go," Max replied as he unclasped the hook of my bra, allowing my breasts to fall heavily. His eyes went dark as he scooped them up with his hands and brought his face to one nipple, sucking gently, before attending to the other.

I climbed on top of him, my knees sinking into the plush mattress. His cock was hard as I hovered over his lap, the head of it bumping against my swollen clit, making me moan. Max buried his face in between my breasts as I lowered myself on him, sinking down inch by inch. I needed to be filled by him. I craved the pressure I felt whenever he was inside me.

"Baby, you're so warm, fuck," he hissed, "you are so goddamn wet."

I was at the stage in my pregnancy where I couldn't get enough of him. One look at his dark eyes and I was ready to jump him. I pressed myself down on him, sinking him in as far as he would go. I tilted my hips forward and back as I ground myself into him as he licked, sucked, and squeezed my breasts.

With one hand on my breast, bringing my nipple into his mouth, Max trailed the other down in between us and pressed his fingers into my clit, swirling gently. The added pressure was enough to put my hips into a frenzy. I brought myself down on Max over and over as he brought me closer to that glorious edge.

My thighs tightened and I stilled just enough for the orgasm to flow through me, my grip tight on the back of his head. My mouth found Max's, our breath warm and our tongues tangled. Wet noises filled the air as my arousal spread over us both.

"Fuck me, Max," I begged.

His hands found their hold on my hips, gripping my skin tightly as he brought his hips up to meet mine. With deep, quick thrusts, Max pounded himself into me. Sweat glistened over his chest as our thighs smacked together.

"Oh, *fuck*, baby," Max groaned as he found his release, pumping himself into me.

My chest heaved and curls stuck to my forehead as we caught our breaths. Max rested his forehead on my chest, his hands wrapped around my waist, rubbing my back gently. I twirled my hips gently on his lap, chasing the high he gave me whenever he was inside me.

"*This* is why you have a young guy around, huh?" he asked with a tease. "So you can get fucked back-to-back."

I laughed into his neck as I felt him stirring inside me.

"It's your fault," I said. "You unlocked this horny side of me I've never seen before."

As Max's hands roamed my back, I placed kisses along his neck and jaw. I was content knowing I had a lifetime of these moments ahead of me. That there was this man who was undeniably obsessed with me and making sure I got the pleasure I craved. I had a feeling Max and I were going to have the time of our lives breaking in this house.

Isabella
Two Years Later

As I stood at Linden Hollow Vineyards, surrounded by the lush greenery and the soft hum of celebration, I couldn't help but marvel at how my life had unfolded. The vineyard, with its rolling hills and picturesque scenery, was the perfect backdrop for our wedding day—a day that had been years in the making.

Most had assumed Max and I would tie the knot before I gave birth, if not at least make it courthouse official. But as the months went by and my due date got closer and closer, the pressure to do what everyone expected me to do subsided. Becoming a mother was the most freeing thing that could've happened to me.

It changed my perspective on everything.

After Max had continued working with the owners of

Linden Hollow to get their wine featured at the Guild and a few local restaurants around the city, they had all but demanded we have our wedding here. The ceremony had been intimate, with just our close friends and family and, of course, our daughter.

Ava, now a glorious, chubby, almost two-year-old, had shifted everything for Max and me. She had come into our lives and had helped me see, with intense clarity, what was actually worth worrying about. When it came to the three of us, I had zero hesitation.

As I watched our daughter toddle around the reception, my heart swelled with an indescribable mix of pride and joy. Ava, with my wild brown curls and deep brown eyes that mirrored Max's, was a constant reminder of the life we had built together. And how exciting the years ahead would be.

Max and I had opened up our reception to more people, giving our moms the chance to invite the people they wanted even if it was to just brag about how beautiful their grand-daughter was. WanderLand Events had been able to design and plan the entire thing, with me serving as creative director of our, now, team of four full-time employees. Emma had lent her design expertise, infusing the day with touches of elegance and whimsy that perfectly complemented the vine-yard's natural beauty.

My eyes found Max's from across the lawn, and he raised his champagne glass as a toast to me from a distance. His eyes didn't leave mine as he made his way through the crowd, ignoring a few people who called his name.

"Tell me I can sneak you away now," he said as his arm

snaked around my waist, his hands gliding over the emerald-colored silk of my simple gown. "I promise I can be quick, and I won't even mess up your hair. I'll just slide up your dress and slip into you from behind . . ."

Heat immediately shot to my core, and I swore I could feel my pulse in between my legs. "The evening is almost over," I said with a smirk.

"My mom is taking Ava tonight," he reminded me. "And I booked us a surprise for tonight," he said.

I raised my eyebrows as I pressed my chest against his.

"But I'd love to get you ready for later," he continued. "I could just slip my fingers into your wet pussy, have you coming on my hand, before we try for baby number two later?"

I chuckled and sipped my Champagne. "Let's say good night to Ava, then I'll let you take me wherever you want, Max Kingsley." I stepped closer to him and stood on my toes so I could whisper in his ear. "You can slip whatever you want inside me later."

Max's groan made me chuckle as I walked away to find our daughter. The reception area glowed around me as I walked through the space. Tables adorned with delicate floral arrangements and vintage lanterns dotted the landscape, while strings of fairy lights cast a warm glow over the guests as the sun set.

I walked through the small dance floor as one of the final songs played. It was a slow number and there were just a few quests left lingering, swaying to the music. My eyes paused as I caught sight of Dominic dancing with Jessie. Her cheek rested on his chest and his face had such a warmth to it that it made my stomach flip.

It always seemed like they were playing a game of cat and mouse, but I never could tell who was the cat and who was the mouse. Dominic had never been one to commit to a relationship or settle down. He lived his life on his terms with zero apology or explanation, but Jessie was a character who had stuck around despite it.

I made my way over to where Ava sat in her Gigi's lap, sleepiness overtaking her. I knelt down to place a kiss on her forehead and say good night. "Thank you for taking her tonight," I told Max's mom, now lovingly referred to as Gigi.

"Of course, dear, we're going to have so much fun, just us girls," Gigi said with a smile. Our parents had been a godsend throughout our transition from barely dating, to homeowners, to parents, and now finally husband and wife. They'd stepped in, without judgment, to help whenever they could, each of them equally obsessed with Ava.

Max joined us to say good night as he reached for my hand. Our things were already loaded in the car, so we slipped out through the small crowd to sneak away. The band was packing up now and guests were milling out to the parking lot. Max and I walked through the sloping lawn to where he had parked on the other side of the main building.

My eyes caught sight of a couple in the throes of making out on the edge of the reception tent and my eyes furrowed in recognition. I shook my head to clear my focus because I was surprised to see that one of the people was Jessie. And the person she was hugging tight and kissing wasn't Dominic, but rather a woman I thought I recognized.

"Is that, *Reagan*?" I asked Max quietly.

Max chuckled, tugging me to his side. I don't know what sort of situation Dominic had gotten himself into, I just hoped he knew there were other players involved.

"I'm not even going to *try* and dissect your brother's love life tonight, Isabella," Max said. "I have way more fun things on my mind."

I grinned up at him. "Oh, yeah? Like baby number two?" I asked.

We'd decided after Ava, that we'd start trying right away for number two. With the surprise that my first pregnancy had been, we'd expected it to happen quickly.

The idea of getting pregnant had turned us a little ravenous for each other. I was perfectly content with our little family, but I was certainly into the idea of Max trying to put a baby in me as much as he wanted to.

"Like pounding into you as much as you'll let me and filling you up with everything I have over and over and over . . ." he said as his hand squeezed my backside firmly.

God, his dirty talk immediately sent signals to the space between my legs.

"Are you going to tell me where you're taking me tonight?" I asked as we finally made it to the car. "Do I need to change?"

"Nope, you're dressed perfectly. Your event team planned something cool and timed it perfectly," he said with a wink.

I furrowed my eyebrows trying to think of all the events

we had on our calendar. But with the wedding, I hadn't been in the office as much as normal the last few weeks. I slid into the passenger seat as Max settled in and led the car out of the parking lot.

His hand rested on my thigh as we made our way back into the city, the traffic lights glowing through the windshield. I turned to him in surprise as we pulled up outside of Vinifera, the wine bar that masked the hidden underbelly of the Mirage Guild.

"Tonight, there's a masquerade party," Max said as he pulled out a small sack from the backseat. "So, we'll wear these and blend in with everyone else. Only your assistant knows we're on the guest list tonight, under different names, obviously." He handed me the mask meant for me.

My fingers traced over the large golden crystal headpiece. It featured an elaborate frontal masklike structure, heavily adorned with a rich tapestry of crystals and beads, creating a dazzling array of sparkles as light caught each facet. The central motif showcased a symmetrical arrangement of larger, marquise-cut crystals, surrounded by clusters of smaller gemstones and beads, giving the illusion of a luxuriant, jeweled crown.

Suspended from the ornate centerpiece were delicate chains of gold, each culminating in a teardrop crystal. These chains draped elegantly down, framing my face and cascading over my cheeks as I slipped it on, catching the light with every movement.

As I ran my fingers over the crystals, they glided smoothly across the cool, faceted surfaces, feeling the weight and craftsmanship of the headpiece. The structure felt secure yet comfortable, designed to stay in place throughout the evening's festivities, allowing me to move with grace and confidence.

"*Fuck*, Isabella," Max whispered from beside me as I turned to face him. I grinned at the sight of him wearing a matching gold crystal mask, albeit far less intricate than mine. With the dim lighting inside the Mirage Guild and the coverage of these masks, I was confident we would be able to remain hidden.

"I'm going to need to get inside you as soon as we get settled," he said through gritted teeth. "I reserved the mirror room for us later, but I don't want to wait."

"Oh my goodness, husband," I said with a tilt of my voice, "are you saying you want to fuck me in front of everyone? Do you want to come inside me while other people watch?"

"*Isabella*," Max said like a warning.

I locked my eyes on him as I reached up my dress to tug down my underwear. I dangled the lace from my fingertip as I tossed it in the backseat. "There, that should make things easier," I said.

"Out of the car," he said as he opened his door, "now."

I chuckled as Max came around to my side and helped me out of the car. "I *love* this side of you, *wife*," he said.

Max gave our keys to the valet and led me through the doors of Vinifera. We passed by chattering tables as we made our way to the bookshelf tucked in the back corner of the building. Max pulled the hidden handle and gently pushed me in over the threshold.

I grinned with the quiet pride of my team at the total transformation of the Mirage Guild. WanderLand was in charge of making sure the club matched the theme of its various events and we had done our job well.

Massive billows of black mesh fabric hung from the walls with hundreds of twinkle lights cascading down. Plumes of cream feathers billowed out of large vases that sat on table-tops and in corners of the floor as guests milled about, each wearing their own disguise.

As we made our way inside, Max holding my hand as he navigated us through the crowd, not a single person looked at us in recognition. Our masks were doing the trick and were exactly what I needed in order to fully get to be myself in this space. Being here, not as someone whose brother and friend owned the space but as a guest, had been on my bucket list since the beginning.

Max had found a way for us to explore our sexual fantasies in a way that kept our anonymity. I took a deep breath, held my head high, and smiled at the thrill of what this evening would bring.

***

I sank down into the plush seat of the curved upholstered booth, my silk dress sliding along the smooth velvet fabric. I smiled at the polished gold plaque on the low marble table in front of us that read "reserved" and took a glass of chilled Champagne from the waiter.

Liam had hired brand-new people to take over my spot and Max's as our roles shifted a couple of years ago. Although Max still worked a few events at the club every now and then, he was mostly needed for private events that WanderLand put together. Having a sommelier on staff was a perk my clients seemed to love.

It was a little odd being in this space as a guest rather than a family member of someone who helped start it. No one here knew who we were or who we knew. It felt freeing. Our sitting area was like its own living room vignette with our small sofa, a low coffee table, a side table with a lamp, and a plush rug underfoot. Surrounding the entire setup was a sheer black curtain that could be kept open or closed.

Looking around at the other couples in their own curved booths put a smile on my face. Guests here at the Mirage Guild truly leaned into the wild out and open vibe of the club. Some couples were more modest in their escapades, sneaking hands under skirts and tongues in mouths. While others were more overt. The curtain gave the illusion of privacy but was sheer enough that people close by could still get glimpses of what was happening inside.

My eyes widened at a threesome going down a few feet away. Two men were roaming their hands all along a woman's body, tugging the material of her top down to reveal her breasts. Their curtain remained open for us to watch. All of our booths sat back from the main attraction, the circle stage at the center of the room. The section Max had reserved for our table was considered one of the semi-private areas of the club.

On the stage, over my shoulder, were performers in their own masquerade attire. While masks covered their faces, not much covered everything else. Blends of thin layers of mesh and metal chains covered parts of their bodies, but for the most part, they were exposed. They walked around the stage in a sort of performance art act where they took choreographed steps toward each other.

Each touch, each move of their body had been planned and designed for this crowd. My eyes found Max's as he waited for me to take it all in and I smiled.

"It's not too much?" he asked.

"No, this was a great idea," I said reassuringly. "Thank you for bringing me here."

"I wasn't lying when I said I wanted to be inside you as soon as possible, Isabella," he said, his voice deep with desire. "I want to come in you now, so I can do it again and again once we're in the mirror room later."

My thighs clenched and my heart pounded. Did he know the effect he had on me? Based on the smirk in his eyes, he must.

"Does it turn you on to hear me talk about how much I want to come inside you?" he asked as he tugged our curtains closed. Having the thin layer of privacy was enough to help me focus on him and not anyone who might be able to see us.

I took a deep breath, trying to calm the burning heat in my chest. I nodded, a blush flooding my cheeks.

"Don't be embarrassed," he replied. "There's something about it that makes me *completely* fearful." He turned toward me, sliding a large hand up my thigh. "All I've been able to think about today is pumping you full of my cum so we can make another baby. I want it spilling down your legs just so I can shove more of it inside."

The moan that escaped my throat was absolutely obscene.

"Come bring those gorgeous tits and put them in my face as you sit on my lap," Max said, tugging at my hips.

I lifted the front hem of my dress, making sure my backside was still covered, as I spread my knees out on either side of Max. His eyes slowly slid up my legs, taking in the garter and lace band I still wore.

"Fucking hell, Isabella," he said as he lifted one of the straps and dropped it, letting it smack gently against my skin. His warm hands gripped my inner thighs and squeezed "I need to be inside you right now," he said, unzipping his dress pants, "I'm going to fucking come as soon as you sit on this cock, then I'm going to make sure you come over and over in the mirror room."

His dirty talk sent tingles down my spine. I watched between us as he reached inside his pants to pull out his hardening cock. Precum glistened his head as he gave himself a few strokes before pressing it against my entrance. I was already so damn wet for him.

Once I felt his head nudge against the right spot, I gripped his neck, brought his face toward my chest, and lowered myself down onto him in one movement. I held steady as I felt him shiver and shake beneath me.

"*Fuuuck*," Max said as I sank down. I lifted myself slightly so I could repeat the movement, and true to his word Max was already close to the edge. Before long I felt him still then twitch inside me as he filled me. I rocked my hips against his lap as he thrust his hips up to give me all of him.

"You might just have to sit here with my cock inside so you so the cum stays where it needs to," Max said with a chuckle, his hands rubbing my back.

I pressed my chest toward his mouth, the only thing not covered by the mask on his face, as I twirled my fingers in his hair. My dress dipped into a v-cut that, especially in this position, pushed my breasts up together. I loved the feel of Max's five o'clock shadow scraping against my skin as he placed warm kisses across my chest.

I lifted my gaze to scan over the room as I straddled his lap. The evening had most definitely kicked up a notch. The men that had been tending to the woman in the booth not far from us were now stroking their cocks as she alternated her attention between the two. The performers on stage had brought out small toys and were in the throes of giving the people in the front row a very good show.

Everything about this space was designed to keep your senses heightened at all times and it was working. My nipples pressed hard against the satin of my dress and my chest was flushed red. My hips moved subconsciously on Max's lap, craving the friction.

"Baby, you keep moving like that and I'm going to have

to pound into you regardless of how many people can see us," Max said roughly as he pressed kisses down my neck.

With a chuckle, I slid off his lap, keeping my legs pressed together so he wouldn't spill out of me. Max shoved his cock back into his pants and stood to sign us in for our private room. I was ready to slip these masks off and spread out. Max walked back over, his hand reaching out for mine. Abandoning our champagne glasses, we walked through the small lounge and over to the room with the lion's head knocker.

Memories of us sneaking back here when the Mirage Guild still hadn't fully opened yet came flooding back to me. It felt like we had lived a lifetime since then but somehow had found ourselves back here. Max used a small brass key to unlock the room and pressed open the heavy door, ushering me inside as he held it open.

My eyes widened at our disheveled look being reflected back to us on every surface. The room was covered, every wall and across the ceiling with large, mirrored panels. Mirrored furniture was spread across the room, making sure an angle of yourself could be seen no matter where you stood. As soon as I heard the click of the door behind me, Max's hands were at my sides, roaming over my belly and up my breasts, slowly walking me back against one of the mirrors.

I reached for my mask and slipped it off, feeling relief from its missing weight, before setting it on top of a nearby dresser. Behind me, Max slung his own mask off and tossed it on the floor, pressing his face into my neck as he pushed the straps of my dress down. His hands found the small zipper at my back and slid the metal down, letting the dress fall and pool at my feet.

A groan slipped from Max's mouth as his eyes roamed over my body. The creamy lace garter still clung to my hips and thighs, my full breasts pushed nearly over the edge of the matching bralette, and my feet still arched high in my velvet heels.

Max was on his knees in an instant, his hand sliding up between my thighs. My body lurched forward as his fingertips grazed the sensitive skin.

"So fucking beautiful holding my cum in between your legs," Max said as his eyes flared. With a smirk, he took his fingers and scooped up the creamy liquid that threatened to spill out of me. "I just need to put some of this back where it belongs."

My moan echoed around the room as Max pushed two of his fingers into my pussy. My shoulder blades pressed into the mirror as my hips pushed out to demand more. Max's mouth was on me in an instant, his tongue flicking out to dance over my clit. As his fingers continued to slowly push into me, Max brought me closer and closer to the edge with his tongue.

"That's it, baby," Max said, his voice muffled between my thighs, "squeeze my fingers."

My entire body shivered, and my thighs flexed as my orgasm rocked through my body. Max slid his fingers out of me and stood, sprinkling kisses over my belly and up my chest as he raised to his full height. His hands reached for the fabric of my bralette, tugging the lace down so my breasts spilled out.

His warm mouth landed on my nipple, his tongue flicking out to tease it. My fingers dug into the back of his hair, pulling him closer. I needed to feel more of him, all of him.

"I already need to be inside you again," Max said as he guided us over to the edge of the bed. The back of my legs hit the soft edge of the mattress as I sat down. Once we had decided to intentionally try for another baby, something had shifted in Max. We'd always had a very active sex life—it's what helped bring us together back then—but this was on another level.

It was like it was a primal need for him to make it happen so he was ready to go, as many times as I could handle it, at a moment's notice. I can't say that I hated it. Max pulled his shirt off over his head, undid his pants, and pulled himself out.

"Watch me slide into you," Max said as his hands gripped my knees and pressed them apart.

My eyes moved to the mirrored ceiling where I could see his hard cock jutting out from his body. Max stood in between my legs and slowly pressed his hips forward. I couldn't take my eyes off us from above as he sunk deeper and deeper.

Max pulled himself almost all the way out, letting only the ridge of the tip of him stretch me. His cock glistened with our arousal as he pushed just his tip into me, hitting the sensitive part of me he knew I loved. He would alternate his movements, sometimes pressing himself as deep in as he could go before pulling himself almost all the way out and not pressing past my entrance.

I was scratching at the skin of his thighs as I tried to bring him closer. Max reached into the pocket of his pants and pulled out a little satin bag I recognized from home. As he wrapped one hand around my knee, Max opened the bag and pulled out a small pink vibrator we liked to use.

Max pressed the on button to the lowest setting and trailed the vibrator over my lips, down my chin and neck, and over my nipples. The entire time Max kept his slow thrust, never pushing himself all the way inside me. I watched in the mirror as his cock stretched me open so he could slide in but instead, he hovered at the edge.

"I'm going to press this against your clit so I can watch you come," Max said as he trailed the vibrator down between my breasts. "I'm not going to press back in all the way until I feel you dripping over the tip of my cock."

I moaned and tried to twist my hips so he'd reach a deeper spot in between my legs, but his hand held my knee firmly.

Max chuckled. "Come first for me baby, then I'll fuck you," he said.

He brought the vibrator down to my clit and turned up the speed a couple of notches. He ran the vibrator over my pussy to get it wet then circled my clit with the firm point. I could already feel my orgasm building up in my belly.

Max continued his leisurely thrust of the tip of his cock

as he used one hand to spread my lips so he could rub the vibrator over me.

"Come for me baby," he said, "so I can shove my cock inside your beautiful pussy. I want to fucking come inside you again, then I'm going to fuck my cum back inside you."

I moaned as the tingle spread up from my toes and reached my thighs. My body quivered and a low moan filled the room as Max pressed the vibrator firmly against my clit as my arousal soaked us both. Just as I started to catch my breath, Max shoved himself all the way inside.

I felt goosebumps on his upper thighs with each thrust of his hips as he came inside me. I could feel the pulse of his cock in between my legs as he stilled. Max pulled himself all the way as he spread my thighs out wide.

"Fuck, you look so beautiful with my cum dripping out of you," Max said as he pushed his cock back inside. "But it belongs inside."

Our wet sounds filled the room as Max pounded into me, my breasts bouncing roughly. I could feel us dripping down my inner thighs and down my ass. My hand patted around the top of the bed before I felt the warm vibrator. I turned it on high and pressed it against my clit as Max fucked me.

Max's large hands held my thighs out wide as his hips thrust wildly. I squirmed beneath him as I rubbed over my swollen clit with the toy.

"Do you like feeling me inside you when you make yourself come?" Max asked.

I nodded, my eyes pressed tight as I felt my buildup

starting in my belly. "Yes," I replied breathily. My moan was loud as I pushed myself over the edge for the third time. It felt explosive and my vision went blurry as I came down from the high.

Max tried to catch his breath as he slid out and sank onto the bed next to me.

"I love trying to make babies with you, Isabella," he said, turning to me and pushing a stray curl out of my face.

I smiled at him and laughed. "You turn into an absolute wild animal, Max," I said.

"And you love it," he said as he turned on his side and ran his hand down my hip.

"I love *you*, husband," I replied.

"Mmm, I love hearing you say that, wife," he said.

"What if we clean up, go back to our toddler-free house, order some pizza, and we can try to make a baby again?" I asked.

"That sounds like the perfect evening," Max said, placing a kiss on my shoulder.

As Max brought me a warm washcloth and pulled out comfy clothes for us to change into from the bag he'd snuck in, my heart swelled. Even just two years ago, I could've never fathomed this was where I'd be. All of the things on my "probably never going to happen" to-do list had all fallen into my lap, and I couldn't imagine them happening with anyone other than the man beside me.

Tomorrow, we'd go back to our reality of parenthood and work, but for now, I let us exist in our own little bubble. One that just so happened to be full of really good sex.

ADDITIONAL TRIGGER WARNING

The following is a spoiler, so please be advised. This story contains a surprise pregnancy. It is unexpected but very much desired. There is zero hiding this from the MMC and he is *all in*. I thought long and hard about having this element included but the reality is - well sometimes surprises sneak in! There is so much that Izzy wants to control and make happen on a perfect timeline but then - whoa - this comes out of nowhere. I hope that I did this (usually love it or hate it) trope justice.

ACKNOWLEDGMENTS

I'm writing these thank-yous with *The Tortured Poets Department* playing in my headphones, so this may or may not be more melancholic than normal ;)

We freaking did it. Again. I will risk being the ultimate cliché and tell you that what they say is true. The sophomore book to your debut series is the fucking hardest. Endless thanks to Caroline Acebo, my incredible editor, for all the times you talked me through my panic about this story. You talk me off ledges and help me dive into tropes that everyone hates - I guess we'll see if it was worth it.

And the rest of my team; Jen Kennan, Kimberly Hunt, Molly Mills - you are the reason this book is even worth looking at. Even though I pushed the deadline 87 million times. Thank you.

To the local bookstores who stock my books, put them on big displays, host release parties...I owe you a million hugs. Specific shout out to Monstera Books and Under the Cover here in Kansas City.

A special thank you to my ARC team for all the love you show my stories - you are why people can even find my book - thank you.

And, to you, dear reader. I'm hoping you didn't throw

this book out the window once it got to 'the trope'. I *really* hesitated to go through this with one but I truly felt like it was what the story called for. I wanted to create an event that has been the reality of more than one person I know (IYKYK) and shift what would be a HUGE surprise into something sweet and endearing.

Finally, to two of my favorite people in the entire world. B and P. I love you both bunches and bunches.

Gabi Salas, the mastermind behind sizzling contemporary romances, believes reading smut is feminist AF. She's the author of the debut series "The Prism Society," a solid one-handed read *wink*. Gabi resides in Kansas City with her husband, hilarious daughter, and a ridiculously cuddly cat named Pepper. When not crafting stories, she's  drowning in honey oat milk lattes, binging smutty novels, or dark and twisty murder podcasts. Connect at gabisalas.com

ALSO BY GABI SALAS

The Prism Society

The Passion Almanac: Magical Meetings

August

December

www.ingramcontent.com/pod-product-compliance
Lightning Source LLC
Chambersburg PA
CBHW021411010826
48972CB00014B/1280